HOUSE OF VAMPIRES AND FLAME

SHADES OF RUIN AND MAGIC

BRIDES SELECTION
BOOK ONE

MEG XUEMEI X

Books by Meg Xuemei X

SHADES OF RUIN AND MAGIC: BRIDES
SELECTION

MONSTERS AFTER DARK SERIES

UNDERWORLD BRIDE TRIALS SERIES

HALF-BLOOD ACADEMY SERIES

DARK FAE KINGS SERIES

THE WAR OF GODS SERIES

OF SHADOWS AND FIRE SERIES

SHIFTER'S WITCH SERIES

About This Book
House of Vampires and Flame

They say monsters are made. I was born one.

With an angelic face and a cursed talent, I eat magic and ask for seconds. When I pass through the land, flowers wither, earth scorches, and colors bleed out—all at the command of my father, the God of Ruin.

I escaped his prison, only to stumble upon a dangerous school ruled by five savage princes. Girls fight to fall into their laps, even though they're all hot mess assholes.

My name is Bobbi, but they call me "Little Bob," mistaking me for a boy. I roll with the punches and pose as a servant boy in Shades Academy to hide from my father. I try my best to fly under the radar, but the Fates keep tossing me into the path of the princes.

That's how I bump into Killian, the enigmatic, ruthless billionaire heir. I want him, but he's the forbidden fruit. He's drawn to me too, like a moth to a flame.

When he doesn't like the burn, he rips off my bodice to betray my secret in front of everyone and forces me to enter the cutthroat game of the Brides Selection.

Sign up to Meg's mailing list to hear about her new releases and get newsletter only bonus scene and a special gift.

Chapter One

S y rode the wolfman, her breasts bouncing like two soft balls, her hips swaying like a boat on waves.

"Fuck me!" the wolfman cried in ecstasy.

"What do you think I'm doing, sugar?" Sy chuckled.

She pounded him into the long blades of grass. The more excited her target was, the more energy she got. She inhaled his arousal, taking as much as she could. It was hard to find a supernatural to feed upon in the mortal realm.

Human males could barely sustain Sy's strength. We'd learned that lesson the hard way. They broke easily. The wolfman, though not ranked among the strongest of his species, was the best we could find.

Beggars can't be choosers, Sy often complained.

She hadn't fed for nearly two months, and I preferred her to feed this way than to gorge on a corpse. It'd been years since we first went on the run, and I still didn't have the stomach for blood and gore. Sy often retreated after she fed, and I had to take over with my humanoid form and clean up her mess.

I peeked out through her eyes and studied the wolfman's lust-distorted face, a bit curious and a lot bored. At least I was kind enough not to yawn when he groaned like a bitch in heat and stared at Sy's glorious breasts.

I dipped my gaze and glimpsed his bristly pubic hair, wet with the cream Sy made.

Shit!

I darted my eyes to the sky, praying for patience and tolerance.

Hurry up, Sy, I urged. *We should be on the road. I got a bad feeling this morning that something bad is going to happen.*

You always have a bad feeling, she said, bouncing on top of the wolfman like a cheerleader, but she was ready to wrap it up. I could feel the approach of her climax.

Relax, she advised. *Just enjoy the moment, as we

don't have many. His cock is a little crooked, like a curved banana but a lot harder, and he has a knot—

Please! I stopped her. *I don't need to know every detail.*

I could feel a small slice of what Sy was experiencing. More often, it was like looking through sunglasses; everything was filtered—the sound, the scent, the pleasure, and the thrill of her hunt.

I'm harvesting the energy for both of us, she said. *We can go for a week without feeding again, so you should not be so grumpy.*

I feed differently, I pointed out.

The wolfman bucked up his hips to thrust deep into Sy, not realizing he was her dish. After Sy finished feeding on his sexual energy, he'd be spent and suffer fatigue for a few days. He wasn't losing much, though, as this was probably his best lay.

He moaned and growled in pleasure, his corn-blue eyes rolling back. Sy laughed, pounding him further into the grass and dirt. The wolfman tried to grab Sy's bouncing breasts, but he had to use both hands to fully grasp one breast. His gaze fixed on her features lustfully, transfixed by her savage beauty.

While I had a golden, innocent look with my cheeks still round with baby fat, Sy was my opposite. She was wild, sultry, mature, and a head taller. A cascade of long, lush hair covered her pointed ears, and a pair of cracked sunglasses hid her glowing golden eyes at my insistence.

Standing out was asking for trouble.

We walked through cities in my form, all innocent and youthful, making folks let down their guard. Just when they underestimated me, a monster could erupt out of me in an instant, all teeth and claws, and sometimes death.

Even when Sy was out, taking over, like sex-feeding on the wolfman right now, I insisted on her not talking too much and not opening her mouth wide to laugh. She liked to purr and giggle during sex, but she could do it with her big mouth shut.

Three of her targets passed out in the past when they saw her rows of jagged, razor-sharp fangs suddenly pop out, which ended up with their cocks going limp and our feeding being undone and our fuel not being filled up.

Very disappointing.

At my nagging, Sy rode the wolfman harder. I rolled my eyes, as that wasn't what I'd meant. I wanted her to pick up speed and get it done, like now, since I was starting to get antsy. It was supposed to be a sprint, not a fucking marathon.

The earthy forest wind ruffled her hair. The

blades of grass whipped her thighs, which clamped down on either side of the man's legs. He'd have bruises later.

"Give it to daddy!" the wolfman cried out.

Sy chuckled, sapping his energy greedily. "Don't bring daddy into this. I hate my daddy."

The wolfman's face paled, his energy drained, but he didn't know why.

"Lady, you've got some strength, and I have to give you that," he said. "How about let's fuck again tomorrow? I didn't get enough sleep last night. The neighbors had loud jazz on!"

"Hang in there a little longer, sugar," Sy crooned, and the wolfman groaned as he put in more effort in order to get through it.

An ominous awareness washed over me. I was always the vigilant one when Sy lost herself in the middle of a sex feast.

My skin buzzed with alarm. I stilled, pricking my ears to hear.

The wind stopped. A clatter, followed by a series of metal clangs and the rustling of grass, then a stench hit my nostrils.

Sy! I warned, panic rising in me.

She leaped off the wolfman, landing in a crouch

beside him. Her pointed ears pricked. Her hearing was superior to mine.

"C'mon, I'm not done!" the wolfman whined.

"You are now," Sy said sharply.

Growling, the wolfman sat up and grabbed Sy's shoulders to push her down so he could mount her. Sy, tougher than the world, swatted his hands away, gripped his hair, and tossed him aside like he weighed nothing. He blinked, slightly shocked at her roughness and super strength.

"Dumb bitch!" he cursed like a loser.

Sy bared her ragged, razor-sharp fangs.

"What the fuck?" The wolfman scrambled back before he gave a snarl, his face about to morph to a werewolf's.

Sy plucked the sunglasses that covered her glowing eyes and chucked them away, not even slightly concerned at the wolfman's shocked and betrayed look. She planted her hands on the grass, claws sliding out of her hands.

Enemies! she hissed in confirmation.

They were coming.

Ruin's agents, the Shriekers, had tracked us down.

Air wheezed out of my lungs. Icy dread filled my

head as terrible memories played before my fluttering eyelids.

Agony drenched me as Ruin, my father, fed upon me, absorbing part of my essence and sucking my bone marrow to nourish himself.

I writhed in the pit and stared at the dark sky helplessly, praying for it to be over, praying for death to take me. Then Sy was there, shoving me to the background and letting him feed on her instead. When she nearly broke, I'd surface, taking over and enduring every second of pain, torment, and endless horror.

A cacophony of shrieks and clattering came closer.

You ready, Sy? I asked.

Ready for what? she growled.

Chapter Two

The wolfman tore his gaze from Sy's breasts and fangs as she crouched like a lioness, ready to pounce on the monstrous creatures surging toward us.

"Fuck off," my voice commanded through Sy's mouth.

The wolfman didn't need to be told twice. He ran as fast as he could, abandoning his pants. His bare ass got all hairy, then a brown wolf came out, loping through the grass.

Three Shrieker scouts, Sy informed me.

Which meant a larger group wasn't far behind.

Shriekers knew no fear, and they had one single purpose—serve Ruin. They'd been hunting me for eight years now, ever since I'd escaped their master at the age of eleven.

They were monster and machine blended into one, put together by my father's foul magic. These abominations had demonic faces, scaled necks, and rattlesnake tongues. Their scorpion-like claws and legs were part machinery. Those were the basic packages of Shrieker soldiers. Some of them were upgraded with lethal tentacles.

I called them Shriekers because they shrieked like hundreds of nails scratching through glass when they found their mark.

The scouts closed in on us, one female and two males. Amid the Shriekers' ranks, a female gave the orders.

"Princess," the female greeted, parting its black slit lips to reveal four rows of serrated teeth. "You've sunk so low. Master would disapprove."

The Shriekers never called my father God of Ruin outside his realm, as he didn't want the world to learn about his existence before he returned to his former glory. And to completely recover and regain his form, he'd need to feed on me. I was born for that purpose alone—to drain the magic from the land for him, then to be fed on by him endlessly.

My throat closed in fear while icy hatred burned in my chest.

Sy leapt from her crouch, her claws extending and swinging toward the female's left eye. The female let out a shriek and jerked its head back, but Sy had gotten the monstrous eyeball with the tip of her claws.

"Hello to you too, nameless," she said with a sweet smile. Sy was most vicious when she beamed and acted friendly. "Here's our gift to you, love." She flung the dark eyeball at the female Shrieker's demonic face.

The female shrieked again and leapt back in shock, not expecting us to have leveled up. In the absence of being tortured and fed upon daily, we'd gained incredible strength.

"You're too strong, Princess," it hissed. "Master must know!"

"If you can live to tell Daddy," Sy mocked.

The female lunged, its claws swiping down at our head. Sy jumped out of range of its strike and dashed toward the male Shrieker to her left. The male thrust a scorpion leg at our chest; Sy side-stepped to the right in a flash, then leapt several feet and crouched on its back.

Without a moment of hesitation, she

embedded her claws into its skull, shattering its bones and scrambling its brain tissue. Its black blood shot out like thick grime when Sy yanked out her claws.

Well done, Sy! I cheered her. *One down. Two to go!*

I can count, she said smugly.

The remaining male Shrieker charged us, and Sy sailed from the back of its dead pal to meet the challenge. She twisted in the air, about to stab its neck, but a dozen tentacles burst out of its shoulders and caught us in their vise-grip.

Sy slashed at the tentacles that choked us, but they wouldn't release us, threatening to crush our ribcage. The Shrieker's piercing shrieks rang in our ears, and the female joined in. All I wanted was to clamp my hands over my ears to stop the terrible sound.

Sy gnashed her teeth and hacked at our captor frantically, her arms weakening, her breath wheezing. Pain exploded in our chest and spread everywhere until we couldn't tell the source of the agony. I could feel two ribs on our left side cave in and crack. We sucked in a ragged breath, praying they wouldn't pierce our lungs.

Sy's arms went limp at the press of the tentacles.

"Master said to maim but not to kill the princess," the female Shrieker hissed.

"Yes," the male Shrieker hissed back. "We must cripple the princess to bring her back to Master."

Cold panic seized Sy and me. For a second, we couldn't hear or feel anything but the roaring fear that pounded into our bones. We'd rather die than be captured and delivered to that hellhole of ultimate horror. We'd have to find a way to end us on the road once our fate of captivity was sealed.

Then a shot of rage erupted into flames within me.

No, we wouldn't be done today! Being born into slavery, we hadn't really lived. Even after we'd escaped, we'd been constantly looking over our shoulder while living on the streets.

The world swam and stars blurred in front of my eyelids as the Shrieker tightened its grip, its tentacles binding us. The female stalked toward us, its snake tongue darting out as it hissed smugly.

If we blacked out, we'd be done.

Sy, I cried. *I'm taking over.*

Clawing through my blurry vision, I surfaced and shifted. My smaller humanoid form slipped through the tentacles and alighted on the grass. Whenever we were in my humanoid form, my current clothes came with me. While I was barefoot, I had an old shirt on and loose trousers.

Without hesitation, I extracted Deathsong, a dagger forged by my father with his black magic, from the sheath dangling on my waistband. I'd stolen it from him when I made my escape. The dagger was a terrible thing to have, as it brought up horrible memories, but it was a necessary evil. It was the most effective weapon to kill a Shrieker.

The now one-eyed female Shrieker prowled forward, shoving away the male to get to me. I rolled away but was a touch slow, and its claws tore through my trousers and impaled my thigh.

Pain lanced through me. I slashed my dagger blindly at the Shrieker and tore myself away from its claws, blood gushing out of my wound.

The Shriekers sniffed at the scent of my blood and shrieked in excitement and glee. My blood was nectar to all monsters.

Run! Sy urged. *Let me out. I'm faster.*

We won't be able to run far, not while we're bleeding like this, I said in dismay. *And you know it's too risky to shift now.*

When I shifted, it was instant, but when Sy tried, the transition always took three and a half seconds. The Shriekers could get to us in a blink, and in the middle of Sy shifting and taking over, we were as helpless as a toddler.

Let's end this, I said.

I lunged at the female Shrieker, and it lashed out with its massive tentacles. My black dagger cleaved the tip of a tentacle, but its other tentacles slammed into my wounded leg. I flew backward like a rag doll, crashing into the wall of an abandoned factory a dozen yards away.

A whimper escaped my lips as pain shot through me.

"Deathsong!" the female shrieked. "You stole it from Master!"

"To slay you," I offered.

It clucked its rattlesnake tongue and stalked toward me. "I'll make you suffer, Princess."

It stiffened before lurching, eerie darkness swirling in its remaining eye that now glowed crimson. The surrounding air chilled instantly, icy fear slithering up my spine.

The God of Ruin peeked out of the female's eye, fixing his merciless dark gaze on me.

"What has become of you, Daughter?" His voice, soft, deep, and musical, came out of the Shrieker's mouth.

The hair on the back of my neck stood on end,

my palms suddenly slick with cold sweat. I hadn't heard his voice for years, and I'd prayed to never hear it again.

He inhaled in ragged relief. "I've found you, and you'll never leave again, little one. I regret that my agents will have to maim you to bring you back to me, so you won't be foolish enough to run away again. All is forgiven, Daughter. When you return home, I'll put you back together, as you're the apple of my eye."

Get up! Get up! Sy snarled at me, as I was paralyzed with fear.

The female Shrieker stepped closer. It was now three feet from me, its tentacles and claws reaching for me.

I rolled to my knees, every move shooting a spike of pain through me. I let out a hiss of agony as I slammed my palms onto the grass, my fingernails digging into the soil beneath.

The limited magic from the land trickled into me like icy drizzle—it didn't have much, but it would have to do. Borrowed magic buzzed and waltzed on my skin. Five hundred acres of the land around me was bleached of color, scorched and blackened instantly. The weeds and grass withered.

This was another reason why I was better

equipped than Sy to fight Ruin's agents when outnumbered and needing a quick exit. Sy was a stronger fighter, but she couldn't absorb magic like I'd just done.

I hated to drain the land and leech its last magic, but I had no choice. I lowered my head. Probably every villain said the same thing.

"You'll never fucking have me again!" I roared.

Magic blasted out of me in a current of dark light, spearing the female Shrieker. It jolted like a puppet, a half-shriek tearing out of its mouth as my father abandoned his vessel. The male turned its scorpion legs and ran, but my dark light rushed over it, reducing it to a pile of ashes as well.

The wind picked up, sweeping the ashes through the dead weeds and grass before it stilled. For a moment, it was eerily quiet, then a cacophony of shrieks vibrated in the air.

The horde was approaching. I looked at the remaining corpse. I'd used all the borrowed magic to burn the two Shriekers. I had no more to erase the final evidence, and I didn't want to take more from the land. Every time I siphoned magic from any place, my soul grew blacker.

I trembled as the pain returned, my rush of adrenaline receding.

I tore a sleeve off my shirt and made a tourniquet around my wounded leg to slow the bleeding. Then I used the wolfman's discarded pants to clean up the blood on my leg, trying my best not to leave a blood trail as I fled.

The sun was setting, the last ray of sunlight getting into my eyes with its remnants of summer heat. I squinted to survey the contours of the land ahead, the twilight casting rusty gold light on the distant woods, as if the battle and killing had never happened here.

A song dinged in my head, calling me forward; the scent of magic beckoned me to go beyond the woods while my enemies' shrieks grew closer.

A horde was coming.

I half-dragged myself and half-limped toward the woods while holding my side to ease the pain from my cracked ribs. I put my weight on my good leg so I wouldn't bleed too heavily.

It felt like it took forever to cross the dim woods, every breath laden with pain, yet I dared not slow down, desperate to get clear of the Shriekers.

Sy wanted to take over since she could run faster, but I had a feeling that she should sit this one out. She drew way more attention than me and would court disaster.

I reached the end of the woods, only to stop cold. Panting, I pressed my forehead against an ash tree to catch my breath.

A field of weeds decorated with bones and skulls extended in front of me, cut short by broken columns and shattered walls.

"We can't turn back now," I said. "The Shriekers will be lying in wait."

Why can't we ever get a break? Sy said in dismay.

"At least you got your fix!"

Not exactly. It's like a cheap, watered-down drink. It's so hard to find a strong male to fuck and feed on.

I raised a fist. "Quiet."

Piercing shrieks and clattering approached from the other end of the woods. The horde had arrived. They were fast.

We should climb a tree and hide, Sy said, knowing that we were in no shape to fight.

Magic tugged at me from the ruin. As I looked over, something shifted.

The glamour dropped in front of me. A shimmer replaced the shattered, blackened walls. The spells had been so potent that at first sight I hadn't detected that they concealed a portal.

Not many beings could see through the disguise; even Sy wasn't able to tear off the glamour. But I was *the* magic eater; power attracted me like a shooting star.

The other side might be a trap too, Sy grunted, not happy that I pointed out what she was lacking.

"We don't have a choice," I said. "Fingers crossed that it'll be a place where we can hide from Ruin and his agents for a few days."

Sy made a show of crossing her claws.

I started to run again, dragging my wounded leg to cross the ruin, and threw myself at the shimmer. Sy yelped, ready for impact, as she still saw the broken wall.

After a terrible falling sensation, we were through.

I laughed as we alighted on the lush grass at the foot of a hill, gazing up at the radiant ivory tower in the distance.

Chapter Three

I watched in awe as mist and light swirled around the ivory tower. The scent of magic drifted like aged wine from across the hill. Even here, magic bathed us like the last strains of twilight.

If you're thinking what I'm thinking, Sy said, *I believe we've entered Mist of Cinder.*

The last immortal realm that Ruin had been so desperate to find.

While I was under his thumb, I'd tried my best to avoid searching for the realm, and his agents couldn't detect magic without me. I knew what would happen to the last magical realm and me if Ruin ever sunk his claws into it.

Now that I'd just bumped into Mist of Cinder,

would I lead Ruin to the last patch of magical land? I took a deep breath as a sudden burden dropped on my shoulders and chills slithered up my spine. I didn't want to be responsible for destroying Mist of Cinder.

We'll leave if Father breaches this place, Sy said.

I nodded. Without me, Ruin wouldn't be able to bleed this land dry.

Right now, let's settle in here. In Mist of Cinder, we'll grow stronger, Sy said, liking Cinder already, while I collapsed on the long, lush grass.

On this side of the hill, I didn't sense anyone in my proximity. My instincts told me that the Shriekers wouldn't be able to pass through the Veil even if they sensed or found it.

I sank deep into the grass. With the long stalks concealing my body, I closed my eyes for a nap to speed up my healing.

I wasn't sure how long I'd been out until Sy poked me awake.

"Why?" I asked, blinking my sleepy eyes, then the scent of stewed rabbit wafted toward my nostrils.

You need to feed, Sy said.

In the wake of the setting sun, a splatter of pink and orange splashed across the sky, twilight tinting the ivory tower. The long stalks of grass waved in the breeze, and magic rose from the soil, calling to me.

The delicious smell of stew wafted in my direction again, and my stomach grumbled.

I rolled to a sitting position, checking my injured leg. It'd stopped bleeding, and the wound had sealed while I regenerated in my sleep. My ribcage still throbbed in pain, but it was more like an irritation now. I'd had much worse.

I climbed to the top of the hill. The view in front of me took my breath away.

Blooming gardens encompassed shining buildings, houses, and shops, with the ivory tower shining like a jewel. To the far east, a verdant forest stretched, trees and blossoms waving in the wind. A large lake glinting like a vast gem dominated the far west.

This was the most beautiful place I'd ever visited, the air brimming with pure magic, wine, spring rain, and a flowery scent. I tilted my head as I listened to the sound of laughter and chatting that brought the new town to life.

It's the campus of a school, Sy corrected. *It's big.*

"Let's go," I said as I hid Deathsong, my dagger, within a shrub that bore pink flowers before scrambling down the hill.

Pressing myself against the walls and sticking to the shadows, I watched students my age stroll along the paths toward different buildings. Girls wore white tops, red skirts, and high stockings; boys had gray-and-blue jackets and slacks.

I'd need new clothes to blend in. Mine were in tatters.

When I spotted an older woman in a servant's uniform walking toward a russet building, dipping her gaze to the ground, I trailed after her. She passed by the framed golden letters "Jubilee Haven" etched on the wall and entered through a side door.

I waited for several seconds before striding toward the same entry.

It was magically warded. In fact, the whole three-story building was warded, but no wards could stop me. I turned the handle, offensive magic alighting on my fingertips. I brushed it off as if it were a spiderweb.

I slid into the building and closed the door behind me. Luckily, I didn't meet anyone, so no one stopped me. I gingerly crossed the hall and paused at the base of the stairs that led all the way down. From my experience, servants usually dwelled in basements, and no one guarded their humble quarters.

What kind of thief would be dumb enough to rob a servant?

The current one. Sy grinned, but she approved my thinking as I sprang into action.

I took the steps two at a time and reached the bottom floor. There were several rooms on either side. I headed left and pushed on the first door. It was locked. I could get it open, but it would take time and effort, so I moved on. I got lucky with the third door.

I slid into the room.

Just as I assumed, it was a servant room with a bed and minimal furniture. I went straight for the open closet. Three sets of male servant uniforms that were obviously two sizes too big for me hung on the rack.

With a sigh, I worked on shrugging off my blood-tainted, tattered shirt and pants and putting on the servant's uniform. At least it was clean. I also found a cord to tie the pants at the waist so they wouldn't fall off.

The servant had two spare pairs of shoes, so I took the liberty of inserting my bare feet into the nicer pair. They were an inch and a half too long, but it wasn't the time to be picky. I swiftly cleaned myself up a little to make sure no blood was left on me, then I wrapped my old clothes into a roll, snuck out of the room, and dumped my dirty clothes into the trash can at the other end of the corridor.

My stomach grumbling, I rushed up the stairs. It was time to hunt for food.

A plan formed. I'd pose as a new servant who came to the kitchen to ask for a full plate of food for my master. If the kitchen staff asked me which master, I'd scowl to intimidate them. Under usual circumstances, I always did my homework first to make things go smoothly. But right now, I was spent, and I needed fuel urgently.

I jogged faster, the scent of delicious stew nearly making me cry with joy. Not wanting to bump into anyone and raise suspicion, I avoided the main hall and detoured to the back of the kitchen, following the smell.

I paused at the double swing-doors, took a deep breath, and raised my chin, ready to dive in and demand a plate of food for my "master."

Just as I was about to shove the door open, I spotted a blur of movement in my periphery. Before I could react, a strong hand grabbed my throat, slamming me against the wall by the doors.

The impact knocked the breath out of my lungs. I snarled, my fists striking out, but they were both caught and strung up above my head. Next, I found myself glaring up at cruel eyes, a gorgeous face, and sensual lips.

My opponent was tall and well-built, dressed in a white button-up shirt and a pair of dark trousers. Silky blond hair flowed down to his broad shoulders.

"My, my," he purred, his lips curled up. "Look who I caught."

How had he gotten past both Sy and me?

We're spent, and we were distracted by the delicious smell of stew and cakes, Sy said, not even slightly concerned that a stranger had cornered us.

She peeked out and nodded in approval at his good looks and strong frame. She always had a weakness for powerful men.

"Who are you?" I demanded as I tried to even out my breathing. My heart rammed into my bruised ribcage.

"'Now that's interesting," he said, a predatory smile widening on his lips and sending a bad shiver to the nape of my neck.

I'd blurted out the wrong question.

He tilted his head and studied me like I was an intriguing pet. "I followed your trail. You vanished for a minute before reappearing again. I was almost afraid that you might slip through my fingers."

I frowned at him, as I hadn't felt anyone tracking me. Was I getting rusty, or was he too good?

"Why did you follow me?" I grated. "That's stupid."

"Stupid?" He let out a low chuckle. "No one dares to talk to me that way. I've killed for lesser slights. You obviously don't know who I am."

"I asked and you refused to tell me," I said. "Now let go of me. My master sent me to fetch food for him."

"Which master?" he asked, a taunting smirk dancing below his pale blue eyes.

Fuck, he was persistent!

"I'm not at liberty to say," I said, thinning my lips. "But if he learns that you interrupted me and delayed his mealtime, you'll get whipped. Let me go now, and we can forget all about it."

He grinned as if he'd just won a prize. "He'll whip me? That's kinky. Do you promise?"

Shit! He was toying with me, which could only mean one thing—he must be a *power* here. Just looking at his designer shirt and expensive shoes, anyone could tell that he wasn't some nobody.

This time, I might not be able to bluff my way out.

"I won't tell. I won't get you into trouble," I said, my voice softening a notch to show him my submissive side as I changed my strategy. "Let me go, please."

"What's your name, boy?"

I wasn't a boy, but I bit my tongue. I understood where he got the impression.

My short golden hair was curled like a horde of soft snails. Also, I was dressed in an oversized stolen male servant's uniform, and I spoke in a low, husky voice, as I didn't want to draw any more attention to myself.

"My name?" My voice remained husky. "Why do you want to know?"

"Don't be difficult, boy." He smirked. "You do have a name, don't you?"

Tell him your name, Sy urged. *He's a good mark and powerful. We haven't met such a quality. We can fuck him later.*

Quit fucking everything that moves, I scoffed.

"I'm Bob—Bobbi," I offered. "Now will you let me get on with my business, sir? It's urgent!"

"Little Bob, you smell good," he said and sniffed my scent deeply.

I always smelled good to monsters.

His nostrils flared. His irises dilated. His fangs popped out. My heart thundered.

Shit, he was no sir; he was a vamp—

"Today is your lucky day, little Bob. I usually don't ask my meal's name."

Faster than a shock, he sank his fangs into the side of my neck, piercing my throbbing vein. It dawned on me that he'd smelled my blood in the wind, lured by its scent and power, and tracked me all the way here before I could sneak into the kitchen to get some solid food into my stomach.

My blood flowed from my veins into his mouth. While he swallowed a mouthful, groaning in great satisfaction, panic clawed at the back of my throat. I shoved him, but he pinned me against the wall with his vampire strength.

The leech is going to kill us, Sy! I shouted in alarm.

Sy tried to break out of my skin, but somehow, she was subdued.

It's his venom, she said in dismay.

Even if she came out, she might not be able to overpower this vampire.

The double doors were suddenly flung open, and a male server stepped out of the kitchen, holding a tray. A big female with an air of authority followed him out.

The pair noticed us, and their eyes widened in alarm.

I writhed, indicating I was an unwilling victim and hoping they could lend me a hand.

They dropped their gazes quickly and bowed deeply. "Your Highness, have a good day!" they murmured before scrambling away down the corridor.

Shit! I was being fed upon by a vampire prince! In every world and every realm, vampires were always the worst predators, perching at the top of the food chain.

The female glanced back over her shoulder at the vampire prince in longing, as if she longed to replace me.

Be my fucking guest!

While I was thinking this bitter thought, pleasure rocked my body unexpectedly.

It isn't so bad now, is it? Sy purred like a feline, utterly forgetting that we were being fed upon.

When my father consumed us, it'd been like our essence being chipped away and our bone marrow being drained. Every feeding had left us completely hollowed out.

This opposite experience disarmed Sy. It didn't feel like being fed on, more like a fair trade—giving a pint of blood in exchange for incredible pleasure.

Perhaps I shouldn't blame Sy so hard. A vampire's bite was meant to disarm their prey; their venom in the victim's bloodstream offered a pleasurable experience. Sy was my primary self who had no sexual inhibition. She was probably a sex addict, even if she sugarcoated it as feeding.

Yet no matter how wonderous the pleasure was, it couldn't disarm me like it did Sy.

A cocktail of lust, fear, and rage washed over me, then my strength returned, pumping into my backbone, freeing my limbs from being paralyzed by the vampire's venom.

"Fuck off, leech!"

I heaved up my knee and rammed it into his nuts while my body still hummed with arousal from Sy.

The vampire prince yelped, not expecting his meal to break his spell, let alone fight back fiercely. It must be a first for him that he failed to immobilize his prey. In fact, he was so surprised that his fangs retracted from my neck. But I knew he wasn't just going to let me go. The deranged hunger in his eyes told me that he'd descend upon me again, and soon. My blood was too delicious for him to pass on.

"You dare?" he snarled. "Do you know who I am, boy?"

His fangs that had blazed white before he'd sunk them into my neck and broken my skin were now tainted red with my blood. I wanted to punish him and drag him down, but there was no time. I needed to get away from him right now.

"I don't know who the fuck you are, blood-sucker, and I couldn't care less," I said.

I blasted out my last reserve of magic taken from the land earlier at the vampire.

A gust of wind tossed him away from me, my hair whipping around my face. In the meanwhile, the double doors flew open, dish after dish sailing toward the vampire. Shouts rose from inside the kitchen as a fire broke out, shelves fell with utensils and jars of ingredients tumbling to the floor, and pans and plates darted through the door to attack my opponent.

"What the fuck?" the vampire prince cried out angrily.

He avoided most of the onslaught with his super reflexes and lunged at me. I dropped lower and dove through the doors, letting him grab empty air while flying plates and spoons zoomed over my head toward him.

The vampire cursed.

A clamor broke out in the kitchen as the chef and his team tried to locate the source of the chaos while endeavoring to catch flying pans and plates. They scowled at me when they saw me, then lifted their scowls and replaced them with looks of reverence as they spotted who was chasing me.

"Incoming!" I yelled my warning as I zipped through the space to avoid crashing into anyone. "Out of the way!"

I had to jump onto a long table to avoid colliding with a group of service people in uniform.

"Out of the fucking way!" the vampire prince bellowed at the kitchen staff, closing in on me.

As I ran across the table, I caught sight of freshly baked rolls in a large basket. I scooped up two of them and sailed through the open front door while commanding the last of the wind to slam the door in the vampire's face.

I was out of the kitchen, a roll in each hand. Blood still dripped from the tiny puncture wounds on my neck. My arms swung hard, my legs pumping as fast as I could manage. I wound up in the dining hall.

It wasn't dinner time yet. Still, a few teenage girls and boys in their school uniforms lingered. Their heads snapped toward me as I sprang toward the arched entrance. Before I charged out, I heard the girls volunteering the information eagerly.

"Prince Louis," a girl asked, "are you looking for the servant boy?"

"Prince Louis," another girl called. "He went for the main entrance. There he is!"

"Do you require assistance, Your Highness?" several chimed in.

I pulled strength from Sy. It was a trick between us; it would last only for a few seconds, but those seconds had saved my ass a handful of times.

Out of Jubilee Haven, I zoomed toward its back and ran past a building shaped like a squatting duck before I halted at the north side of a courtyard. In its center, five towering sculptures that represented different superior supernaturals guarded an ancient tree that bore white and blue blossoms.

A blue-haired girl, close to my age, sat on a bench not far from one of the sculptures that held a magic wand in his hand. She raised her gaze from a hardcover book and smiled at me. Then, closing the book on her lap, she pointed her wand toward an orange dome behind her.

"Go there," the witch said.

The shimmering letters "Pathfinder" swirled on the façade of the dome.

"Why did you help me?" I asked in suspicion, but I didn't wait for an answer, as I heard the quiet and swift footfalls of the vampire prince.

I shot into the dome and prayed it wasn't a tomb.

Chapter Four

"What's the first rule of Mist of Cinder?" The mature and sultry voice of an older female from one of the rooms floated to the hallway where I stood.

The building of Pathfinder turned out to be a maze of classrooms. I'd made a few turns and come to this section. Classrooms lined the corridor on both sides. Obviously, classes were in session, as most of the rooms were occupied.

Several students offered tentative answers, but they were all shot down by the teacher. I looked on. Both the front and back doors to her class appeared open and inviting. I snuck toward the back door, interested in knowing the first rule, or all the rules, as

I might stay in this place for a while before I'd have to move again.

I ducked low and slid into the back of the room when the teacher, who wore a bright pink dress, turned her back to write something on the chalkboard.

I sat behind the door, settling in and letting out a breath of relief. With a room of students confusing my scent, I doubted that goddamned vampire would be able to track me down and single me out.

"Weed out the weak," a girl said.

"The stronger has every right to crush the weaker!" a boy added.

Well, the rule wasn't that different from that of the mortal realm. Supernaturals just didn't sugarcoat it like in human society, where the greedy morons and hypocrites ruled.

I took a big bite from my freshly baked roll and barely chewed it before swallowing. I was starving. I should've grabbed some cheese and a bottle of water as well. But then, I'd been desperate to get away from that powerful bloodsucker.

"The strong rule the weak, as it's the natural order." The teacher stared at her pupils. Her pale silver eyes were so wide apart that they must constantly miss each other. Her ash blonde hair passed her slender shoulders, not covering her pointed ears. She was a fae. "Each one of you belongs to a house, so you'll have certain protection from the head of your house against stronger predators from other houses. But bear in mind, as freshmen, you're the bottom feeders."

That's good, Sy whispered. *We're strong. Let's prey on the weak, and we don't even have to apologize.*

When she apologized, she usually ate them.

The teacher waved an electronic tablet in her hand. "Now, why were you enrolled in the Shades Academy?" she asked. "Let me hear some good reasons."

"We're here to learn magic, spells, glamour, shifting, potions—" a serious-looking girl said dutifully.

"Stop quoting the textbook," a boy two rows behind her said.

Half of the class snickered.

"Being the bride to the prince heir of one of the most esteemed, powerful bloodlines," a redhaired girl said, her voice laced with confidence and privilege. "That's why I'm here, why all of us are here."

Other girls giggled.

"That's not why I'm here," a boy with spiky hair said. Was he a wizard? "It's so unfair; every girl wants to marry a prince."

"The school's byname is Brides Selection Academy, is it not?" the redhead continued, ignoring the spiky-haired boy. "I'm so in the right place, as I was born to rule by the side of one of the prince heirs. May the best woman win!"

The two girls sitting on either side of her nodded vehemently. They were the redhead's wingwomen.

A mating school? Sy perked up. *We're here to stay! I'll have my pick. No more warning me to be cautious, and no more slut-shaming!*

That last statement was aimed toward me.

"Which prince is your favorite, Lady America?" someone shouted.

The redhead laughed like a high-class lady. Well, she was one. "The winner who fights for me."

She thought she was the shit.

"Lady America of the House of Fae is correct," the teacher said. "Finding one's true mate is not a laughing matter. The corruption from the mortal realm has started to seep into Mist of Cinder. Magic is fading faster in the realm. It's our duty to do everything in our power to preserve it, and thus the Brides Selection is the solution to protect the last magical realm. Can anyone tell me why?"

"An ancient oracle predicted the chosen one born of powerful fated mates will bring back the wild magic of old to all five kingdoms," America said, flipping her red hair over her shoulder. "One of the prince heirs is destined to find his powerful fated mate, give birth to the chosen, fulfill the prophecy, and be anointed the High King of Mist of Cinder."

"A fairytale," someone murmured.

"It's not," the teacher said. "The realm is connected to the High King, but the seat has been vacant for a millennium."

"Little Bob!" the vampire prince bellowed from the hallway.

Shit! I nearly choked on a chunk of bread.

A few doors not too far away banged open one after another.

"Have you seen my servant boy?" the vampire prince demanded. "Short with blond curls. Everyone should recognize him with his two-toned freak eyes."

I scramble to my feet, pressed myself against the wall, and pulled the door closer to me to better conceal myself.

"Prince Louis," the fae teacher said in a revered gasp. "What an honor—"

Fuck, he was at the front of the class!

"I'm looking for my new servant boy, Professor Longweed," the prince interrupted rudely. "He tried to run away. Anyone who hides him from me will suffer my wrath!"

Chairs scratched. I could feel the class turning to look at the back. My heart rammed into my chest.

"If we see him, we'll report to Your Highness," several students promised.

"Prince Louis," America said in a honeyed voice. "I'd love to assist your search for your lost pet. And it'll be my pleasure to seize and return him to you."

"Quiet! I heard something!" the vampire prince called. "Huh, whose heart is beating so fast?"

He strolled toward the back of the classroom, whistling.

Shit! He could hear my rapid heartbeat above everyone else's. He was gunning for me!

I slid out of the back door, ready to burst out of the classroom.

The vampire was there in a blur and kicked the door shut to cut off my escape route.

"There you are, little Bob!" He stepped into my path with a smug smile. "I'd have gotten to you earlier if that little witch hadn't pointed me to the wrong building. When I came out of it to punish her, she'd already run away. It'd be a sad day if I let you get away, wouldn't it?"

He grabbed the back collar of my servant

uniform and yanked me toward him. I yelped and slapped his face with the remaining roll.

"Really, little Bob?" He sighed and swatted the roll away from his face.

He wrapped a strong arm around my waist, binding my arms to my sides and pinning me against him. His other hand seized my entire ear and dragged me to the center of the room by it. Obviously, my curly hair was too short, silky, and slick for him to grab.

I tried not to whimper at the pain while fighting to get him to release my ear. I had a low tolerance to pain, which made my days of torture at my father's hand even more insufferable.

The entire class glared at me, stunned and disgusted, as they'd just discovered that a servant had dared to sneak into their class.

"That hurts!" I yelled.

"Serves you right!" said the vampire prince, but he let go of my ear.

Instead, he grabbed my chin and lifted it for everyone to take a good look at me, so they could shame me.

Every angry eye trained on my wildly curly golden hair and my dirty bare feet. I'd lost the oversized shoes on the run from this damned vampire prince.

I pouted, hating to be the center of attention, but Sy preened. For her, there was no such thing as bad publicity.

"What are you doing in my class, servant boy?" Professor Longweed scolded. "Answer to Prince Louis and me humbly!"

I struggled to break free of the vampire prince's vise-grip. I tried to maneuver to bring my knee up to his nuts, but he expected it and pinned me against him. I lifted my foot to stomp on his, then I was suddenly lifted into the air as the vampire's hand clutched my throat and squeezed.

I gagged, trying to pry his hand off my throat.

He chuckled. "Our little Bob is a wild cat, utterly disrespectful and untamed."

"I'm not your fucking servant." I managed to wheeze my words out. "I demand you release me immediately, or you'll regret it!"

The class let out a collective gasp. I bet no one had ever dared to curse at the vampire prince right in front of his face.

"Will I?" he sighed. "Now you even deny my ownership. If you don't belong to my house, then which house do you belong to?"

"A good house!" I said.

The vampire chortled. The professor and her class all snickered on cue. Then I realized the first rule in Mist of Cinder. These people couldn't care less about being good.

"A powerful house," I amended.

The vampire prince arched an eyebrow and taunted. "Which powerful house, little Bob?"

"Fuck you," I said.

The class growled on behalf of the vampire prince.

"If I were you, I'd be very careful what comes out of your mouth next, little Bob," purred the vampire viciously.

He still held me in the air by the throat as if I were a goose. If he wanted to punish me, he could break my neck in front of everyone.

Fear bubbled up my throat, but I managed to put on a bored expression. It was futile to struggle, so I didn't bother; it'd only excite a predator like him.

"Allow me to show your insolent servant boy the consequences of slighting an heir, Prince Louis," America offered, flashing him a syrupy smile before narrowing her blue eyes on me like I was less than dirt.

He gave her an appreciative glance. The Fae chick

was a classic beauty with a creamy heart-shaped face and perfect full lips. Her reddish hair cascaded down her elegant shoulders in flowing waves. She could be one of those chicks who combed her hair a thousand times a day.

"I'd be honored to teach Little Bob a lesson with magic." The girls now fought over the task of punishing me.

Suckers must've thought my name was Little Bob.

Louis clicked his tongue in delight. "It appears that no one likes you, little Bob. However, I'm going to give you the chance to decide which house you'll join. Choose wisely, or I'll let those pups dole out harsh punishments on you. I'd hate to dirty my hands, as I've got a date tonight."

"What date? With whom?" I asked, waving a hand at the class. "These little sluts are all giving you moon eyes. They want to get fucked by you, especially that redhead."

My honest statement elicited hisses and snarls from almost everyone, and their teacher looked aghast, but Louis laughed, which sounded sensual, amused, and nasty all at once.

He turned to the angry class and snapped his fingers. "All right, newbies, have your fun and let our little Bob have a taste of magic. But remember not to damage him too badly, as I still have use for him."

He'd gone through this much trouble to chase and discipline a low servant like me. My blood must taste too good, or he'd have offed me already with his bare hands, even though he claimed that he wouldn't dirty his hands.

"My pleasure." America rose to her noble feet, purring for the vampire prince and hissing at me.

The entire class stood up, their hands out, aiming at me. Their teacher smiled and nodded in approval.

"Bring it on, little shits," I said.

"You're dead, servant boy!"

A fireball formed between America's palms, and I squinted at her. "Is that a firebug?"

She tossed the fireball at me with a smirk, aiming to make me bald while showing off her skill.

I could easily eat her fire then toss it back at her, tit for tat, but I restrained myself from being too aggressive and thus exposing myself, so I remained still. Only my eyelids fluttered a couple of times to acknowledge her offensive magic.

The fireball sank into my golden curls, probably tainting them red before vanishing. A few hot sparks fell on Louis's head and singed a strand of his blond hair.

"What the fuck? Watch it!" he snapped, his free hand swatting ash from his head.

"I'm so, so sorry, Your Highness." America widened her eyes and called out her apologies. "Let me try again."

I let out a low chuckle. "Nice try, fae chick. Next, you'll singe off the big bad vampire's eyebrows. He might want to keep them for his date tonight, so he can get laid."

Professor Longweed and the class gasped at my slight. This bunch weren't good sports.

"That's it, little Bob!" Louis announced. "I'm done protecting you."

He dropped me to the ground and secured me in front of him, using me as target practice for the students and a shield for him. "It's open season. Let's see what you got for little Bob. Do not disappoint me."

The students cheered, flinging their magic—fire, wind, and spells, mostly—at me all at once. The collective magic passed through me without leaving a ding. A couple of them tried earth magic on me, but their thorned vines withered before reaching me.

"Wow, look how powerful you little shits are," I

offered while trying my best to remain passive instead of absorbing their magic. "I'm impressed."

A low profile was the best way to live another day. No one needed to know that I could take their magic into me, cook it my way, then throw it right back at the original users, letting them have a good taste of their own medicine.

If they knew what I could do and word got out, Ruin would know exactly where to find me. Also, if I used too much of my ability, I'd leave a blazing magical bonfire for my father's agents to trace me.

Silence shocked the class until Louis broke it with his dry chuckle. "Aren't you full of surprises, little Bob?"

The students threw their hands up and shot their offensive magic at me once again. The spells fell off me like dust motes, but some went astray and hit Louis.

He raised his shield and snarled. "Cease fire, little shits!"

The assault on me stopped. The class glared at me, then stared at their hands in confusion, then glared at me again.

"It can't be," Professor Longweed gasped, staring at me as if she'd just discovered a rare bug. "I thought Echo, the null, was a myth, and here he is! The servant boy is a null who can neutralize and cancel magic. I'd love to study him!"

Like that was going to happen.

"Not going to happen. He's my servant, mine!" The vampire prince spun me and gave me a long onceover. "We had fun, little Bob. Now let's return to my house."

"I'm not going anywhere except the place I want to go," I said and rammed my fist toward his eye.

The vampire ducked at incredible speed, and I took the chance to burst into a run. I raced out of Pathfinder and laughed a little when I believed that I'd ditched the vampire prince.

The witch who'd pointed me toward the classrooms was no longer on the bench.

I didn't stop but sprang across the courtyard just as students started streaming toward Jubilee Haven. I needed more food, but I wouldn't risk being caught by the vampire prince again.

Stars filled the night sky, more vivid and brilliant than in the mortal realm.

I zoomed through the woods between buildings. Crystal witch-lights hung on the redwoods and white pine trees. I would return and get a couple of crystals for myself. But right now, I needed to put more distance between me and that vampire.

Then I'd need a new plan to find shelter and secure food for the night.

I looked over my shoulder to see if the vampire was still trailing me. Convinced that I'd lost him, I let out a gleeful chuckle, only to find my body slamming into a hard obstacle.

A clean male scent mixed with pine and winter rain hit my nostrils, powerful and intoxicating, before I jerked away from a broad chest of hard muscles.

"Watch yourself!" I growled, massaging my tender cheek.

"There she is," the male purred.

I narrowed my eyes and lifted my gaze from a powerful frame to a striking face that only existed in a dark fantasy until this second.

His face lit up. His lips tugged up, so carnal that it would stop an old lady's heartbeat. Younger women didn't stand a chance at resisting their wicked temptation. Yes, this male was temptation and sin incarnate.

Suddenly, I was not immune either. As if I had been struck by dark lightning, lust like I'd never felt before swirled to life and coursed through my heated bloodstream.

His expression changed; it was no longer amused

but stunned, as if the sky had poured out a meteor shower and trapped him in the midst of its flame, smoke, and destruction. Heat rose in his storm-blue eyes that were no longer like the cold winter sun.

We stared at each other, then before I knew it, my pussy was slick with wet heat and my whole body hummed with a burning need.

What the fuck?

Mate material! Sy peeked out in approval, then preened as the stranger's intense, dangerous gaze pinned us in place, as if he could see through me and sense Sy like no other could.

Woo, powerful! Sy tilted her head to study him further.

The longer I stood in his presence, the deeper my desire went. It was like my sexuality just awoke with the intensity of a thousand fucking suns. For the first time, I understood Sy's urge, even though I had no need for sexual feeding.

He's most delicious, isn't he? Let's fuck him, right here, right now, Sy urged, licking her lips. *Want me to do it?*

Fuck off, I told her.

She blinked. *I thought you'd be over slut-shaming me now that you've just found a fuckable male yourself.*

"Who are you?" the powerful male demanded, his deep, rich voice sending a shiver of renewed need down to my toes.

Even his voice had an effect on me. Before I knew it, I was beaming at him, my skin buzzing with pleasure at his rapt attention. Unable to help myself, I reached for him, and he let me, gazing at me expectantly, as if I was a delicious puzzle.

Before my fingertips touched his taut chest to explore him, a sudden gust of wind shuffled the trees around us and stirred up dried leaves and pine needles. A blur dashed toward me, then strong hands grabbed my shoulders possessively.

"Killian, I see that you're stalking my new servant boy. He's tried to run away from me twice today." Louis swept me off my feet and tossed me over his shoulder, all in a swift move.

I'd been so captivated by Killian that I'd forgotten everything else, so now I was caught in my pursuer's net again.

Louis shot toward the end of the woods before the stumped Killian could demand an answer. Trees and bushes blurred by as the vampire sped on, carrying me like I was precious cargo.

I couldn't kick him since he'd grabbed my legs, so

I pounded my fists into his back, but it was like hitting a giant rock and bruised only my muscles.

"Good massage, little Bob." He chuckled. We were out of the woods and under the starlit sky. "You'll need more training though to hit all the right spots."

One day, I'd let Sy out to finish him off, and then we'd see if he still fancied our massage.

"You'll regret kidnapping me, vampire!" I issued a threat.

"What if I give you a promotion in my house?" he offered.

What?

Let's hear him out, Sy advised. *We need to get a foot in the door here. This is a good place for us. If we aren't happy, we can always run.*

I stopped punching the vampire. "What promotion?"

"You'll be my squire instead of a servant," he said. "It's a very big promotion."

"Does it come with good pay and decent health insurance coverage without co-pay for every visit?" I asked, intrigued.

Not that I needed any health coverage, but I wanted to make sure that I wasn't being taken advantage of. I didn't want my new boss to be a cheap scumbag like some human employers.

"That can be arranged." But his voice was laced with disdain, as if talking about money was beneath him.

"Why squire? You aren't a knight, and you certainly don't look like one, sir."

"I'm a prince!" He sounded offended.

"So, you want me to carry your shield, accompany you to tournaments, and ensure your honorable burial if you're killed?"

"Your most important duty is to provide me with nutrition," he hissed.

I blinked. "You want me to hang out in the kitchen, swing my cock around, and order the chefs to bring you daily meals with sufficient protein and vitamin C?"

"You're the nutrition," he said shamelessly. "I'll drink your blood daily."

"Bloody hell! No way!" I shouted.

"We can do it the hard way or the easy way," he threatened. "For your contribution of blood, you'll receive good benefits besides my protection, food, shelter, and good pay."

"I don't need your protection, sir," I said. "There're beings much worse than you out there, but I can protect myself well. However, I'll accept food and accommodation. I also expect to get paid biweekly for being your squire."

He dropped me like a sack of potatoes, a magnificent maroon building looming ahead. We stared at each other. I massaged my stiff hip, and he narrowed his eyes in displeasure.

"There're beings much worse than me out there?" he demanded.

"You have no idea, sir," I said, shaking my head. "The universe is a big, scary place."

He snorted. "I'm one of the most powerful, terrifying superior beings in this realm."

"No offense, sir, but I'm not interested in whose dick is the biggest," I said, then hurried on at his scowl. "Let's get down to business then. You won't drink from me daily. My blood is very precious, and I don't give it away easily. We can go for once a week."

"Twice a week," he said firmly. "That's my final offer."

"Fine, but I must insist on you not taking more than necessary during each session, sir."

"You drive a ridiculous bargain, little Bob," he growled. "If other servants dared to be so insolent, they'd be dead at my feet by now."

He meant it. I should never forget for one second that he was a predator.

So are we, Sy chimed in. *We'll handle him.*

"You said you promoted me to squire," I argued. "Besides, I have a rare commodity that's worth more than gold." I pumped my fist to drive the point home. "I get to call the shots!"

"Do you now?" he asked drily.

"Being fed upon isn't my favorite," I said testily. "I can't believe that I'm even agreeing to this!"

"Then I must have one more test run and see if this commodity is worth all the trouble," he said, and he brought my wrist up before I could pull away and sank his fangs into my throbbing vein.

"What the—" Before I could ram my other fist into his face, he released me.

"You passed the test, little Bob," he said with a dreamy smile. "Now come."

He led me toward the maroon building inside a sleek steel gate and fence. That must be his lair.

Suddenly, a dark thought came over me. Sex predators roamed the human world since their society deteriorated two decades ago. Everyone was out for themselves now. The foundation of "do the right thing" had long since been shredded and left in the dust.

"One more thing, sir," I called urgently.

"What now?" he asked with irritation.

"Vow on your mother's soul you aren't going to molest me!"

"What the fuck?" he grated, then shook his head. "I'm not a little boy molester." I glared at him at the insult, as I wasn't a little boy. "I won't touch you even if you beg me," he added with a half-snarl. "And my mother has no soul. Now be very careful what comes out of your stupid mouth next, little Bob. I might be in a good mood today, but my patience is running thin with you."

I nodded. I had that kind of negative effect on people, but it wasn't entirely my fault. I had a terrible childhood.

"Sorry about your mom, sir," I said.

He was still better off than me. At least he recognized that his mommy didn't have a soul. I didn't even know who my mother was and didn't care to know. Whoever mated with the worst predator, birthed a monster, and left me for Ruin to consume daily wasn't worth two shits.

He braked before the gate to the maroon building, where the crimson words "House of Vampires" stood out above the frame of the twin doors.

Chapter Five

"Go on," Prince Louis said with a wicked smirk. "That's the house I rule. You'll live there as a member of my household."

The gated stone building in the center of a lush lawn occupied half of the street, a narrow high window in each room designed to admit minimal sunlight.

Everyone knew that the sun weakened vampires.

Vampires hung around the splendid building, many of them wearing students' uniforms. We'd passed a few who were patrolling the perimeter and moved like fast shadows. A human eye wouldn't spot them, but I wasn't exactly a human.

I could detect all supernaturals just fine.

The vampires in sight bowed to their prince before sliding their attention to me. As Louis purred his encouragement and urged me on, his underlings flashed mean smiles, as if they all expected me to fail big time and be tonight's entertainment.

I squinted, studying the house, and saw why the vamps thought I'd fall on my ass.

The building was heavily warded. The vampires didn't take their security lightly. Other than wards and spells, I could sense that the magical house was also sentient. It wouldn't accept an outsider. It'd do more than spit out an intruder, as it was the blood-suckers' first defense.

Not being given a list of the house rules, I had no way of knowing how the magical vampire house would decide whether to admit someone. But I understood magic, and no spells and wards could stop me.

The gathering vampires, including their prince, waited eagerly for me to make a big fool of myself and to get a good laugh. They hadn't a clue what I could do.

"You're the prince, sir." I glanced at Louis and insisted, "You go first."

He chuckled, not missing the sly calculation in my

eyes. The gate slid open for him automatically, and he strode through like he owned the land. I followed him gingerly, not meeting any trouble yet. The vampires' smirks didn't drop, which meant shit was coming.

We crossed the lawn. I liked the soft grass under my bare feet, and the wind sent a sweet, flowery scent from the cherry trees that adorned the landscape. As we reached the bloodstone stairs, the transparent metal doors swung open for the vampire prince, magic greeting him. He strolled in, very much at home.

I halted by the doors, tilting my head and regarding the red sheen of light over the doorway. I doubted that even the vampire prince could see the color of magic as I did.

Louis turned, wiggling a finger to beckon me forward.

"Come, little Bob," he said. There was an undertone of menace in his invitation. "We don't have the whole day, do we?"

Even though we'd struck a verbal deal, I was still an outsider in the vampire world. I knew that; the prince knew it too. There must be a ritual to initiate me into the house, but he wasn't doing it. The prince wanted to punish me for my bold bargain with him and intended to let his magic house put me in my place.

I'd once seen a local Chicago witch coven's magical house repulse and drive away humans, and when anyone still insisted on entering the house, it'd maim them. If the invaders carried on with sinister intent, the house would kill them.

Magical houses were all territorial.

"Chop-chop, little Bob," Louis called impatiently. "What are you waiting for?"

"Just taking a moment to enjoy the view and smell the cherry blossoms, sir," I said and jogged through the doors that stood open deceptively while the prince stood behind them.

No resistance. No rejection. It was as if I were a ghost. And then I was on the other side of the door, joining the prince.

A flicker of surprise flashed in his eyes before he frowned, then smirked again. He'd gotten his money's worth, as I'd proven to be more than met the eye. I hoped that he wouldn't get a bad, bold idea by sending me to do his dirty work or spy on his rivals, since if I could enter his house without being initiated, I could just as easily get into other houses.

The vampires around widened their eyes in surprise. Their grins dropped.

The interior appeared even more splendid than the exterior. The hall looked like a five-star hotel, yet more luxurious. The color tones were creamy white and soft gray. Large round columns in the lounge served as decoration while providing security coverage.

If enemies breached their house, the vampires could hide behind the columns while regrouping to take down their foes.

My gaze swept across the hall. An older vampire was playing a piano solo in the north corner. Two beautiful vampire women armed to their teeth stood behind an upscale front desk. A few vampires perched on the gray sofa under chandeliers, chatting quietly and sipping blood from glasses. The male vampires were dressed in suits and the women in gowns.

Every eye turned to their prince before snagging hungrily on me. They could smell my blood, which always smelled damn good to monsters. Sy bolted up, on high alert. As fatigued as we were, we'd have a hard time fighting off a horde of vampires if they all came at me at once.

Louis turned his hard stare on his underlings and snarled in warning, a crimson ring forming in his eyes, and the other vampires either averted their gazes or schooled their expressions to tone down their hungry looks.

The prince motioned for me to step closer to him, and I inched toward him. His hand lashed out, gripping my shoulder. His fangs slid out, glinting white under the chandelier light. Before I could shove him off or run back out of the door, he sank his fangs into the side of my neck. His venom pumped into my bloodstream at rapid speed as he attempted to mark me as his.

"What the fuck? This is the third time in a row! You need to chill!" I struggled while Sy moaned at the pleasure.

Louis retracted his fangs and sealed the two tiny wounds on my neck.

"Stop fucking fighting me, little Bob," he ordered. "I've marked you with my scent, which should warn everyone off. No one will dare to touch you, as you're *mine* now. Words will spread." He swept another warning stare across the hall. "They all know how I punish anyone who tries to poach my valuable possessions."

The vampires in the hall bowed in acknowledgement of their prince's declaration.

Louis clapped, and a blonde woman with a high ponytail dressed in a blue shirt and smart pants rushed forward, an electronic tablet in her hand. Clearly, she was an assistant.

"Your Highness." She bowed to the vampire prince before glancing at me.

"Here's my new squire," Louis said. "Make sure the boy bathes thoroughly. I don't want my meal to smell."

I glared at him. I'd been on the road a lot, running and killing the Shriekers and then running from him.

"You didn't complain when you sank your teeth into my neck, sir," I said in my husky voice.

The assistant blinked and looked at her boss for cues as to how to treat me, or maybe she was waiting for him to strike me down.

"See, our little Bob not only stinks; he knows no manners." Louis shook his head with a smirk. "You'll make sure he learns the rules, Drusilla."

I frowned at him. "What rules?"

He shot away at super vampire speed before his assistant nodded dutifully. "Yes, Your Highness."

"He's gone," I told her.

"Of course," she said. "Follow me, Little Bob."

Drusilla turned, not looking back at me, as she expected me to follow her.

"Actually, it's Bobb—" I didn't finish saying my real name, as a new idea hit me.

It'd work to my advantage if everyone mistook me for a boy. Ruin's ears and eyes reached far. If his agents or associates ever got into Mist of Cinder, they'd be looking for a girl me. I'd be a lot safer staying a boy.

I followed her across the hall to the elevators. We got in one of the two elevators, and she pressed B1.

"What's B1 about?" I asked. "Where exactly are we going?"

"B1 is the floor where servants reside," Drusilla said, not looking at me.

"Fine," I shrugged. I was good so long as I had a bed to sleep in and a roof above my head.

"Right now, we don't have a vacant room on the fourth or fifth floor, where the prince's close circle and squires take up residence. Feeders dwell on the third floor. The top floor belongs to the prince only."

"I don't mind staying with other servants," I said.

The elevator stopped, a ding sounded, and the door opened. I followed her out.

"You're only a half-vampire, aren't you?" I asked.

Her eyes tensed up. "Even you can tell?"

"Yeah. I haven't met many like you."

"They call a half-vampire like me a dhampir," she said, leading me down the long corridor.

"I didn't know vampires could reproduce the natural way," I admitted.

"Not in the mortal world. But here, very powerful vampires can. It's getting hard since magic has started fading." She sighed wistfully. "Our numbers have reduced greatly. The elders think magic will taper out in less than a century if we can't find a way to keep the magic in the realm."

My gut lurched. Had my father and I caused the magic to weaken in Mist of Cinder as well while I'd been draining magic from the mortal cities for Ruin for a decade?

"Our prince is the only natural-born pureblood vampire in centuries," Drusilla said, her eyes shining with longing and sadness. "There's hope if His Highness finds his true mate in the Brides Selection."

Was she in love with Prince Louis? She'd be in for a world of hurt then.

"Hope is a dangerous thing," I offered.

Guilt settled in my chest, weighing me down. As soon as Ruin was out there, no realm would be safe. And as long as I existed, magic wasn't safe either.

She glanced at me. "What are you?"

"The fuck I know," I said.

"Mind your attitude, boy," she warned without heat.

"Sorry."

"You might be half-human and half something else. No matter, you're still one step above humans. They're placed at the bottom of the food chain in the realm. Even so, few want to leave Mist of Cinder. Magic attracts them too, and they have a long life here." She then turned to frown at me and scowled deeply at my dirty bare feet. "Why am I telling you all this?"

"You want me to survive," I offered. "You aren't as mean as the others."

"Then you need to grow some sense, Little Bob. I hope you last. Maybe you will. I saw you barge into the house before Prince Louis initiated you. How did you do that? And the prince has never personally escorted any of his courtiers before."

"I'm his squire, not a courtier," I confessed. "I'll be carrying his flag, and when he's killed, I'll make sure he gets an honorable burial."

"Squire is just a fancy name for his entourage or top donors."

"Fuck! He didn't tell me that. He said it was a big promotion."

I looked sour. Drusilla laughed and shook her head. "Okay, here's the gist you need to understand. There are five kingdoms in Mist of Cinder, and each kingdom has a magical house in the academy where the Brides Selection is held. Currently, all the prince heirs, the most sought-after bachelors, dwell in the academy and are hunting for their true mates. Each house only admits their own kind unless the head of the house initiates an extra member of a different species into the house, including human servants. Basically, each house has a two-step authentication entry rule in place, except for the House of Chaos, where they take misfits, hybrids, outcasts from other houses, the unknown, and even a few demons into their ranks."

"Maybe I should head over to the House of Chaos then."

"It sounds easy to be initiated into the chaos house," Drusilla said. "But its house rules are stricter than those of other houses. Two terrifying ghosts guard the entrance diligently, one of them a poltergeist." She gave me a sharp look. "If you know what's good for you, you'll stay away from that house, especially their formidable prince. He has cold eyes and the coldest heart. You go into his house without permission, and you come out in a body bag."

"Shit." I widened my eyes. "I don't like the sound of that. Last time, I slept in a body bag to stay safe, and it got carried to a morgue at midnight. When a technician zipped open the bag, I blinked at him after being woken up. He gave a frightful scream and dropped to the floor, passing out just like that. A grown man!"

Drusilla rolled her eyes at me and stopped in front of a nondescript door. She pushed it open and gestured for me to enter.

"Lady first," I said as I started to practice being a boy.

"It's your room," she said.

I stepped in tentatively.

"Bathroom and showers are in the servants' common room at the left end of the hallway," she said. "I'll have a maid bring you a couple of new outfits to get you settled in."

"Thanks, Drusilla." I lingered in the doorway and blurted out just when she turned to leave, "By the way, do you know who the hell Killian is?"

She turned back to look at me. "You already met him?"

I nodded. "A few minutes before Prince Louis

snatched me in the woods. Killian demanded to know who I was."

"Were you in trouble?"

I bit my lip and gave her a puppy-dog look. "I'm always in trouble."

"Well, you don't want to get into trouble with Prince Killian of the House of Chaos, boy. If you offend him, even our prince won't step in for you, no matter how fond he is of you. The realm doesn't want another house war. The previous one almost leveled Mist of Cinder. The prince heirs are the most powerful beings, and every single woman wants to land one in the Brides Selection. But people like us who have no chance in the Selection will try every-thing not to catch the heirs' attention, which will only bring you a world of hurt."

"So true, Drusilla." I nodded gingerly. "I caught Prince Louis's eye, so he dragged me here to be a squire. But I've accepted my fate since he promised to pay me for my hard work and provide good health care coverage that might even include dental and vision."

Not that I needed it.

"This isn't the mortal realm, Little Bob. There's no such thing as health insurance."

I bristled. "The prince lied to me?"

She waved a hand dismissively. "You should count yourself lucky that he only lied to you. Anyway, if you see Prince Killian, even from afar, run as fast as you can. Got it? Stay under his radar."

Shit, I'd already caught his attention, but he'd caught mine as well.

He wants to fuck you. Sy perked up. *As do you. There's strong chemistry between you two—*

I flushed. *We don't want to fuck a prince.*

Liar, she crooned. *He's very powerful. A wet dream for us to fuck.*

"You've got a talent, Little Bob." Drusilla sighed and walked off. "Don't waste it."

I closed the door, turned on the light, and took in my small room that had basic furniture with a bed. I didn't need much. As long as I wasn't constantly being hunted by Shriekers, I counted it as a blessing. Having no belongings only freed me. I didn't grow attached, and I could leave at any second with the clothes on my back.

I strode toward the one-pane window to check my reflection in the glass—my cheeks were round with vibrant youth, my lips full and pale. My two-toned eyes, one green and the other sapphire, so different from Sy's violent golden ones, didn't look so distinguished in the dim light.

I touched my pale golden face dusted with a few freckles like stardust. I still couldn't see myself as a boy, but my low, husky voice and the messy, soft golden curls piled on top of my head might've given everyone the wrong impression.

Or it could be my natural camouflage that misled everyone. I was a born chameleon.

"I have to be a boy from now on," I told Sy.

Sy grinned. *You got this.*

"If they find out, it'll be shit. These supernatural aren't nice folks, and they're dangerous."

As are we, Sy offered. *And we eat them.*

Chapter Six

I'd scrubbed myself clean in the servants' public bathhouse last night. I'd waited until everyone had gone to bed. I'd also found my way to the kitchen and eaten so much that I almost popped.

Then I'd gone to bed, binding my breasts and sleeping in clean clothes.

I sighed in contentment and dug my nose into the pillow, shutting out the faint light coming through the small window. The servants' quarters were one floor below the ground, but we still got a window overlooking the cherry trees and lavender bushes outside.

Something prodded my ribs. I wiggled away and burrowed further toward the wall.

"Little Bob," a voice called.

Why couldn't they just forget about me and let me sleep a couple more hours? I ignored the calling and folded the pillow to cover my ears. But then someone tugged my pillow away by force.

"Bob! Little Bob!" a deep voice bellowed against my ear.

Arrgh!

I drove my elbow back but hit empty air. On instinct, I bolted up. I hadn't extracted Deathsong, my dagger, from the hill. I was planning to do it at some point. With no weapon at my disposal, I grabbed the blanket, pressed it against my chest, and found myself peeking up at the sneering face of the vampire prince.

"Why me?" I asked, lifting a hand to rub the sleep away from my puffy eyes. "What are you doing here?" I demanded before adding "sir" in a rush.

He peeled his lips back in a snarl, not pleased at me questioning him. I scrambled back from him at the sight of his fangs, my back hitting the wall.

"Cool—calm down." I'd almost said "cool your tits," which would get him to backhand me.

He pointed two fingers at his eyes, which were narrowed to slits. "This is my calm version."

"I humbly think you're in the wrong place, sir. This is my room."

"No longer," he said confidently. "You're being relocated to my floor, so I'll always have immediate access to you."

My brows creased. "Is that necessary?"

"Yes," he snapped. "You have no sense, little Bob. I won't take the risk of your untimely demise due to your idiocy."

Fuck, he really liked my blood.

"But sir, you live on the sixth floor," I offered, licking my parched lips. "I'm afraid of heights."

"No more excuses!" he said. "C'mon, let's get moving. Pack your stuff!"

"I have no stuff," I said.

"Good. Then let's go."

I immediately regretted speaking too quickly.

"Sir, I'm sorry that I misspoke," I said. "I do have some stuff to pack. Maybe you can wait outside and—"

"Nonsense. Leave it behind. Drusilla can pick it up for you."

I bit my lip. "But I need to clean myself up first. You said you didn't like your squire smelling and bringing shame to you."

"I don't give a fuck about being shamed. And who dares to shame me?"

"But sir—"

He gave me a onceover, appreciation glinting in his eyes. Then he leaned in to sniff my scent. I ducked, but there wasn't enough space, and he ruffled my curls. I swatted his hand away. He only chuckled.

"You've cleaned up nicely, and you smell delicious," he said. "Water, food, and rest can do wonders. I've provided all three for you. Now it's time for me to have my breakfast."

Alarm shot up my spine.

"Let me go to the kitchen to fetch you something to eat right away, sir!"

"You're my breakfast."

"But you had my blood three times yesterday! Our deal is twice a week!"

"Yesterday was but a sampling—an appetizer. Today will be counted as a formal meal." He stepped toward the door without looking back at me. "No more stalling or I'll backhand you and inflict pain on you. You don't want that, do you?'

"No, sir," I said, stuffing my feet into a pair of new shoes and following him out.

My uniform was wrinkled, but if the prince didn't mind shame, then why should I?

"Where are we going, sir?" I asked uneasily.

"My private feeding rooms. You need to get used to me drinking from you in different settings. But in the future, I'll mostly take your blood in my suite."

"Uh, sir." I cleared my throat. "I think it's best if I have my breakfast first, or I won't provide good nutrition for you. You won't enjoy it if I faint due to my hunger while you drink from me." I then snapped to attention. "Allow me to report for duty after my breakfast, sir. I'll make sure to eat an iron-rich meal."

"Relax, squire," he said lazily. "Drusilla will bring your breakfast to the feeding room."

Fuck.

I sighed. I couldn't get out of it then. I'd tried. Might as well just get it over with so I could get on with the rest of my day. I bowed my head, hunched my shoulders, and trailed after him in defeat.

Don't worry, Sy offered. *We'll get through this. It won't be too bad.*

She liked the pleasure the feeding brought. I hoped she wouldn't be reduced to a junkie.

We'll stop him if he goes too far, she added with a low chuckle. *When he meets my fangs, we'll see who's *feeding whom. We'll give him a nasty surprise and laugh at the look on his handsome face.*

We got into an elevator, and Louis smiled at me —his food—fondly. I didn't smile back. I doubted any meat on the plate would smile back at the one about to eat it.

The elevator stopped at the fourth floor, and the prince led me like a butcher leading a sheep to an artfully decorated banquet room.

Feedings were already going on in the hall. Over a dozen vampires had their fangs buried in their human donors' necks or wrists. Some kinky ones were sucking from young human women's inner thighs.

On a raised stage, a lovely redheaded woman was playing the violin passionately.

It was sickening.

As soon as I stepped into the hall after the vampire prince, all eyes snapped in our direction. Prince Louis dragged me out from behind him, slung an arm over my shoulder, and pinned me to his side. I wanted to shrug him off but decided against it at his warning look.

I didn't need a mirror to see how my face had paled.

Every vampire stared at me with intense hunger;

some of them abandoned their feeding to focus on me. They could smell my potent blood that was like nothing they'd ever tasted. My divine blood was irresistible to monsters.

Half of them rose to their feet, their fangs flashing crimson. A red ring formed and glowed in every vampire's eyes. One nod from their prince and they'd all descend on me like bloody vultures.

My heart pounded, my eyes turned hard and inhuman, and my sweaty palms pressed against my thighs.

A cold, sharp smile formed on the vampire prince's face but didn't reach his pale blue eyes.

He turned to me and quirked an eyebrow. "Not impressed, little Bob?"

"I didn't fucking sign up for this," I said, my voice and face devoid of any emotion.

I was most dangerous when I had a blank face while Sy was most lethal when she smiled sweetly.

One wrong move from the vamps and I'd suck the magic out of this place and collapse the House of Vampires. And with the magic I took, I'd destroy as many vampires as I could but save Louis for last. I'd set Sy on him to shred him to ribbons.

Even if I survived the battle, I'd have to leave Mist

of Cinder, the last haven for me, with more hunters on my heels.

I stood as still as an ice statue. I would not act rashly, but I was ready to react at a moment's notice. After years of existing on the brink of death, my survival instinct had trained me to read the room first. But once I was on the move and turned into a killing machine, no force could stop me. Sy and I wouldn't hesitate, and we'd slaughter any living things in our war path.

The vamps thought I was prey? They had no idea what kind of predator they'd brought amidst them.

"Of course not, little Bob," Louis said, his voice booming loud enough for every vampire to hear. "I parade you to show everyone whom you belong to. You're exclusive to me. Anyone else who brings their teeth near you will be severely punished, and anyone who dares to take a drop of your blood will suffer my wrath and beg for death."

The vampires bowed to their prince and resumed their feeding with less zeal, their hungry gazes still trailing me, as if they were imagining their meals were me.

I shuddered.

"They can look but not touch?" I asked.

"Exactly." Louis smirked in satisfaction. "You really think I'd share you?"

"Who knows what runs through your vamp mind," I grunted.

He raised his knuckles and cuffed the back of my head. I yelped. I was a notch too slow to duck.

"Sir, all the blood donors seem to be humans," I said as he led me deeper into the hall. "I don't see any supernatural feeders."

"Humans are our primary food source," Louis explained. "Supernaturals are like a delicacy. The new law forbids us from forcefully feeding on any supernatural that belongs to the other houses, unless we want to break the truce. Also, it's less complicated to feed on humans, as they don't fight back. It's a great deal for the human blood donors in the realm. Other than getting paid, they'll have a prolonged life, not to mention the pleasure they can't get anywhere else."

"You're talking about junkies." I stared at him hard. "And I'm a lone supernatural who hasn't found a house to protect me, so you took advantage of me, sir."

"If I were you, I wouldn't talk back to my superior like you are my equal," he growled. "I saved you from the life of a petty thief." He paused to ponder for a second while regarding me. "You don't know what kind you are, do you? You have no house to join except mine. So, quit bitching and be grateful that I'm offering you protection and shelter while you're under the contract."

"I get the shorter end of the stick," I insisted. "We need to renegotiate the contract."

"Don't be stupid," he said and steered me toward a secluded room at the end of the hall.

The private room had landscape paintings on the wall above the fireplace, live plants in the corners, and a large sofa in the center.

A variety of dishes—scrambled eggs, sausage, bread, and fruits—were spread out beside a pot of steamy coffee on the table.

My eyes going wide in glee, I dashed past the prince, nearly bumping him to the side. I squatted to pour myself a mug of coffee, adding half a glass of cream and five spoons of brown sugar. I heard that only serial killers drank pure black coffee, so I made sure never ever to drink black coffee again.

I took a long swig of the coffee, smiling, before I spotted a smoked chicken leg and went for it.

"Table manners, little Bob!" Louis shouted just as my teeth tore a strip of chicken meat into my mouth.

I glanced at him then at the table, noticing

another empty mug. I nodded, put down the remaining drumstick on the plate, and poured coffee for the prince. If he drank the coffee, he wouldn't need blood, right? Who drank blood in the early morning anyway?

"For you, sir," I said respectfully.

I'd chewed the meat in record time and swallowed it before I opened my mouth to speak. I had manners!

I pushed the mug of black coffee a bit further from my side, hoping the prince wouldn't notice the grease left on the handle by my fingers that held the drumstick.

"I'll have to let Drusilla teach you etiquette." He rubbed his temple, as if he had a headache, and sighed.

"No need, sir," I said after swallowing a mouthful of bread that I barely chewed. "Education costs money. And I have enough street smarts to last me a lifetime."

"It's necessary in my court!" he grated, settling down on the sofa beside me, too close to me. "And let me fucking worry about money and resources. I'm a billionaire ruler."

I inched my ass away from him and pointed at those expensive chairs on the other side of the radius nesting table. "There're enough chairs around."

Some folks were just annoying. I'd once snuck into a theater that played an afternoon action movie. There were hundreds of empty seats, and the next sucker coming in just had to sit right next to me.

"We don't need to sit next to each other, sir," I offered honestly.

"How dare you give me directions, squire?" The prince smacked me in the back of my head, again, too fast for me to react, but then I was eating.

I yapped, and he hissed, "No more nonsense," and sank his fangs into my neck.

I didn't fight him off. It was coming sooner or later anyway.

His fangs dug deeper into my veins, and I felt my precious blood flowing into him. My skin tightened, then tingled. Pleasure rippled within me, and Sy latched onto it, drinking it all in. She moaned instead of me, wanting to fuck badly. I had to give it my all to rein her in, so she wouldn't break out of my skin and land on Louis's lap.

As he kept drinking from me greedily, the pleasure increased, dancing on my nerve endings. He gripped me to him, and I reached out, about to trace my greasy fingers across his taut chest, not caring that I would ruin his expensive designer shirt, only to stop at the last second. I folded my arms across my chest, hugging myself, and put a stop to my foolishness.

Yet I couldn't stop Sy's lustful moans from tearing out of the back of my throat.

Growling, the vampire prince held me tighter, drawing blood from me slowly now. His lust and heat warmed my skin, his hand rubbing up and down my shoulder and forearm intimately while his other hand cupped the back of my head.

"Enough," I said.

He broke the contact, his fangs retracting, and his pale blue eyes were still shining.

"This is unnatural," he murmured to himself. His gaze cut to me, roving over me slowly and sensually. My breath caught. Despite his vile attraction to my blood, he was gorgeous and sexy in every way. "I've never felt this way before." He shook his head. "It's not right. I should not crave your flesh. I was never into men, let alone boys, and I'm not planning to start now."

Even if he was into a male, he wouldn't choose this path. All the prince heirs were competing to find their fated mate to conceive the One foretold by the oracle. None of them would let their lust get in the way of their ambition.

"Are you done, sir? Can I leave now?" I asked while part of me didn't want him to release me.

"I haven't even started," he growled. "I just need to arrange something else, so I won't slip and make a fucking mistake."

He pulled out an electronic tablet from his pocket and typed something on the screen. Then he tossed it to the middle of the sofa, dragged me to him as I nearly fell onto his lap, and grazed his fangs against my wrist.

The vampire prince was no gentleman. He craved my blood and flesh, but he wanted to make sure not to give in to temptation and wake up regretting having fucked a servant boy.

Part of me was disappointed, but the last thing I wanted was for Louis to find out I was a girl.

A knock sounded on the door. Drusilla swung it open and escorted two gorgeous blondes into the room. The prince seemed to have a thing for blondes.

Drusilla's gaze darted to Louis, longing in her hazel eyes. It cooled when she glanced at me. She bowed, withdrew, and shut the door behind her with a tight expression.

The two women made a beeline toward Louis,

swaying their hips for good measure while stripping themselves on the way, so smooth that I had no doubt they'd done this too many times. Their dresses and bras scattered on the floor. Then their panties dropped to their feet as well, their breasts and pussies bared. One of them was completely shaved like a bare turkey; the other had pubic hair curled around her pink pussy.

"What the fuck is going on, sir?" I inquired, my face flushing. "I don't want to be a part of this."

Louis barely gave them a glance before he fixed his gaze on me.

"You *are* a part of this, little Bob," he ordered. "You're my squire."

The two women were on him the next instant. They unbuttoned his shirt. Then Blonde Number Two moved to the back of the sofa and massaged his bare chest from behind, her perky breasts rubbing his blond head erotically. I had to admit that the vampire prince had a nice chest, all taut muscles and smooth as silk. He was gifted with great abs that didn't even fold or wrinkle as he lounged on the sofa.

Blonde Number One batted her lashes and zipped open the prince's fly. His cock sprang free. It was long, thick, and hard as a rock. She gave it an appreciative study before bending her head and taking it into her parted lips. The prince sucked in a breath and sank his fangs into my wrist.

He sucked me, and she sucked him, running her mouth up and down his shaft eagerly.

I shoved down a moan of pleasure caused by his venom.

"Will you hurry up please, sir?" I asked in a husky, surly voice. "You've had enough of my blood! Now this is taking too long."

The women stared at me, stunned at my boldness and impoliteness.

Louis lifted his lips from my wrist and growled, not pleased that I'd interrupted his enjoyment. "You have some place to go, little Bob?"

"I don't want to see you get sucked," I said as I lifted my chin stubbornly.

"Is that so?" he asked, a wicked smirk forming on his lips. "You want to see me fuck then."

He pulled Blonde Number One's head off his cock by her hair and commanded her, "Sit on me. Little Bob wants to see how I fuck."

The blonde climbed onto the sofa and straddled him, her pussy rubbing his length, but they hadn't joined yet.

"That's not what I said," I argued, yet I couldn't

tear my eyes away from their act. "I want to get out of here, sir."

"Can't take a little heat, squire?" Louis taunted as he licked the last trace of blood from my wrist; it was so intimate and sensual that I shivered, especially as I watched him buck up his hips and thrust into the blonde's pink flesh.

She arched her back and screamed in pleasure, her hands cupping her own breasts. The prince thrust in and out of her rapidly, his blue eyes fixing on me instead of her. He was getting off with me watching him.

"Have you fucked a woman before, little Bob?" he purred.

"No!" I grimaced. "It's gross. I don't like fucking."

Louis smirked. "Maybe you couldn't get any girl with your tiny dick?"

The two bimbos threw their heads back and laughed.

I glared at him. I didn't need to be insulted just because he didn't like his reactions to me. I bet he thought it was beneath him to be drawn to a servant boy.

"Why would you say something so insane?" I scolded him.

The bimbos gasped. No one talked to the fearful, powerful prince this way, but I'd had enough.

"You." He jerked his chin at the blonde in his lap. "Go give little Bob a treat while I fuck your friend."

She pouted while he plucked her off his length roughly and grabbed the other blonde who'd been massaging his neck and the half of his face that she could reach with her big boobs. He flipped her over to this side, bent her over, and nudged his cock at her entrance. He rubbed the head of his cock along her slit, as if showing me the ropes, before driving deep into her.

Then he started pounding in and out of her pussy repetitively. The woman moaned loudly for the whole world to hear. The wet sound of flesh slapping flesh grated on my nerves. Heat emitted from Sy, warming my face in an uncomfortable way. She wanted to join the threesome. She thought she could do better than the two bimbos.

I hissed, reining her in, and shook my head. Sy was too primal.

"More! Your Highness, yes, more! It feels so, so good!" Blonde Number Two screamed in pleasure, but the prince wasn't paying attention to her.

While he screwed her mechanically, he looked on

with more interest as Blonde Number One came to harass me.

"My little darling virgin," she crooned.

"Fuck off," I told her.

Louis laughed and thrust harder into Blonde Number Two, getting off on the game.

"Don't worry, Little Bob," Blonde Number One offered sultrily, about to cup my groin. "We're going to have a blast!"

I shoved her away, and she tumbled into the prince and her friend. Louis withdrew and remained standing since he was very strong, but the two bimbos tangled on the sofa then slid to the ground.

"The stupid boy's got some strength," Blonde One complained. "And he's so rude!"

"You're being rude, little Bob," the prince said. "You don't want to fuck, then don't fuck. But come closer. I need to have a drink from your neck while I fuck them both. Your blood makes me hard as a rock."

"Fuck it! You already took more than you should have," I said bitterly. "And now I'm dizzy. I'm not going to take more abuse, sir. I'm getting the fuck out of here."

No more free porn? Sy asked in disappointment.

I grabbed the basket of rolls, tossed two peaches

into it, and threw the door open. A horde of vampires gathered outside, fucking frantically and drinking at the same time. Their prince taking my blood had caused a feeding frenzy.

I froze for a second before I kicked my way through, then I put on my top speed to zigzag amid the entwined bodies and zoom across the hall toward the exit.

"Come back, little Bob!" the prince bellowed behind me. "I'm not done with you!"

Chapter Seven

When I was off duty from being the vampire prince's favorite walking blood bag, life in the House of Vampires wasn't all dark, even though danger followed me everywhere.

All those leeches craved my blood more than any other's. Their prince had warned them off me, but some younger vamps still lost control and came after me. Louis had had to kill two of his subjects to set an example within the first week. I now mostly went out during high noon when the vamps were the weakest.

I'd gone back to the hill and withdrawn Death-song. Vampires were sneaky, and I felt safer carrying a weapon around in case they jumped on me when I least expected. I'd lingered near the portal as long as I could to make sure none of the Shriekers got in. The Veil would prevent them from breaking in, but nothing was guaranteed in this world, so I'd never let my guard down.

Louis liked to have me around. I amused him. He brought me everywhere he went along with his security detail, which was required since he was the prince heir, especially when he left the academy grounds.

He went to bars and strip clubs a lot, one of his vices. I wouldn't complain about exploring different scenarios as long as he didn't make me watch him fuck or try to get a bonus drink from me. Sometimes, I served more like his wingman than his squire. No chicks who were sane would pick me over him. I made him look damn good.

As his squire, I got to dress in a white wool tunic and nice pants, the best material I'd ever worn. Drusilla dressed even better. She donned an exquisite silk gown with a belt from the shoulder to her hip, like the ancient Greek women. One time, I pulled at the fabric around her waist just to feel the material— I appreciated the fine things in life even though I hadn't been given any good stuff—and she swatted my hand away with a scowl on her face. I bet if the prince did the same, she'd throw herself at him and beg to be fucked.

Other than the prince, she was mostly in charge of me. She prohibited me from wearing a wrinkled outfit and unpolished shoes, saying I'd bring shame to His Highness.

"It's not like the prince wears my wrinkled clothes; I'm wearing them. So how can I bring shame to him?" I argued.

"How dare you think the prince would wear a servant's clothes?" she scolded.

Drusilla was not always unkind to me. She was just stuck up, like everyone else. The whole realm was about power, then getting more power.

"What we do and say reflects on the prince!" she added.

"That's a lot of responsibilities," I said. "And if all of what we say and do reflects on the prince, he'll look like a piece of shit."

Drusilla tried to hit me, but I ducked.

The vampire prince and his entourage, me included, strolled through the woods toward the Jubilee Haven, the main dining hall for all students and faculty, one of my favorite haunts. Food comforted me. I'd put on some good weight after being in the realm for a week.

I sidled up to Louis at his summons, trying to match his long strides with my own sprints. I had shorter legs, if he hadn't noticed already, but he didn't care, as selfish as he was. But at least I wasn't panting due to years of practice being on the run. If I sweated, panted, or my heart pounded too hard, the scent of my blood would become even more potent. The last thing I wanted was to tempt the prince at my own expense.

"How dare you say that I'm not a good, diligent student!?" Louis growled at me.

I could feel holes burning into the back of my head as the guards scowled at me. They didn't like it that I had a mouth on me. They also craved my blood, but they had more discipline. I bet that they hoped their prince would get bored of me and toss me aside one day, preferably sooner rather than later, so they could all swarm me, draining me dry.

I'd prayed for the sunlight to toast the vampires so I could sleep longer in the morning, but the local vampires were much stronger than their brethren in the mortal realm and thus could withstand the morning sun. Only they couldn't run around under the direct sunlight at high noon.

"But sir." I gazed up at the prince. He was dressed as usual—a white button-up designer shirt with expensive slacks that hugged his powerful legs. "Didn't you say you liked me to speak my mind? You said it was quite refreshing."

"Now you keep track of my words?" he demanded.

"Only the important ones, sir. I also write things down, including when you take my blood, for our records, even though I have a photographic memory."

He growled.

"Having a photographic memory isn't all blessing," I offered in a hurry. "I'd rather unsee many things and erase bad memories." I gave him a meaningful look, as I really wanted to erase the ones when he banged two chicks at once.

Sy, on the other hand, voted to keep them as a stimulation for her next feeding, so she could compare notes. We'd always been on the run in the past and hadn't had much chance to access the internet, or Sy would've spent all the time watching porn.

"What makes you think I'm a bad student?" He

still sounded irritated, like a belligerent puppy who wouldn't let go of a bone.

"I checked your schedules, sir. You never follow them. You skip a lot of classes. Other students would've been expelled."

"Dare you judge me, little Bob?"

"No judgment here, sir. I swear on my mother's black soul," I said huskily. "What I was saying is it's good to be fucking powerful in the realm. You can stomp anyone lower than you like a bug and then walk away with a career criminal smile on your face."

He nodded before narrowing his eyes on me, as he couldn't decide if I was complimenting him or being sarcastic.

"Shut up," he said just as a raven appeared out of nowhere, diving toward me at a sharp speed, its claws out. I moved in a flash and ducked behind Louis.

The prince's hand lashed out, faster than committing a sin, and clutched the raven's neck before the guards could shoot forward to shield their prince. I peeked out from behind the prince's broad back. The black bird stared straight at me, darkness swirling in its eyes.

Shit! It carried Ruin's signature.

How had it followed me here? Had Ruin built other creatures besides Shriekers since I'd fled? He hadn't needed to use others when he had me. My father could possess his foul creatures. A chill slithered up my spine. My heart pounded. If Ruin had spotted me through the raven, I wouldn't allow him to spy further. And if he hadn't, I wouldn't allow the raven to report back.

A hidden silver needle slid into my hand from my wrist, and I hurled it into the raven, piercing both eyes from the left angle before anyone could stop me.

I'd stolen the needle from a boutique bookstore at the edge of the campus commercial district. The bookstore sold weapons in the back of the shop, borrowing the idea of "knowledge is a weapon."

Two vampire guards, one of them the captain, lunged at me and threw me to the ground even after I'd raised my hands in surrender to show them that I'd meant their prince no harm. My jaw hit a rock on the hard dirt, which made me bite my tongue. Blood seeped into my mouth, and I pressed my lips together hard so no vampires would smell a drop of my blood.

With the guards on either side of me pinning me down, I still managed to tilt and lift my head to check out the raven. A breath of relief left my nostrils as I saw its limp body in the vampire prince's strong hand. Black blood streamed from its eyes, tainting its shiny black feathers and pooling in the space between the prince's thumb and forefinger.

"What the fuck, little Bob?" Louis snarled.

I swallowed my own blood before answering from the ground. "It was a spy!"

"How do you know?" he demanded.

"It was trying to attack you, sir," I said. There, I'd tried to shift his attention.

"Is that why you used His Highness as a shield?" snarled the captain, whose name was Gunnar—a bad name. "Where's your loyalty, you little shit?"

"The prince can handle himself well," I said. "He did, didn't he? And what use would I be to the high sir if the raven raked me blind? Did you see the size of its claws?"

"It might be a spy from the House of Mages or even the House of Chaos," Louis grated, a dark, pissed-off look on his face. "The Shifter House hates us more, but they're more straightforward than Cade and Killian."

"Sir! Gunnar still has his big foot pressed on my back, and the dirt is getting into my mouth!" I called. I could throw off the guards, but it was best that they let me go by their good will.

Louis waved a hand impatiently. "Release little

Bob. I don't want to hear his constant bitching. That boy is a nuisance."

He tossed the raven at a guard. "Take it to the witches on our payroll and find out if this creature was a familiar from any house. We'll get to the bottom of this!"

"Yes, Your Highness," the guard said, bowed, and took off.

Gunnar lifted his foot reluctantly, and his pal released my wrists that were pinned behind my back as well.

A rush of wind went under me, trying to pull me up.

Air magic.

In Mist of Cinder, powerful vampires were graced with the air element, unlike their weaker counterparts in the human realm, where centuries of technology had suppressed magic. When magic felt unwelcome, it slipped away.

Louis was one of the most powerful immortals, but even he didn't flaunt his magic often, since it would drain his reservoir.

After all, magic was no longer in endless supply as in the good old days.

That was one of the reasons that the heirs were all in a race to find their true mate and hopefully conceive the One, who was prophesized to bring back the wild magic of old, so the realm could have endless magic again.

The prince had forgotten that no magic worked on me, or more likely he thought he was special. I didn't want him to lose face in front of his minions, especially since he would for sure take it out on me, so I acted like I was yanked up by his air magic and was at his mercy.

"I'm going to prove you wrong, little Bob." The prince sneered at me.

"But sir, I didn't do anything wrong," I objected, picking a couple of sticks and dried weeds from my tunic.

"I'm an excellent senior student," he declared. "I'll go to all the classes today after meeting with those jerkass heirs from the other houses for breakfast."

I blinked in confusion. What did it have to do with me?

"Run along, little Bob," he ordered. "You already made me late, and my rivals will be whining like juveniles."

Chapter Eight

Jubilee Haven hall could hold over two thousand students. The ceiling was arched and high, the floor was white marble, and the dining tables were made of hard maple wood.

Louis swaggered across the hall like he owned the place. He might as well be swinging his cock around naked as well, since all the students snapped their eyes to him, tracking his movements, their food forgotten. Royalty had that kind of effect.

My gaze swept to the steamy buffet dishes on the long tables, my mouth wet. Before I could dart across the hall toward one of the tables, Gunnar grabbed the collar of my tunic and yanked me back.

"What did we say about table manners, Little Bob?" he hissed, showing his fangs. "We aren't here to eat. We're attending to His Highness. You serve him, and I guard him."

"Then when will we get to eat?" I asked.

"You'll eat when you're told to!" he said.

"That sucks, man. I don't like this job anymore," I murmured to myself.

Gunnar slapped the back of my head. I got so annoyed at being denied food, so his sloppy slapping didn't bring out my good nature. Hissing, I turned to punch his throat, but I didn't land it, as he shoulder-shoved me. I stumbled, so my fist crashed into his shoulder bone, which was like hitting a rock.

A head and a half taller, Gunnar enjoyed towering over me to intimidate me. No matter the weather, he always wore a trench coat, which hid a dozen weapons and spells inside.

I scowled at him, but he rolled his eyes.

"Prince Louis is scheduled to drink from me tomorrow," I said. "I gotta get some iron-rich food into my stomach before it's too late!"

"You'll eat after the prince goes to his class," Gunnar said. "Now quit acting like an annoying chihuahua."

I looked over my shoulder. The rest of the entourage had peeled off, so it was just Gunnar and me, trailing behind the prince at a respectful distance.

"Where did they go?" I asked.

"It's none of your business, chihuahua. You don't even have a rank."

"Then why am I on duty?" I asked. "I'm not even a bodyguard. I don't fight like you guys because I'm just not vicious."

"Oh, you're damn vicious. You're just impotent," Gunnar said dismissively. "You should consider yourself extremely lucky to be among a select few who have the honor of serving His Highness."

He was full of shit, but if I said so, he'd punch me, so I gave him the side-eye. That was my new passive-aggressive approach.

"Shut up, focus on your task, and do as you're told!" he added.

He hadn't told me anything useful.

We followed the prince toward a winding staircase to the open second floor. My gaze snagged to the center, where an exclusive buffet table covered by fine white linen stood. A variety of dishes perched on top of elaborate holders with magical fire beneath to keep the food warm. Three servers in nice uniforms stood on either end of the table.

"So, we get to eat here later?" I whispered, grinning ear-to-ear.

"Not you, chihuahua," Gunnar sneered. "This is the princes' private dining area. If you try to be a good dog, you might get some crumbs from the princes' table. His Highness has been lenient with you, but it won't last. He'll get tired of you."

I sneered back. It wasn't like I wanted to stick around forever.

I'd noticed two gorgeous men lounging on the chairs that half-circled a golden table with symbols of the star charts adorning its edge before my coveting glance fell on the food.

They were drinking coffee while overlooking the assembly on the ground dining floor, without a care in the world.

Louis strode to join them at a lazy pace; it could only mean that the two were prince heirs as well. The one to the left of the table had a striking face and amber eyes brimming with ambition. A tattoo of giant paws crawled down his left temple. He must be the shifter prince then.

The other male who faced him was lankier than the bulky shifter prince. He had dark skin that was close to bronze and reddish hair like deep ruby wine.

I liked his fashion sense. He wore a wool sweater paired with a scarf.

I lifted my foot to follow Louis toward his table. The coffee smelled delicious. He barely ate solid food, so I could eat it for him as his squire. Why waste food? But Gunnar yanked me back by the collar of my tunic again.

I scowled, but I was no match for him while I had to lie low, so I let him shove me to stand at ten o'clock from where the princes sat and enjoyed their food and drinks, laughing.

The redheaded prince's turquoise eyes trained on me for a second too long before he winked and turned to Louis as the vampire prince took a seat beside him, opposite the shifter prince.

What was the point of me standing here to watch them eat and drink? I glanced at Gunnar, then mimicked his posture with my feet wide apart and my hands clasped in front of me.

I made a tweak or two though. While he puffed up his chest, I hunched my shoulders. We looked ridiculous together, like a fly beside a pig.

He soon noticed that, peeked down at me, and hissed. I pulled my lips back and hissed back. His face turned beet-red with anger, but there was nothing he could do to me in front of the princes.

"Don't look at me, man," I said. "Look at the prince. His Highness might summon us at any time. I'm the little squire and you're the big squirrel."

"I'm the captain, dumbass," he snapped.

I shook my head. "That doesn't make sense, Captain Dumbass. Prince Louis isn't a king yet, so you can't be the captain of the guard."

"You'll pay for this, chihuahua!" he threatened.

I ignored him. He wasn't worth it. Then the display from the dining hall on the first floor caught my attention. The female students looked up at the upstairs thrones where the royals perched, openly showing their interests. Some girls giggled loudly to draw the princes' attention to them. A group of females paraded in the center of the hall where the princes had a clear view. The princes did glance at the parade. Even though their interest was minimal, more girls joined the parade.

I grinned, waiting for catfights.

"You're late as usual, Louis," the shifter prince said. "I wouldn't be surprised if one day you're late even for your own funeral."

"Bitter I got more ladies' love, Silas?" Louis smirked.

"Right, your fated mate is waiting down there," Silas snorted.

Louis arched an eyebrow. "I'm not worried. But are you? Everyone knows my house is one of the richest and mightiest in the realm. No wonder females from other houses line up to hook up with vampires."

"Keep telling yourself that," Silas said, but his amber eyes flashed with anger.

House rivalry. Louis might've lured away some of Silas's lovers. These things happened, since Louis screwed a lot and changed partners every night.

"Kilian is actually richer than you, Louis," Cade chimed in with a smirk, a dimple deepening on his cheek. "Last I heard, his stock in the mortal realm skyrocketed again."

My heart skipped a beat as I recalled our encounter. I'd never reacted that way toward anyone before, let alone felt a true connection. He'd seemed surprised at the electric thing humming between us and demanded I tell him my name before Louis had whisked me away.

I'd learned from Drusilla that Killian was the prince heir of the House of Chaos. She'd warned me to run from his path if I spotted from afar that he was coming.

I hadn't seen him since. But just thinking of his

smoldering eyes roving over me made me wet, and I wasn't even as slutty as Sy.

As soon as Killian's name was dropped, my interest was piqued. I pricked my ears, listening in attentively.

"That bastard has all the luck," Silas said through his clenched teeth, jealousy searing his eyes. For a second there, I thought that a wolf might emerge from him.

"His fiancée might be the next High Queen," Cade continued, a hint of warning in his voice.

Silas narrowed his eyes. "You think so?"

"We've all heard how powerful she is," Cade said.

"If that happens, none of us will have a chance to be the High King except Killian," Louis drawled.

My heart sank, which was a stupid reaction. Why had I even felt that way toward the prince of the House of Chaos? He had a woman already. Well, now it was crystal clear that he was taken, so I should forget all about him. Even if he wasn't taken, I could never have a chance with him. He was a prince, and I was a servant boy from a vampire house.

I'd forgotten myself and craved something that I could never have. Sy's way was simpler. No real attraction. No attachment. Just fuck and run after the feeding.

"He can't be the fucking High King that way." Silas narrowed his eyes. "The rule is clear. Only the heir who finds his fated mate and brings back the wild magic with her will be the next High King to bond to the realm. The strongest rules!"

"Try not to dream too hard that you're the strongest, Silas," Louis retorted. "I for one am fine without a High King to rule us all. The position has been vacant for centuries. It can wait a few more centuries or forever. Queen Lilith's house isn't even acknowledged in Mist of Cinder."

"Once Killian marries her, their houses will merge," Cade said, drinking his coffee, and my sensitive nostrils smelled whiskey in it. "If she happens to be his fated mate and they produce the offspring who's the prophesized one, the high crowns will be theirs. Rumor has it that they'll get married once Killian graduates."

"It'll be like a year from now," Louis said. "Why wait?"

"Killian doesn't want to get married too soon."

Louis smirked knowingly. "Of course. He wants to fuck as many women as he can before he gets tied down."

"Actually, he can't," Cade said. "I heard that she's bonded him."

Don't worry, Sy offered, sensing my dark mood. *We can still fuck him. We aren't like others. Rules don't apply to us.*

Stop, Sy! I hissed inwardly. *What kind of person are you, thinking like that?*

One of a kind? she answered. *I'm not a dreamer like you. I'm pragmatic.*

I'm not a dreamer! I nearly yelled at her. *We wouldn't have survived this long if I'd been a dreamer!*

Cool your tits, she said. *You're only upset because the chaos prince has other love interests.*

Distracted by Sy, I missed out on a few key points the princes had discussed and caught the last question, "You think Queen Lilith is really his true mate?"

Cade shrugged. "Who knows. It doesn't matter. Females still drool over him in droves. Who doesn't want to taste forbidden fruit?"

"Fuck forbidden fruit if I ain't it." Louis yawned. "Can we not gossip about Killian all the time? That arrogant fucker doesn't even bother to show his ass here anymore. Anyway, where is our good fae Rowan?"

Rowan must be the prince of the House of Fae. Cade, the redhead, must be the prince heir from the

House of Mages. Silas was the heir from the House of Shifters. Louis seemed to get along with the mage prince just fine. From their body language, he and Silas weren't each other's fanboys. Vampires and shifters were natural enemies.

"Perhaps you should go out more often instead of indulging in blood orgies," Silas offered, "then you'd hear the most current news."

Louis glared at the shifter prince. "You have first-hand intel because you and your goons have been sniffing everywhere where your noses don't belong."

"Like your minions don't sneak around my back-yard," Silas snorted.

"Guys, guys, let's not get into another pissing match," Cade said and lifted a hand to show the Hawaiian Aloha sign. "If one more war breaks out in the realm, we'll all be done. There was a reason that the five of us grew up together. We should be bros. Well, here's what happened with Rowan. A fae was murdered outside the Veil, probably a week ago. The body was found yesterday. Rowan has been leading the investigation."

My heart skipped a beat.

It fit the timeline when I escaped the Shriekers. When I fled into Mist of Cinder, I hadn't encoun-tered anyone on the other side of the Veil. The

Shriekers must have chased me to the portal, but they couldn't see through the glamour. If they realized that there was a portal there and I'd gone through, Ruin would send an army to come after me, and the realm would no longer be safe since Ruin and his agents would eventually find a way to breach the Veil.

Icy fear sank its claw into my chest and seized my heart. My mouth suddenly felt as dry as the desert sand.

"What was a fae doing outside the Veil?" Louis frowned. "It's been a backup door that no one has been allowed to use for centuries."

"It doesn't matter anymore," Cade said tensely. "There was a sighting of monsters in the forest outside the academy."

I swallowed the bile at the back of my throat. I couldn't allow the Shriekers to get in. I needed a plan.

I wiped cold sweat from my palms on my pants. Nothing could rile me up like Ruin and his Shriekers. It was a conditioned fear coming from a decade of being tormented and seeing no hope.

My heart was pounding wildly. Prince Louis would hear it, and I bet the shifter prince's hearing was superior too. They'd turn their attention to me.

If I didn't leave the scene now, I was going to bring suspicions my way.

"I need a bathroom break, like right now," I whispered urgently to Gunnar.

I was courteous to inform him, but he didn't seem to appreciate it, as he bared his fangs at me. I doubted he'd ever dealt with his fellow vampire sentinels needing to poop.

"Hold it in!" he ordered, as if it were a piece of cake.

He wasn't even my direct superior, but he'd taken it upon himself to boss me around.

I widened my eyes incredulously. "But I need to shit, man!"

Repulsion rippled across his strong vampire face. "Who say things so crudely like that?! You're a disgusting chihuahua!"

"Fuck it," I said huskily and aggressively. "You don't want me to stink up this upscale room where the princes dine, do you?"

He snarled at me, his face turning purple. I turned on my heels, and he lunged at me. This time, I'd expected his moves and ducked swiftly, letting him seize a handful of empty air. I shot toward the stairs and scrambled down.

As I looked over my shoulder, Gunnar had an

ugly snarl on his lips that might park there permanently if he wasn't careful. He couldn't risk chasing me without drawing his fickle boss's attention. He'd be punished more than me if he disturbed the princes' heated debate now.

I reached the foot of the stairs in no time, scanning the hall in front of me. Dozens of chicks still paraded back and forth on the floor, showing their cleavage and swaying their hips to offer the princes the best views.

Good. I silently urged them to keep the princes horny. I recognized America among them, the front runner fae chick who had tossed fireballs at me to impress Louis.

I bet if those chicks weren't required to wear their school uniforms—shirts with pretty skirts and stockings—they wouldn't mind being naked to lure the princes.

I moved along the far end of the hall, the only blind spot from where the princes sat, heading toward a buffet table. Then luck struck again as I spotted a student with a baseball cap on his head. I snuck up on him while he focused on digging into a pile of hash browns on his plate. I snatched his cap at lightning speed, hiding it under my armpit, and zoomed away.

I heard him cry from a dozen tables behind me, "Where's my hat? Anyone see my hat?"

At a safe distance, I watched him give up looking and go back to his meal, brooding. I put the cap on, picked up a large tray, and piled plates of food onto it. The more, the merrier.

A few students scowled at me, knowing I wasn't one of them from my gear. But I dressed well as a squire, so no one came to challenge me. It wasn't a good idea to offend a squire and thus risk offending his prince.

Fake it to make it.

So, I moved like I was swinging my cock and found a corner table, enjoying my breakfast. After the scare from the princes' talk upstairs, I urgently needed some comfort food to calm my nerves, so I could think up some backup plans.

Halfway through the meal, I had narrowed it down to three plans.

Plan A: run. But where could I run? And I was so tired of running.

Plan B: go out to hunt the Shriekers. But they'd be waiting for me. I couldn't fight an army while my true power was still locked. Ruin had bespelled me to make sure that I'd never fight back or be capable of anything other than being a magic eater and his vessel. No other spells could work on me, but he was a god.

I needed to find a way to purge his hex on me. With me growing stronger every day in Mist of Cinder, in time, I might just make it happen.

So, I had to stick to Plan C. Hide and lie low while forging a path to free my true power. While I lurked here, I'd find any opportunity to hang out on this side of the Veil. If any Shriekers came through, I'd pick them off one by one like a vigilante.

I was a boy now. Even if Ruin's agent infiltrated this realm, they'd be looking for a girl. There were many other perks to being a boy. If I did some ruthless, dumb things, I'd mostly get some smacks to the back of my head from someone's knuckles. They wouldn't whip me since I was Prince Louis's squire.

Act like a boy!

At the thought, I filled my mouth with half of my omelet, ready to chew it loudly, before I spat it out into an empty bowl. I didn't like onion, as it had been my main dish when I was my father's captive. Why did the cook put onions in it?

"Hey, it's you!" A polite voice greeted me.

I raised my head and narrowed my eyes on a blue-haired girl, the witch who had pointed me in the direction of the classrooms when Louis was in hot pursuit of me.

I didn't return her smile.

"So, you're with the House of Vamps now," she said.

I scowled at her. "Yeah, thanks for leading the vamp prince to me."

Louis had dragged me to stand in front of the entire class by my ear to humiliate me, and those little shits had tossed their elemental magic at me to kiss his ass.

"He'd marked your scent already," she said. "It was inevitable, but it's only a phase. I saw it in the tealeaf reading the day before I met you."

"You're a psychic now?" I snorted, yet my pulse spiked.

Did the self-proclaimed oracle know I was a girl? It'd be inconvenient. I needed to be quick on my feet and think of an exit strategy.

"Not exactly," she said. "My tealeaf reading has only eight-three percent accuracy. But next year, I'll be enrolled in the crystal ball reading class to improve my odds. Professor Rainy is the best divination teacher. Anyway, I think I was destined to meet you. I'm Bea. May I sit with you?"

"It's a free country, isn't it?" I asked. "Sit with

me at your own risk though, since I'm looked down on here. And I'm not sharing my breakfast with you, just so you know. You'll have to get your own plate."

She smiled at me again as she glanced at the plates of food spread over the table, threatening to weigh it down.

"Don't worry." She smiled. "I ate already. I usually eat lightly so I won't need to go to the gym to lose weight."

I gave her a onceover. She was a little chubby but on the cute side. She shouldn't worry about some extra pounds. There were a lot worse things to worry about.

"Are you saying that you're too lazy to work out?" I asked. Not that I went to the gym either.

"It won't help to go to the gym," Bea said. "We witches come in all sizes and shapes, unlike other supernatural species. Vampires were made from the gene pool of only the young and the best looking. Fae are born beautiful. Shifters have a great metabolism. My kind have human genes, even though we have a lot more magic in our veins. Even after evolution, we still share their fragility."

"I don't understand why everyone is obsessed with a slim body image. So the wind can blow them away?" I shook my head. "Each to their own. I don't eat lightly. I eat heavily since my body needs it. Also, from my experience, food is not always guaranteed. I never know when I'll have my next meal. So, when I have access to food, I eat as much as I can until I nearly pop. It's the same with shelter—when I have a bed to sleep in, I try to get a full sleep."

"I'm sorry. You must've had a hard life." She sat down across from me and set her wand on the table. "What's your name?"

"There he is!" Gunnar shouted angrily from the stairs. "That damn chihuahua!"

Unfortunately, he'd found me, as had Prince Louis. The prince zoomed toward me like a hurricane.

"Shit!" I cursed. "I haven't even finished my breakfast." I regarded the witch ruefully. "Go! They're a mean bunch. You don't want to be seen sitting with me now."

Bea turned to look at the coming prince and left my table in a hurry. But she didn't go too far; she stopped several tables away and hid behind a tall boy.

Every eye looked our way, fixing on the vampire prince. The girls wanted him and the boys wanted to be him.

Prince Louis shot toward me, halted beside me, and regarded the dishes spread over the table.

"You're a glutton, little Bob," he said.

My face reddened in humiliation.

"I'm eating for two!" I argued in my husky voice. "I've got to prepare for giving you iron-rich blood tomorrow. It's a burden which I'll have to bear alone."

"How dare you!" Gunnar hissed. "You're on the job."

"But I'm not good at it," I said. "You aren't good at it either. I caught you sleeping on the job."

"That's a lie!" Gunnar said menacingly, then dropped the attitude when he noticed his boss frowning at him. "Next time you must say 'may I have your permission to leave, Your Highness.'"

"Say may I have your permission to leave, Your Highness," I said.

A few giggles came our way, including Bea's.

"You're a disgrace, Little Bob!" Gunnar said. "You have no discipline. Now get off your lazy ass and attend to His Highness properly!"

"Okay, okay, I'll attend to His Highness," I said. "Let me box the food to go first. I don't want to waste it."

From the look Gunnar gave me, he was planning to strike me, but he restrained himself at the prince's warning look. After all, I was no one's pet but the prince's.

"Just grab an apple to go," Louis ordered. "No more shenanigans, little Bob. My patience has a limit. My tolerance has an expiration date, and it expires now. For making me late for class, I'll require an extra feeding tonight as a suitable punishment."

I rushed to his side, not even snatching an apple. "Let's hurry up, sir."

The prince led the way out of the hall, strutting like a peacock, commanding the attention of the room as if it was his birthright. I lowered my head and hunched my shoulders to follow him.

"That's my hat," the former owner of the cap said in a small voice as we passed his table.

"Take it then." I tossed it at him. "You won't get into any girl's pants for being cheap."

Gunnar glared at me. "That's a new low!"

"Look who's a negative Nancy. Not me." I smirked at him, then snatched a peach from the last table we passed.

Chapter Nine

Prince Louis's first class of the morning was held in a private park owned by the Sun Harbor club house, which only the prince heirs had access to, though they could bring their entourage with them.

It was a bright glass house with violet vines streaked along the walls. High fences of ivory wood surrounded the perimeter, warded to keep the commoners out.

Gunnar demanded I be grateful that I was allowed to step my worthless foot into this exclusive club and watch the elites practice dangerous magic while serving Prince Louis.

He cursed at me when he caught me rolling my eyes.

Around thirty students gathered around a giant male, his back toward us, and hung on to his every word. As I gave the male another glance, a switch suddenly flipped in me. My heart thundered, my chest tight with pressure.

I would recognize that powerful frame anywhere, even though I'd been in his presence for only a few seconds.

Shit!

Killian, the prince heir of the House of Chaos, was here.

His power pulsed in the air, stronger than anyone else's. It found me right away, spearing me at the speed of light. I staggered back a pace in shock. No power, other than my father's, had been able to affect me. But Killian's called me, and my core magic answered in desperation yet still couldn't break out of its icy cage.

I drew in a sharp breath, instantly aware of the danger the chaos prince posed to me. I needed to get out of here before he pounced.

As if being summoned by the Fates, Prince Killian suddenly turned his head, his gaze homing in on me. He'd sensed me, and the uncanny connection between us sparked to life like a livewire.

Surprise flashed across his gorgeous face, as if he

hadn't expected it to happen again either. I had an effect on him too, and he liked it no more than I liked his effect on me. An undercurrent of dark rage seethed beneath his controlled manner, but I could feel its damaging power.

While my nerves spiked on high alert at the danger, a thrill strummed in my veins at the hunt.

His dark gaze pinned me, then roved over me, trying to peel off my secrets. His heat, even from across the practice field, stroked my skin and caressed me. Before I knew it, I was slick, my pussy aching with need.

I wanted to fuck the heir of the House of Chaos, even though the sensible part of me warned me that he was an apex predator and screamed for me to run before he could come for me, because when he came, it'd be too late for me.

Yet my feet were glued to the ground, my eyes fixed on him in challenge while I kept wondering how it would feel to have his cock buried deep inside me.

When Sy fucked, I'd felt pleasure through her, but it was like feeling it through a thick glass door or wearing gloves.

Our gazes locked. While his harsh, masculine beauty touched me in a way no other man had done,

I pulled my lips back in a silent snarl to show him that he'd be messing with the wrong chick—the wrong boy—if he tried to pounce on me, despite the formidable power oozing from his every mighty pore.

I'd never allow myself to be anyone's easy pickings again. With the vampire prince, it was a temporary arrangement while I needed a foothold in Mist of Cinder. Now that I'd met the strongest immortal in this realm so far, I knew I should steer clear of him at all costs, but the part of me that had gotten hooked by him at first sight only wanted to get closer, wanting to have a taste of his starlight, even though I'd get burned.

Seeing my snarl, the prince of the House of Chaos smirked, which was unexpected. It wasn't a kind smile by any means but dominating, while his intense gaze gave me one last caress that was more like a squeeze.

My heart skittered, and my pussy became so slick that I felt my face burning with embarrassment.

Then he turned away from me, as if nothing had happened and I no longer existed, and barked instructions to his fan club.

The tension, however, didn't drop. His groupies had followed his gaze. Luckily, they merely stared at

Louis, probably thinking the two princes had gotten into a pissing match. I, a servant boy, of course was beneath the prince's notice and theirs too.

Silas and Cade, who stood some distance from Killian and his groupies and bent their heads in a hushed discussion, turned and looked straight at me as well before darting their glances at Louis, confusion resting on their faces before they blinked it away.

I attracted monsters and powerful beings. This was a bad situation for me to be in the presence of four princes, four predators.

The tension broke when Louis was suddenly on the move. He cleared his throat, letting his power ripple off him, and marched toward the gathering.

I didn't want any of the princes paying attention to me again, so I looked away and scanned my surroundings until I spotted a long table at the edge of the grass field between a column of purple trees. On the table were several steel vats of gelato. Two servers stood behind the table, spooning ice cream into paper cups.

I let out a gleeful squeal and sprang in that direction but made it only two steps before I got yanked back by Gunnar.

"You won't be allowed out of my sight for one

second, and you won't be excused, not even for a real bathroom break," he vowed. "I'll make a proper squire out of you!"

"You don't need to do this, man," I said in dismay. "You don't need to be such a tight butt. There's ice cream there. I'll go fetch you a cup as well, I promise."

"The ice cream and refreshments are for the princes only," he hissed.

"You can't know that," I protested. "I don't see any sign that says it. And there is enough for everyone."

"There are certain etiquettes and unspoken rules," he lectured. "You're not the privileged class. You're at the bottom of the food chain. Blame it on your birth father, chihuahua."

Oh, I could blame my father for every fucking thing, on and on and on.

"Stay right here and look ahead," he instructed. "But don't stare at the princes. Every now and then, look in the direction of His Highness and see to his needs."

"He won't need us," I said. "He has his pals over there, and they'll get into a contest of showing whose dick is bigger."

He smacked his large hand against the side of my

head. "Shut up and start learning! Be useful for once!"

"What's there to learn?" I murmured to myself.

Maybe I should hope for Prince Louis to be killed, so I could get out of the contract after I did my one last deed of making sure he got an honorable burial.

We can kill him, and then I'll eat him, Sy offered. *It'll be a shame though to waste him like that.*

The prince was sexy as hell. Sy lusted after him as well. She didn't go after him only because he was too close to home. For her, there were two categories—fuck them or kill them.

Occasionally, she did both.

I wasn't going to be a total hypocrite. Sy fucked to feed, and I benefited from the energy she harvested as well. Sy was a predator, through and through, but she wasn't a sexual predator. Our body needed to feed that way, but she never forced anyone. It was more like luring her targets—or victims, in some cases—but no one could really resist her seduction.

We're not that desperate yet, I told her. *But maybe we should kill Gunnar. He has a nasty personality, so I don't think he'll be missed.*

Should we fuck him first then? Sy consulted.

Ew! I scolded her.

I don't like wasting resources, she laughed.

The students spread over the practice field and split off into twos or threes. It seemed there were five or six of them from each house, based on the crests on their uniforms. They were doing mostly elemental magic, like conjuring fireballs, wind, or water, and tossing it at their opponents.

After a while, a patch of grass was seared by fire. Lots of spots were soaked with pools of water. My favorite was their earth magic. I liked to watch vines shoot out of the ground and grab their opponents in an iron grip.

Within minutes, I'd figured out each house's magical brand.

Vampires owned air magic. Shifters were affiliated with water. Two elemental magics graced the fae house, so a fae either possessed fire or earth. Mages, however, had better luck in diversity. Some mages could wield fire, some were proficient at conjuring ice or wind. However, they had to use spells to make their elemental magic work.

That was why the spellcasters and potions masters mostly came from the mages' house. Fae were good at potions too, but they couldn't compete against the mages in spells. Ancient fae could store spells and magic in artifacts, but the art had been lost a millennium ago.

My dormant magic was more powerful than any supernatural's, except for Killian, probably, since I couldn't exactly make out his power, which was a first, and a challenge.

Watching the students practice magic from the sideline, I was both thrilled and anxious.

I needed to figure out how to get hold of my core power if I wanted to last in this realm and face my father in the end. I couldn't hide or run forever. He'd find me eventually.

We can learn in the academy, I told Sy.

You do the learning, she said. *I'm watching the hot boys.*

I laughed when a boy got hit by earth magic and was strung upside down by an ankle. He yelped, conjuring his water magic, but it wasn't any help in getting him down.

"Are you amused, squire?" Gunnar asked.

"It's funny," I said.

"You're not here to have fun, squire!" he scolded.

"That dude should've shot his strong water at his opponent to make her lose focus, then he'd be able to get down. If he knows how, he should also manipulate the water within the brunette and choke her, but then he's no good when he's panicking like that. Fear kills."

"What do you know about magic?" Gunnar sneered. "I told you to learn, not to pretend to be something that you're not and make ignorant comments!"

"Yeah, yeah," I said.

He had no fucking idea that I was every magic user's worst nightmare and their greatest enemy. But I wasn't foolish enough to show my hand.

Gunnar was right about learning, though. I needed to observe closely how the students summoned their magic. I was living on borrowed time unless I could harness my own magic; then I'd stand a fighting chance against Ruin.

"Let me aid you." America rushed toward the trapped boy as she noticed the princes were all looking on at his struggle with light amusement.

It seemed that they were mostly supervising the students, bickering with each other, fishing for information, or exploiting the others' weakness. Drusilla had given me a crash course on the heirs and the house rivalries in the realm. None of the princes wanted to show the other houses what was up their sleeves.

America stood in front of the unfortunate student, waiting for all eyes to fall on her.

This was the perfect opening to get all the princes' attention. She'd paraded herself shamelessly in Jubilee Haven earlier. This time, her aim was toward Killian. She batted her blue eyes at him, even though he wasn't even available. Seducing him was like cheating with a married man, though he wasn't exactly married. Not yet anyway.

But that fae chick didn't seem to care. The two top buttons of her uniform were open to reveal more of her cleavage.

What a slut!

I glared at her.

Maybe I should snuff out her magic and embarrass her in front of everyone?

Do it, Sy encouraged. *Don't let her take your man.*

He isn't my man! I folded my arms across my chest.

America tossed her fireballs at the vines that gripped the boy's ankle, burning the vines, and the boy tumbled down to the ground with a yelp. America laughed at his expense, and others joined her.

Sympathy wasn't an admired quality in Mist of

Cinder. It was perceived as weakness. I'd learned that when I snuck into the class. Only power was respected.

America didn't achieve the result she wanted, as none of the princes paid her much attention. Cade and Silas put their heads together again. The mage prince said something, and the shifter prince darted a suspicious glance at the chaos prince.

Out of earshot of Cade and Silas, Killian and Louis were trading information.

At my summons, Sy came as close to the surface as she could get, and her superior hearing aided me.

"So, you got yourself a new pet, Louis?" Killian asked, nodding in my direction.

I bristled. I didn't mind others calling me that, but such an insult from his sensual mouth hit me like a brick.

I lashed out without a second thought, my dark wind setting forth to suck out his magic and render him fatigued. He'd be replenished in a few hours, considering how powerful he was. There was a difference between siphoning the land and supernatural beings. The acreage would be barren after being drained of its magic. Supernatural beings could survive if I didn't absorb their essence, and their magic would return, unless I harvested every drop from their very core.

I was being reckless, but the arrogant Prince of Chaos wouldn't know what had hit him. He wouldn't expect a low servant like me to be able to sip his energy like it was juice.

As my dark wind creeped over his skin, ready for a drink, his magic composed of starlight—something I'd never encountered before—rushed to meet my wind, flirting with it.

What the fuck?

How could this happen?

My siphon power and his starlight entwined in a dance. Heat burned in my core, liquid fire licking between my thighs.

I jerked back, my lips parted, and I instantly withdrew my siphon power.

"Not exactly a pet. He'd be the worst pet," Louis said with a chortle, glancing my way before returning his attention to his frenemy. "Everyone notices that boy. There's something about him."

"Where did you find her—" Killian's gaze slid over me, and my heart skipped an icy beat. "—him?"

He corrected it, but it sounded false. When I'd first bumped into him in the woods, he'd said, "There she is!"

The way he smirked knowingly at me might hint that he knew about my disguise. He was playing with me, getting me worked up. Everything about the prince of the House of Chaos spelled disaster waiting to happen.

"He's too pretty to be a boy, Louis," Killian added.

Louis frowned. "I've been thinking the same."

My heart raced erratically.

"But then, who cares if your squire is a boy or a girl," Killian said, "as long as he knows how to take your directions and does what you ask him, right?"

Asshole!

"Here's the thing though, Killian," Louis confessed in a low voice, and I bet he didn't know that I could hear him. "My squire, little Bob, mostly doesn't follow instructions. He's one of the crankiest creatures I've ever come across. He's like a skittish, growling chihuahua on his best days. He bares his teeth even more often than me, and I'm a powerful vampire prince."

"You haven't told me where you grabbed him," Killian said.

"Why are you so interested in my servant boy?" Louis narrowed his pale blue eyes. "Isn't it a bit unusual, especially for you, Prince Killian?"

"Don't be ridiculous, Louis," Killian said. "I might need a new squire, fresh blood and all."

"Are you planning to poach my squire?" Louis grated.

"Now you're paranoid," Killian said lazily. "All I'm trying to tell you is that there're spies in our midst, and you know that too. We should check out everyone's background, especially our new pets, squires, and guards', since they follow us everywhere."

"Well," Louis retorted, "I and my house are more likely to be spied on by minions from other houses, including yours, rather than being spied on by my new squire. If little Bob is a spy, he's the lousiest spy. His all-time favorite thing to do is to raid the kitchen. The amount of food he can consume is shocking. He eats like there's no tomorrow, and the damn boy is always hungry. I've heard too many complaints about him."

I seethed. He was making me look bad in front of Killian.

And you shouldn't look down at people just because they eat a lot!

My body needed to consume a lot of energy, and Sy needed to feed so we wouldn't be forced to drink magic and drain the realm. It was like I was born with a void that constantly needed to be filled, considering who fathered me.

Yet I didn't want to be the villain in the story that hurt people and the land if I could help it. It was bad enough that Sy needed to feed the way she did.

"Yet you keep him around," said Killian.

"He's something, and he has something to give." Louis eyed the chaos prince slyly. "And you're awfully interested in my new squire. I want to know the real reason."

Killian stared at the vampire prince. "There's no real reason. If you don't want to share, beat it. Don't accuse me for nothing."

"Temper, Killian." Louis laughed. "What happened to you lately? We barely see you anymore. What about the houses' cooperative spirit? Under a lot of stress because of the approach of your wedding? Shouldn't you be in a fabulous mood, groom-to-be?"

Rage seethed in me and scorched the back of my throat, as if the idea of the prince of the House of Chaos getting married didn't sit well with me. The next moment, I was taken aback. I shouldn't have this kind of stupid, possessive reaction. Why should I care whom he went to bed with? I might've felt an intense, unnatural link to him that I'd never felt with anyone else, but it could mean nothing. It could be one-sided. Mostly, it could be a dumb crush.

"Fuck off," Killian said.

"Hmm, I see, you don't like talking about your own wedding," Louis said. "Your engagement has been the gossip of the month. Let me in on something, then I'll be more willing to share whatever you want to know."

"I won't get married before graduation," Killian said grimly. "Who the fuck wants to be tied down in their twenties?"

"Well, we'll want to if we find our fated mates," Louis said. "Isn't this the whole point of hanging out in this academy, where every eligible female in the realm is placed in the Brides Selection? We are all in a race to find our true mate, mate her, and produce the right powerful heir, and then one of us lucky bastards will rise to be the High King."

"Take the High King's throne if you want or can," Killian sneered. "Like I give a fuck."

"You're a sour grape, Killian," Louis clucked his tongue, "since you can't swim with us sharks in the pool of the Brides Selection. You're no longer allowed to hunt. You're so bitter that you don't show your ass at our breakfast anymore. But think of it this way: if Queen Lilith turns out to be your fated mate, you'll be ahead of us all. Is she your true mate, Killian? Have you tried her out?"

I strained my ears to listen, acid in my blood, ice in my heart. And I had no reason to react this way.

Killian smiled coldly. "Why are you so fucking interested in my mating life?"

"Everyone is interested in your mating life." Louis smirked. "C'mon, Killian. If you want to trade information, let's trade fairly. You've never asked about anyone else who works for me except my new squire. You never even care about me. But little Bob has a special talent other than his blood tasting like nectar from a god."

My heart skipped a beat. My breath hitched.

Killian hesitated for a second, then sighed. "I want to postpone the wedding even after my graduation, but I'm not sure if it can be done. My hands are tied. You know how my father is." His jaw clenched. "That's all I can tell you."

"Tell me one thing that I truly want to know," Louis drawled. "Is it true that your dragon will come out only when he recognizes his fated mate? Are you even a dragon?"

"You'll never know, Louis," Killian snorted cynically. "You and the other heirs gossip like old church ladies. Don't you have better things to do?"

Prince Louis clapped Killian's shoulder as if he forgave his attitude already. "There's no reason to be defensive. You shouldn't be sulky either. Queen Lilith is a great beauty, not to mention powerful."

"Back to your pet squire," Killian demanded.

"His origin is unknown." Louis shrugged. "He was in bad shape when I caught him. He must be from the slum in the realm."

Killian frowned at him. "When did you become sloppy, man? Don't you drink from everyone before initiating them into your house to see their memories?"

Fuck!

A powerful vampire could see his target's memories when he drank directly from his victim or donor's veins. I had forgotten this fact and threat because no one had taken blood from me before, not even my father.

I shifted from foot to foot, my nerves on edge. If things went south, I would have to run in the next second.

"Little Bob is immune to my magic," Louis said.

"Immune how?" Killian asked eagerly, and I focused on their conversation.

"While his blood tastes like the purest magic, like

ambrosia directly from a god's veins, I can't see his memories," Louis confessed.

I let out a relieved breath, and tension left my shoulders. He wasn't wrong about the taste of my blood, only he didn't really know about my true origin. He should consider himself lucky that he was clueless. If he knew about my dark secret, Sy wouldn't risk letting him live.

"I've been pondering on this," the vampire prince continued. "He's also proven to be immune to others' magic. A whole class threw their magic at him, and he just brushed it off. He can pass wards like they aren't even there. The boy has a hot temper and a foul mouth, and he doesn't fear me." The vampire prince shook his head. "He only worries about his own needs. He might be even more self-serving than you, Killian."

My face burned in anger and humiliation as they kept trashing me. Maybe I should do something to shut them up!

"On the other hand, that boy is refreshing, as he's unlike any other," Louis said. "I caught him when he tried to steal food from the kitchen in a stolen servant's uniform. I took pity on him and took him under my wing to give him a chance to turn over a new leaf. He's raw material that needs a lot of work.

He thought being my squire meant carrying my sword and flag, then making sure to bury me honorably after I'm killed."

Killian blinked, then laughed while glancing in my direction. "She—he said that?"

He'd used the pronoun "she" to refer to me three times now. I doubted it was a slip of the tongue. Somehow, I suspected that he did it intentionally. But how could he tell that I was a girl while others never questioned that I was a boy? After being a boy for a week, I'd mostly forgotten that I was still a girl. I took great care when I had to use the bathroom or take a shower. I also bound my chest good and solid.

Hearing Killian's laughter, everyone turned to look in his direction in surprise.

"Hey man, it's good to see you laugh." Louis smirked. "You barely crack a smile these days. It's like you've got this twisted, dark storm of rage living within you."

"Fuck off, Louis," Killian said, glaring at the students, who all quickly found other places to look.

"And you know what?" Louis chuckled. "My new squire is incorrigible, yet he's surprisingly shy when it comes to fucking."

His eyes on fire, Killian leaned toward Louis, like

a shark smelling blood, menace rolling off him. My heart stuttered.

"You fucked your squire?" he growled threateningly.

"Fuck no!" Louis said, glaring at Killian. "What the fuck is wrong with you, asshole? I don't fuck boys. I just made him watch me fuck while I drank from him, and he hated it."

Killian studied the vampire prince intently, then a wicked smirk ghosted his mouth. My stomach flipped. Heat coursed through my bloodstream as I stared at his lips, thinking of what those sensual lips could do to a woman.

"I have a way for your squire to get rid of his shyness," Killian drawled.

Louis arched a brow. "No offense, but I don't want you to get involved. Plus, his shyness blended with his obnoxiousness is quite endearing."

"The boy is a virgin," Killian said. "His behavior is that of someone who tightly guards his or her virginity."

Once again, he said "her." Did he know I was eavesdropping, so he was toying with me and making me sweat? Thank goodness, Louis didn't catch any of that but nodded.

"He needs proper sex education. Send your

women to seduce him," Killian said, intent on planting bad ideas in Louis's head.

"I tried," Louis said. "He's incredibly rude to them. Last time, he punched a blonde, knocking her teeth out when she didn't take no for an answer but made an aggressive advance on him. He's petite, but he's got some surprising strength, and he's damn fast."

Laugh lines appeared around Killian's storm-blue eyes as he laughed again.

I clenched my teeth, not as amused as he was.

"Make it a game," Killian said, and Louis's eyes flashed in intrigue. "Reward the first one who sucks his little cock."

That motherfucker turned in my direction and winked while I was shaking with anger, my face burning beet-red.

I needed to get the hell out of here before I lost my shit, but Gunnar stood too close to me. I made it half a step before he clamped his hand down on my shoulder.

"Where do you think you're going?" he growled. "And what did I say about not staring at the princes like an idiot?" he scolded.

"I'm just going to fix my shoelaces," I said, dropping to re-tie my shoelaces, as I planned to bolt as soon as Gunnar looked away. That vampire barely blinked.

A shadow creeped over me, and I squinted up at Prince Louis, who frowned down at me with a hungry look in his eyes. He'd shot over here with his silent vampire speed.

I could barely ditch one vampire, and now I had two.

"What's the matter, little Bob?" the prince asked. "Why do you have a bulldog look on your face?"

He was teasing me. He didn't punish me for every bold and stupid thing I did or said because I amused him, besides my blood nourishing him more than any other's blood.

"I'm not used to working long hours, sir," I said, slowly rising to my feet so I wouldn't feel the blood rushing to my head. My plan of bowing out had failed already. "I probably should join the union. I wonder if there's a supernatural labor union." My voice turned to a whimper. "I need to take a break. You don't want to drink from me tomorrow and taste sorrow and fatigue. Also, to be honest with you, sir, I've been in Gunnar's company for way too long, which isn't good for my mental health."

"You're lazy and you have no discipline in your

bones!" Gunnar barked. "You're the worst squire in history."

"What history? And whose history are you talking about?" I barked back. "You need to give me a better definition, *Captain.*"

Gunnar bared his fangs as if he planned to strike me. "I'll give you a better definition, chihuahua!"

"Please, but before you do," I turned to sneer at him, "you should know that history is never accurate, since the winners wrote it, and they didn't become queens and kings because they were nice. They slaughtered everyone who stood in their way and had different opinions."

Gunnar narrowed his eyes and opened his mouth.

"Shut the fuck up, both of you," Louis ordered. "I can't believe I have to deal with you two bickering nonstop in this humid weather."

The weather was perfect with a gentle breeze and warm sunlight. The vampire prince was so spoiled.

"It's so humid that my brain hurts," I said. "Permission to be excused, high sir?"

"You can't even get my title right, squire." Prince Louis sighed. "You'll be excused for the rest of the day under one condition."

Life and suspicion both swirled back into my dull eyes. "What is it, sir?"

"I get a drink from you tonight," he said.

"But what about tomorrow?" I asked. "We're scheduled for tomorrow. Are we moving up the date?"

"No, little Bob," said the prince. "Tomorrow is still on. Tonight's drink will be compensation for you cutting short your working hours."

My lips thinned, but I had no choice. The longer I stayed here, the sooner the prince of the House of Chaos would figure me out or make me slip. He'd riled me up enough!

"Then tonight shall be an appetizer," I said. "We'll have to measure the volume properly this time, so there won't be any chance of overdose."

"A snack then," he agreed.

"And I'll need a full disclosure of my job description, working hours, and compensation," I said. "I'll need to review a written contract and have a copy on record."

"You dare, squire?!" Gunnar snarled for his boss's sake.

"Let's indulge our little Bob," Louis said with dark amusement. "He's young, and he has a lot to learn." He turned to me. "I'll have an attorney draft it up for you. Happy now?"

"Thank you, sir." I beamed at him and pointed at the ice cream table. "May I have a cup of ice cream after I'm excused, good sir?"

Louis shrugged, not interested in the ice cream at all. "Knock yourself out, squire."

Gunnar's lips twisted with displeasure at me. Yet there was nothing he could do to stop me.

I flashed him a smile. "Sucks to be you, dude."

Without waiting for his retort or threat, I shot toward the ice cream table.

"A dozen cups of ice cream to go for Prince Louis, all sorts of flavors, please," I placed my order.

I looked over my shoulder while the servers scooped the ice cream and put the cups in a box. Among all the people, my gaze found the prince of the House of Chaos right away, only to see him smirking at me, looking utterly amused.

I snapped my head back, took the box of ice cream, and zoomed out of Sun Harbor with my heart pounding in my chest, sweat under my armpits, and liquid heat pooling between my thighs.

Chapter Ten

I was on my third cup of ice cream when I detoured to the main courtyard. I wanted to get familiar with every street, alley, and land-mark in this campus town.

I spooned the rest of the ice cream from the cup into my mouth, grinning, which dropped as soon as I thought of giving my blood to the leech prince tonight. I soon shook it off, as I'd learned not to cash in the bad in advance.

The years in the pit being drained to within an inch of my life had taught me an important lesson—never let bad people steal your laughter. That was how you beat your enemies. Never allow them to have that power over you. Don't talk about them over and over and thus let them live in your headspace. Treat them like they were nothing, and you'd get to move on to a better life. It wasn't easy, but keeping doing that, you'd get rid of a victim mentality.

And you'd be stronger.

Then, you'd need to find a way to vanquish your enemy to be truly safe and free.

Some wounds may never heal. I would have this terror living inside me as long as Ruin was out there, but I made sure to laugh whenever I had a damn good time.

Like this moment, while I was enjoying ice cream and sunlight, I reminded myself not to let anyone steal my joy, not even the vamp and chaos princes.

My mind drifted to Killian again. I needed to stay far away from him. He was too hot for his own good and too dangerous.

A blur of motion passed by my periphery, and I snapped my head around.

A girl sprang in my direction, her blue hair going wild in the wind, worry tightening her pixie features.

It was Bea, the witch!

A group of seven students—fae, witches, mage, shifter, and siren—were chasing her, shouting in elation, thrilled at the hunt.

A boy and a girl outraced her, cutting off her

escape route. The rest of the gang hemmed her in like a pack of coyotes, ready to tear flesh and taste the blood of their prey.

"Where are you running, freak?" A siren chick, who smelled of seaweed, stepped into Bea's path.

"Leave me alone!" Bea cried out, her trembling left hand thrusting a wand in front of her, her right arm hugging a thick book against her chest.

"What can your toothpick do?" a small-nosed witch snorted, pointing her more refined wand at Bea.

I tilted my head as I recognized this witch as the fake blonde who sat on America's other side in the class I'd stumbled into while fleeing from Louis. I could bleach the color out of her hair with a snap of my fingers.

This mean witch was stuck up, and she, like the others, mistook Bea as lesser. I sniffed again just to make sure. Yep, Bea was more powerful, but she had a block, just like me.

"I've never bothered any of you," Bea said. "I've been keeping to myself."

"You should never have gotten into this elite school and brought down the reputation of our house," the mage boy who had outraced her shouted. "You're defective. Go into exile, like your father!"

"It's not like I wanted to be here," Bea protested. "It's mandatory for every coming-of-age supernatural to join the school and expand the pool of the Brides Selections."

"So, you think you can be one of the brides and land a prince?" the fake blonde witch snorted, and the gang snickered.

"You're putting words in my mouth," Bea said. "I don't have your kind of agenda or ambition. I'm here to learn magic, so I can find a proper job after I graduate from the academy."

"Yet you drool over Prince Cade every time he passes by the house," the fake blonde witch hissed.

"I don't drool," Bea said. "But since when is it against the law to look?"

"How dare you talk back to us? Do you know who I am?" a rich fae brat barked, his arm around the fake blonde witch's shoulders.

Huh, that was how the fake blonde witch got accepted into the gang that seemed to be trying to police the school.

"Who are you?" Bea asked, and I chuckled.

The fae boy darted forward and shoved Bea with such force that she fell to the ground. Her precious book dropped and flipped open at the middle.

"Book of Shadows!" the fake blonde witch

hissed, envy glinting in her eyes. "Where did you get it? A low witch like you should not have that book!"

"It's a grimoire from my grandmother," Bea said as she crawled toward the book, but the siren girl kicked the book away.

Bea waved her wand, sending a gust of wind with sparks of fire toward the siren chick, flinging her into a bench. The other bullies threw up their shields. At the same time, their magic—fire, ice, wind, and water—joined, hurling toward her.

If the collective magic hit Bea, she'd be maimed if not killed. The students hadn't held back. Bea was a nobody here, like me. I doubted anyone would even be charged for murdering a *less* powerful supernatural in the Shades Academy.

I tossed out my dark wind, neutralizing the gang's collective magic. Not a single spark of their offensive powers reached Bea while I held them hostage.

The bullies traded a look of disbelief and threw up their hands again. Nothing. Their magic didn't obey them. They looked around in anger and panic, seeking a target.

Some students had stopped, forming a small crowd to watch the fight, but many students kept going about their own business, passing through the courtyard. Not one of them came forward to help Bea.

"What the fuck?" a small-eyed, dark-skinned shifter boy called. "What did you do to us, freak? What kind of witchcraft is this?"

He had water magic. Instead of it going somewhere else, the water drenched his pants, almost like he'd peed himself. I hid a smile.

He and the mage boy lunged at Bea. The mage had his hand on Bea's shoulder to keep her down; the shifter put his foot on Bea's thigh.

"It must be a spell from the Book of Shadows," said the fake blonde witch. "That book is forbidden. I'll take the book for safekeeping; the rest of you can drag her to Lady America. Her ladyship will want to interrogate this low witch since she hasn't paid homage to our lady."

"Don't take my book, please," Bea cried as she struggled to break free. "Take everything else. It's all I have of my grandmother!"

Fake Blonde stepped toward the book, bending to extricate it. Before she could get her hands on the book, I released the hijacked air magic. A strong wind suddenly lifted the book and slammed it into her face. The witch yipped, and the book flew over her head and rose into the air until it floated beyond anyone's reach.

"She's using black magic! Punish her!" the fake blonde witch shouted while covering her bleeding nose with a hand.

The shifter lifted his foot from Bea's thigh to kick her, a smile on his face. Shifters loved violence even more than vampires.

No, you don't, I murmured under my breath and released the magic I held. It slammed into the bullies around Bea, and the gang fell over each other on the ground. Bea widened her eyes while searching the crowd until she spotted me.

I winked at her, finishing half of the fourth cup of ice cream.

The bullies shot up, growling and cursing.

"It's the servant boy messing with us!" the fake blonde witch called, stabbing her finger at me as recognition lit her eyes. "His name is Little Bob! Professor Longweed said he's an Echo, a null who can cancel out magic. Prince Louis beat him into submission in class last time! He deserved it and more!"

Her narrative wasn't exactly true. Louis had dragged me to the center of the classroom by my ear, but he hadn't hit me.

"Hello, Fake Blonde." I clucked my tongue and shook my head. "The dye doesn't even look good on you, and I see the dark roots all over."

She shot daggers at me, but her other hand that didn't cover her bleeding nose automatically went to touch the top of her head.

"We're going to beat the crap out of this little shit!" the shifter said.

"But he belongs to Prince Louis," another witch said. "Will we get into trouble?"

"He's only a stupid servant," the fae boy said arrogantly. "I don't think Prince Louis would mind us putting this Little Bob in his place. And he's a freak. Look at his two-toned eyes."

I laughed. "And you bunch of cunts think you're the shit."

Bea's eyes went even wider at my bold, crude insult at her bullies, but more than a few bystanders snickered.

The gang looked astounded and utterly offended that a servant dared to mock them, then all of them cursed at me. Five of them stalked toward me, coming to teach me a violent lesson.

"Leave him alone!" Bea cried, but she was pinned to the ground. The mage grabbed her wand and yanked it out of her hand.

"Apologize and beg, Little Bob," the shifter yelled, "and—"

"In what order?" I interrupted him rudely, then raised my hands in surrender as he came near me. "Wow, wow, you look so big, shifter boy. Chill. Sorry about my mouth, okay? I was wrong. You lot aren't shit." I paused. "You're clowns." He snarled, and I smiled. "I'd love to apologize and beg, but I'm not good at either. So, one of you will have to teach me. You can write it down and read it for me, then I'll repeat it. How's that?"

"You're dead meat!" the shifter bellowed.

The gang—the pack of coyotes—assaulted me as one. I ducked a blow, faster than they could believe. My boot kicked out, making solid contact with the shifter's soft nuts.

He doubled over to cup his groin, yowling in pain; the others stared at me in surprise, tentatively halting their advance on me.

"That move was classic in any book, don't you agree?" I asked the gang. "And it never gets old. Even if a dude tries to protect his balls from the front, you can always shoot to his back and kick him between his legs from behind. It's actually more satisfying, and I'm talking from personal experience."

The gang gaped at me as if I'd grown two heads.

"Anyone else want an apology?" I asked gleefully.

"Maim him! Put him down!" the fae boy bellowed.

The gang lunged at me from all directions. I turned and twisted in the limited space as I shot into their ranks. I slammed the cup that was still a quarter full of ice cream into the nose of the fake blonde witch while she tried to toss her useless magic at me.

The cup stuck to her bleeding nose, and the green ice cream smeared her face.

"Oops," I said. "I can't find a trash can, so you'll do. But don't sweat. It's mocha. Not my favorite. Do you know what's my favorite? Peach!" At the same time, my leg flew up and booted the side of her face to send her away from me. "Be gone, fake blonde witch."

The gang divided into two groups. Group A tried again to conjure their magic to throw at me but to no avail. Group B tried to overpower me with kicks, punches, and sheer numbers. It worked poorly as well.

They relied too much on their magic, so they seldom practiced martial arts. After I fled Ruin, I'd taken it upon myself to educate myself in every way possible, including leveling up my fighting skills. I never took my borrowed time or freedom for granted.

I reached Bea and punched the mage restraining her in the teeth while yanking Bea's wand out of his hand. I returned it to her as I helped her up.

"This doesn't belong to you, Sweet Tooth." I smiled at him as he held his jaw and howled in pain.

"Pussies," I murmured.

The crowd grew bigger. I didn't want to linger and draw more attention, and I especially didn't want Gunnar to catch up with me.

"Let's go." I grabbed Bea and pulled her up to run with me.

"My book!" she cried. "I need to get my book!"

Not missing a beat, I flicked my wrist, and the book fell into my arms. I put the box of remaining ice cream on top of it, not slowing my pace.

"I'll catch you, and I'll fuck you up!" the shifter boy called after us.

"Promise, coyote!" I called back over my shoulder.

"I'm a panther!" he shouted. "And you'll wish you were never born, servant boy!"

"You and me both," I shot back. "I already wish I was never born. But since I was born, I can't go back, so I'm going to grab life by its horns and enjoy every fucking second. Are you with me, coyote?"

He snarled. Not a good sport.

"We need to get out of here!" the fae boy called in warning. "Prince Killian is coming!"

They ceased to pursue me, but I only pumped more strength into my legs. I didn't have it in me to face the chaos prince twice in a day.

"This way, Little Bob!" Bea steered me east, past a white stone building that had *Infinite Library of Mist of Cinder* etched on its façade, guarded by two sphinx sculptures on either side of the arched steel-blue door.

"Are we going to hide in the library?" I asked her. "I don't have a library card, but maybe we can share yours?"

"We're going to the mages' café," she said.

"But a mage and two witches from your house just attacked you," I said. "They'll follow us there."

"They won't attack me in Snowflake unless they want to be banished," Bea said confidently.

"Whatever you say." I shrugged and joined her

walking past the library. "I don't have a place to go anyway."

An amber building loomed ahead; the House of Mages basked in the golden rays of the sun. I'd snuck in once. The interior design appeared more casual than that of other houses. Indoor plants and herbs blended seamlessly with comfortable chairs. The high walls were lined with shelves of books, ancient and new. Mages wanted to show the world that they were the keepers of arcane knowledge.

"I'd have invited you to the House of Mages," she said, "but the house rules are strict. You aren't a witch or mage, so you won't be able to pass the magical requirement to enter my house. Even if you were my kind, you'd still need to be initiated by Prince Cade to be accepted by our house."

"Hmm," I said.

She smiled at me encouragingly. "But let's enjoy tea at Snowflake."

"Prince Louis hasn't paid me yet," I told her, then I hit my forehead with the heel of my palm. "Shit. I should've bargained for weekly pay rather than biweekly. I'll re-negotiate the terms tonight. I won't let him keep taking advantage of me."

"My treat, Little Bob," Bea said.

I perked up. "You're rich?"

She shook her head, her smile staying. "Food and drinks aren't expensive in the academy."

We walked away from the building of the House of Mages.

"But are you sure you want to have tea with a servant boy?" I pointed out the class difference between us.

"A brave boy who saved me. Buying you a drink is the least I can do."

I beamed. "Is this going to be the start of a beautiful friendship?"

"As long as you don't hit on me," Bea teased.

I spread my arms. "I'm not into chicks."

"You're gay, Little Bob?" she asked gleefully. "That's awesome. I've always wanted a gay bff!"

"I'm not gay, not that I'm against it or something."

"It's fine, Little Bob!" She pressed a hand on mine. "You can trust me and come out of the closet. I'm your friend, or I will be."

"There's no fucking closet," I said in a low, husky voice.

The sun was at ten o'clock in the sky, shining on a cluster of upscale shops curved around tree-lined streets. They stretched over two and a half blocks between the House of Mages, Infinite

Library, and Mouline, the art and performance center.

Bea and I merged into the flow of students, becoming one of the hundred faces in the campus business district.

"Hey," I suddenly thought of something, "you think you can help me change my looks with some spells or potions?"

"I know a few spells for disguises. What do you want to change?"

"I don't want to have these golden curls like snails parked on my head. No one takes me seriously, you know? Do you think you can get me straight dark hair, so I'll have a sophisticated look?"

"Then it won't be you, Little Bob," she said. "Your golden curls are perfect, just like your long golden eyelashes! Girls would kill to have them."

I frowned at her suspiciously. She laughed and led me by the hand into Snowflake café.

Just like its name, magical snowflakes drifted from the ceiling, falling on our heads before vanishing. White sand covered the floor, and it didn't stick to my shoes.

Two witches, one older and the other younger, stood behind a glass counter that displayed an array of cakes, cookies, and donuts. They smelled fresh, but I could tell which cakes had spells added. It'd be dangerous for humans and less powerful supernaturals to try them.

I peered at the holographic menu on the board framed on the wall, bouncing on my feet and grinning like a Cheshire cat. I was proud to finally join the ranks of paying customers; that was, if Bea was going to pay for us.

"Hi Sabine, Toby," Bea greeted the witches with a wave of her hand. They smiled at her before fixing their eyes on me again.

The two witches had homed in on me the moment I'd stepped in, their eyes widening and sharpening as if they'd seen something they shouldn't have.

I jerked a thumb toward Bea and offered, "I'm with her."

Bea nodded. "Little Bob is my new friend," she explained and walked me upstairs.

On the second floor, the ceiling was lower, adorned with witch-light crystals like white stars. Bea ambled toward a table in the north corner, but I pointed at the most desirable table in the spacious front center that faced the tall window.

"Let's sit over there," I suggested.

"That's the table for Prince Cade," she said. "No

one dares to sit there unless they want to commit social suicide, or real suicide in some cases."

"Shit, I don't want to commit either." I shook my head, even though I wouldn't even be granted social suicide, since I didn't have a social life to begin with.

"A nice table isn't worth it," she agreed.

But I suspected that Bea might not have many friends either. So now we had banded together to give this social life a try.

We perched on the chairs at the table Bea picked. I put down the thick book on her side and the box of ice cream on mine.

"What do you want?" Bea asked.

"I don't know. Anything is fine. I'm not picky."

She laughed, "I'll order for you then," and pulled out an electronic tablet from her schoolbag.

"What's that?" I asked. I'd seen Drusilla use one to take notes on Louis's orders.

"Spinchat," she said. "Every student has one. It's the equivalent to humans' Facebook and TikTok but cooler, since the device is spelled. The streams are fueled by magic as well, so it's nearly impossible to be hacked."

"But it can be hacked, right?"

She gave me side-eye. "Who would want to do

that? They'd be courting death. Some laws here are very strict, and there are no second chances for those criminals who step into a forbidden area."

"Will you teach me how to use Spinchat? I love all things pop culture and social media."

"Sometimes it's better to stay away from social media," she sighed. "I'll show you how to use Spinchat, but let's order something first."

My legs bounced under the table in excitement. Bea would teach me to be a social media expert. I might even find a new job through it. Being the vampire prince's squire, aka walking blood bag, wasn't a long-term solution.

Bea buried her head in the tablet, swept her thumb over the screen, and then clicked a few items before she put it down on the table. She looked at my expectant expression and laughed again.

All those years on the run and living on the street, it'd always been me looking inside the shop through the window with longing for a mug of steamy coffee or tea with a plate of cake, and more importantly, with a friend to share and laugh with.

My jaw dropped as a tray with two cups of tea and half a dozen cakes on it floated toward our table.

"Here I come, Houston!" I exclaimed and jumped from my seat to welcome the cakes.

I instantly consumed the three cakes on my side, then tried my best to sip the tea the way Bea did, like a lady.

"What are you, Little Bob?" Bea asked abruptly, curiosity lighting her intelligent gray eyes.

I nearly choked on my tea. "What do you mean? I'm just like you!"

"I'm regarded as the lowest in the academy, but I have an ability no one else in my house has, except maybe Prince Cade. I can feel power grades, and you're in the highest caliber. I've never met a magical signature like yours. It's like your magic is as massive as a black hole."

As I'd said, Bea had a potential that she'd never realized. There were several types of magic users in the House of Mages—druids and mages ranked at the top, sorcerers stood on the next rung, and witches were at the bottom. Among the witches, there was a strict hierarchy as well.

Bea was likely registered as a witch, but she was at a mage's level. She'd be more powerful than most mages if she could dig deep into her well of magic and unleash it. When she leveled up to a mage, those bullies who constantly picked on her would have to bow to her. I looked forward to that day.

I'd help her and eat away the elaborate spells that

bound her, but not at our first hangout. I wondered if she knew that she was bound by spells, or if she preferred it that way.

"I'm not a black hole," I protested.

"I felt drawn to you—your power—the first time I saw you in the courtyard," she said. "Others are drawn to you as well, even though they might not know why. Power attracts power. And I was meant to meet you. I was waiting for you on the bench that day after I had a premonition from a tealeaf reading. I was coming toward you again today, since the tealeaves said that we'd cross paths again. Only I didn't expect to be jumped on by America's gang."

"So, your tealeaves failed you."

"They served their purpose, didn't they? You came to my rescue, and now we're here."

I beamed at her. "Eating cakes and building a friendship."

"You'll have to be careful, though, Little Bob." She paused for a second, a shadow in her eyes. "The academy isn't as safe as it appears to be. I saw darkness and danger hovering over you."

That was the story of my life, as I hid a terrible secret that I didn't want anyone to know.

"I know it!" I offered. "All the prince heirs are

dangerous, and Killian is more so. I think he's marked me."

"Marked you how?"

"He fixed his uninvited gaze upon me. He laughed at me when Louis badmouthed me. And then he smirked and winked at me before I ran into you. I was trying to get away from him in Sun Harbor in the first place."

"Sun Harbor is an exclusive club," Bea said. "But you must've been mistaken about Prince Killian. He doesn't do smirks, laughs, or winks; he barely smiles. Actually, no one in the academy has ever seen him smile." She shook her head. "You might be a hot squire to Prince Louis, but I don't think other princes, especially the prince of the House of Chaos, will fix their attention on a servant boy. No offense, though."

She forgot that she'd just said my power grade was off the charts.

"Yeah, whatever," I said. "But I need to find out Killian's weakness, just in case."

"Don't go poking a hornet's nest. Keep your head down."

The chatter around us suddenly quieted down. Potent power rolled into the air.

Pretty boy is here, Sy purred, fully awake now, and I felt the swirling of her lust.

This isn't the time to be in heat! I snapped.

Her heat could muddle my mind.

I need to feed! she protested. *It's been a week!*

You can survive without fucking for a week or two, I said. *We both agreed to lie low for a while. This realm is our best chance to hide from Ruin. We can't just fuck it up!*

I rose from my seat and craned my neck to peek down just as Prince Cade sauntered upstairs, his hands in his pants pocket, his turquoise eyes locking onto me. A wicked smirk hung on his lips, and a delicious dimple sank into his right cheek.

Damn, that man was hot! No wonder Sy was restless.

Cool your tits! I warned as I slumped down in my seat and sank lower to be out of sight.

The mage prince wouldn't be seeking me out, would he? I was nobody. I was a low servant who looked ridiculous with my short golden curls.

Tension left my legs that were about to sprint as I watched Cade stroll to his exclusive table and sit his arrogant ass down on the most comfortable sofa over the brim of my teacup.

"We should get out of here, like sneak out," I whispered to Bea.

She bit her lower lip and nodded. She was shy around her prince.

"You go and I'll follow," I suggested.

"Maybe you should leave first," she whispered back.

"Bob!" someone shouted.

Maybe there was another Bob here. Unable to help myself, I darted my wild gaze around to look for that Bob. No one else answered, and my gaze shot to Cade, only to find him wiggling his pinkie at me, beckoning me to go to him.

It wouldn't end well if I went to him, so I dipped my head and dropped my gaze, pretending that I didn't hear or see him.

"Go!" I urged Bea, who stared at me, a flash of worry in her eyes. She'd heard Cade calling my name as well. Unfortunately, it seemed there was only one Bob here.

"Little Bob!" Cade shouted, his voice unnecessarily loud. "Get your ass here. Right fucking now!"

"Me?" I asked tentatively.

"Who else is Little Bob, Louis's squire?"

"Why me?" I shouted across the room while other patrons stared at me. "I have to leave, sir. I have things to do. Prince Louis needs me to report to him within three minutes. I'm probably late already. If I don't report for duty in time, he might whip me."

Bea and I both got to our feet, ready to flee. But two mages positioned themselves to cut off my exit, the light-skinned one at the top of the stairs, the dark-skinned one heading to my table. Even if I got past the dark-skinned mage and shoved the light-skinned one off the stairs, the war mage patrolling outside the café would still round me up.

All the princes had tight security details on them, even in the academy. The houses didn't take any chance with their heirs.

The dark-skinned mage looked at me and jerked his chin in his prince's direction, which obviously meant, "You want to do this the easy way or the hard way, boy?"

It was inevitable that I had to face his prince then, and I didn't think I'd like the hard way.

"You should go," I told Bea.

She clenched her jaw, her lips pulling down as if they were weighted by anxiety. "I'm with you. Whatever happens, we're in this together."

Warmth swam in my chest. But I hadn't earned her loyalty yet.

I jogged toward the mage prince's table,

hunching my shoulders. His goon escorted me to prevent me from escaping.

"Your Highness," I greeted him. "I'm here at your summons. But we should make it quick. As I said before, Prince Louis is expecting me to report for duty soon."

"What duty?" Cade asked, his ankle across his knee, as if he had all the time in the world.

"I'm not at liberty to say," I said. "It's a confidential house affair."

"You're actually good at lying, Little Bob, but not great," he said. "Sit."

"I didn't do anything wrong, sir," I said.

He gave me a sharp look, and I dropped my ass on the soft bench. Bea stood beside the bench and bowed at the prince. She'd followed me.

"That's not what I heard," Cade said. "You picked a fight and did a number on a few model students in the Trailblazer Courtyard. You kicked a noble fae student in the nuts and blued his balls."

I blinked. "I think I booted a shifter. A coyote? But he said he wasn't a coyote. People lie these days."

The mage standing behind the prince gave me a warning look. I shouldn't have interrupted the prince then. For a servant, the rule was clear: do not speak to your superior unless you're spoken to.

"Who the fuck cares if he's a shifter or a fae." Cade dismissed me with a wave of his hand. He had a gold ring with a large, pure sapphire on top. It must be the priceless house ring, since sapphires and pearls represented the House of Mages. "The more important thing is he won't even be able to fuck a duck's ass for a week." Bea and I shared a look. Then I nodded humbly at the prince to indicate that I acknowledged that was terrible. "And all seven students whom you attacked viciously suffered magical trauma. They haven't been able to summon their magic since you fled the scene."

"Your Highness, that isn't the truth," Bea started, but I gave her a look to stop her.

Shit always hit the fan around me, but I didn't want any of it to drop on Bea. Everyone picked on her already. If she displeased the head of her house, he might kick her out. And then where would she go?

"It was self-defense, high sir," I said. "Those little shits tried to rob me, and I had to protect my interests!"

He arched a brow. "What interests?" he asked, intrigued.

"My ice cream." I sold my blood to Louis for a

dozen of them. "They tried to rob me of my ice cream!"

"Okay then." He nodded. "You gotta respect anyone who'd do anything to defend his ice cream. In fact, I'm impressed with your fighting ability."

Bea widened her eyes, but the worry ebbed out of her gray eyes.

"Thank you, sir," I said, smiling at him. "You seem nicer than the other princes. Now, can I go?"

"Why don't you come work for me instead?" he said. "There's something about you that I can't make out yet."

"I'm a hard worker," I said. "You want me to be your new squire?"

"Why not? It doesn't hurt to add another squire to my pile," he said.

"So, you want me to carry your sword—or in Your Highness's case, your wand? And when you're killed, I'll make sure you get an honorable burial?"

He growled. "What the fuck are you saying, boy?" Menace rolled off the powerful mage prince, all his good nature and playfulness vanishing.

Bea tensed, waving her demure hands in front of her. "Your Highness, Little Bob didn't mean it."

"That's my job for Prince Louis." I shrugged. "I assumed you'd want me for the same."

Cade narrowed his deep turquoise eyes. "Did Louis tell you those were your duties?"

"I asked him if that was what he wanted me to do, since that was what a squire did for his knight in the old days. My prince didn't say otherwise, so I assumed that was it. Yesterday, I requested to have my job description along with my pay written into a contract. I'll have to follow up with His Highness. It's been a week and he hasn't paid me." I bit my lip, anxiety knotting my stomach. "I'm going to see Prince Louis now to get it sorted out."

Think of all those times he made me watch him fuck! I wasn't going to watch it for free anymore! I had bills to pay.

Cade stared at me incredulously, then suddenly roared with laughter while running a hand over his reddish hair.

His mage minions joined in the laughter.

I didn't see how it was funny that Prince Louis hadn't paid me. The rich really had no idea how the poor suffered.

"Aren't you a delight, Little Bob?" he purred.

I gave Bea a look, knowing that she wouldn't be punished since Cade was obviously in a good mood. He was delighted.

"No sir, but I gotta go," I said. "Have a good day."

Without another word, I shot away from his table and flew down the stairs before his mage minions could stop me.

I was out of the door in seconds.

Chapter Eleven

"Prince Louis is gone," Drusilla said as soon as she saw me shooting into the maroon stone building of the House of Vampires.

Was she waiting for me in the lobby to deliver the bad news? Two attendants stood behind the counter, browsing through their tablets, probably on Spinchat.

Bad news traveled fast.

"Gone?" I widened my eyes, shifting my weight from my left foot to the right uncomfortably. "Who killed him?" I shook my head in dismay. "Fuck, I'm too late! Now who is going to reimburse me for my one week's hard work? I'm now worried sick that he might not have told the accountant that I am on the payroll! I just can't get a break, can I?"

And I had to worry about burying him. I hadn't even picked a graveyard for him yet. I was new to this realm!

Drusilla glared at me, which seemed to dilute her moping. As his PA, she usually followed him around. Everyone could see that she had a crush on her boss. Too bad that she had to be the one who kept bringing gorgeous women to his rooms for him to feed on and fuck.

I didn't think that she ever got fucked, even though she was a blonde, and Louis had a thing for blondes. But at least he didn't ask her to watch him fuck, as he demanded of me.

The vampire prince got off on seeing me flush with anger and desire, anger from me and desire from Sy. He could smell her desire and mistook it as mine.

That was one of the reasons that I asked Bea to find some spells and potions to turn my golden curls to straight, dark hair. I wanted to turn him off with my new look.

Drusilla shook her head, her high ponytail swinging, as if she was disappointed in me. Actually, it was more than disappointment. I rocked on my toes and retreated a step, just in case she tried to hit me with the tablet in her hand.

She straightened her silver chalice shirt and smart pants. She always wore pants. One day, I'd tell her that she could try a miniskirt without wearing panties, then sit across from Louis, lifting her foot subtly and crossing her leg a few times while taking notes from him.

I saw an old movie once, and the woman in it got into the cop's pants with that move.

"This isn't about you, Little Bob!" Drusilla scolded, thinning her glossy lips.

I'd steal one of her shiny lipsticks and try it on my lips one of these days.

I was still staring at her lips. "But—"

"You stupid, callous, and self-centered boy!" She raised her voice a notch. "It's a miracle that you've survived for so long."

I tugged up the corner of my lips and smirked at her. "You have no idea, babe."

"Don't ever call me babe again, Little Bob! Don't forget your place!" She scowled. "Prince Louis was called to the realm by the king."

"That's good then, right?" I soaked in the news and let out a breath of relief. I just had to be patient and wait for the prince to come back and pay me then.

"Summoned by the king is never good," Drusilla said.

"Then I hope our prince is alright and the king is forgiving. Maybe His Highness shouldn't fuck everything that moves."

Drusilla looked like she really wanted to slap me, so I took another step away from her.

Mist of Cinder was divided into six regions, ruled by five kings. The House of Vampires ruled the north, the House of Shifters took the south, the House of Mages claimed the east, the House of Chaos made the west their territory, and the center of the realm belonged to the House of Fae, as they were native to the land.

The sixth region was called CrimsonTide, unclaimed by any house. It was the neutral zone and the most dangerous, cutthroat area in Mist of Cinder.

I had studied the map extensively, just in case I had to run one day. I wouldn't want to go back to the human realm, so my best bet was to move deeper into the realm, somewhere like CrimsonTide.

Sy and I would be fine living amid criminals, rebels, and rogues.

Drusilla's expression turned sour, as if she'd

bitten into a lemon. "His Highness ordered me to keep an eye on you while he's away."

My face broke into a big grin. "So, Gunnar and the royal guards accompanied the prince?"

"I wonder why His Highness didn't bring you with him, since you're his new favorite."

She wasn't happy about the prince not bringing her with him. And if she knew I was a girl and the prince's favorite, she might try to murder me in my sleep.

"Maybe he thinks I'm his dirty little secret that he needs to keep away from the king and the rest of the royal family." I shrugged. "So, it's best to keep me here so I won't embarrass him in front of them."

"You'll embarrass him for sure." She nodded. "You need to grow some sense if you know what's good for you."

"Yeah? Will you teach me?" I said, starting to notice a dozen vampires moving closer to me, their hungry gazes homing in on me.

My blood enticed monsters.

The vamps could all smell my delicious blood, which was like nothing they'd ever tried. Some of them still sought an opening to get their fangs into my neck, even after their prince had sent out a warning and marked me as his exclusive food source.

Problem was that Louis's imprint didn't exactly stick, as I ate spells, curses, and magic like candies. I didn't tell him that though. He'd just use it as a legit excuse to drink from me daily to renew his "mark" on me.

Younger or newly made vampires had less control and could barely resist the call of my blood in my proximity. Incidents happened, and Louis had had to kill a few who came after me to set an example, right after I'd stabbed them with Deathsong, which I hid in my boot.

Personally, I wasn't too worried about the vampires jumping on me after a while. They were less scary than Shriekers.

"I'm going back to my room. It's getting crowded here," I said. "But I'll come down for lunch."

With the prince gone, I had the rest of the day for myself. No more accompanying him to see him fuck and then having to find an excuse to depart. He thought it was a game. And now that Killian had put a terrible idea in his head, Louis might just act on it and encourage his harem to come at me to suck my dick.

"You'll give me gray hair, Little Bob." Drusilla

shook her head. "I'm glad Gunnar wants to be in charge of you."

"That's the sweet burden he has to carry," I said and shot toward the elevator.

The prince had put me in the room next to his penthouse on the top floor. I was the only one who had the privilege of staying on this floor, even though I preferred the servant's room first assigned to me by Drusilla. My blood was so rare that Louis became paranoid that I'd be drained by others if he didn't keep me close.

Louis had a lot of quirks and vices, but he never brought women to his suite. He screwed them elsewhere. Only Gunnar, Drusilla, and the prince's old maid were allowed to come up to this floor.

I pushed open the door to my room that was converted from a storage space. It had a window though. The door had no lock, since Louis wanted to make sure that he could stroll in here anytime he wanted.

I'd been extremely careful when I changed my clothes. The vampire prince didn't respect my privacy. But after he and Gunnar both got the treatment of scorpions and spiders falling on them from the top of the doorframe, they were more discreet.

And next time, I promised that they'd get a horde of hornets.

I took off my boots, put them in the closet, and flopped onto the bed.

It was always nice to have a nap before lunch.

Until a shriek pierced my mind and dark mist invaded my head.

Chapter Twelve

The shrieks and wails went on and on, like a fury's cries in the distance.

Cold sweat broke out of my every pore. I was halfway to hyperventilation, which always happened when I sensed Shriekers looming closer.

I rolled off the bed and rushed toward the window, my heart in my throat.

Those abominations had breached the Veil. They were in the academy grounds somewhere.

But how had they gotten in?

They shouldn't have the kind of magic to push through the Veil, but then the mage prince had mentioned that the portal to the academy was their weaker back door.

Last time, the raven, my father's spy, had also gotten in. I'd killed it before it could report back to Ruin. I'd speculated that the raven getting in was because it was a magical creature, unlike Shriekers that were made by my father's dark power.

Chills crept over my bones as a flashback flooded my fluttering eyelids.

Ruin in his half shadowy skeleton and half gorgeous humanoid form latched onto me, sucking the magic I'd brought back into himself. When there was no more magic left in me, he started to dine on my essence. The excruciating pain of being consumed alive made me beg for death.

Yet I couldn't die, even as I diminished and shrank into a mummy-like hollowed form. At six, I'd tried to escape after I was revived, only to be hunted and chained in a deep pit on top of dirt, moss, and bones.

I learned not to rush into action after Ruin's severe punishment, after he'd also let Shriekers feed on me, chewing my flesh and picking on my insides while I endured every second.

I learned to bide my time, planning my great escape meticulously, pretending to be an obedient daughter and servant to please him, enduring being fed upon by him for eleven years. I'd never failed to show my loyalty to him and had passed all his tests.

Until I was strong enough. Until he finally let his guard down. Then one day, in the field while harvesting magic for him, Sy and I slaughtered all his agents that escorted and guarded me.

We'd escaped at the perfect time.

Ruin was getting stronger. One more year and the eater of worlds would mostly recover from being fatally wounded by the two other original gods eons ago, and then he'd venture into our world, consuming it. Everything we knew would be history.

For eight years now, Ruin and his agents had never stopped hunting me. Sy and I had never had a full night of sleep, not even after I'd come to Mist of Cinder, as we were always looking over our shoulder, afraid and paranoid. And when we slept, nightmares came.

I gazed out the window, and Sy peeked out too.

The high noon sun glinted off the top of the ivory tower in the distance. Skyward accommodated a private study, private library, top research center, and meeting rooms that only the prince heirs had access to. It was heavily warded. I hadn't had time to sneak in, but it was on my to-do list.

I looked closer to home, at the cherry blossoms flourishing in the golden rays in the back garden of the House of Vampires. The Shriekers were bold enough to hunt me at noon. Ruin was getting more desperate.

As dread kept rising in me and toxic fear thundered in my chest, rage formed like beating wings.

I'd finally found a place where I could fit in. The magic here was like my kin, and it accepted me instead of fearing me. I'd grown protective of it, but now Father had found me, and he was going to strip me down until I had nothing, no one, and nowhere to go again.

And worse, Ruin would target this realm. Guilt gnawed at my insides, even though sooner or later, I knew he'd find Mist of Cinder, as he'd been hunting for it for a long time. In his glory days as God of Ruin, he hadn't needed to replenish himself with Earth magic, and Mist of Cinder hadn't been separated from the mortal realm back then.

I never asked too much and never thought I could have a future, as I understood I was living on borrowed time. But eight years of freedom was too short, and I hadn't really lived until I came to Mist of Cinder.

It'd only been a week since I came here, and now it was going to be taken away from me.

Wrath rained down on me.

I wouldn't allow it. I wouldn't allow my father to destroy me again.

I'd fight with everything I had to stay in Mist of Cinder, the little haven I'd just found.

I would strike first.

Let's go hunt! Sy hissed.

The thrill of the hunt coursed through our veins, pushing the icy fear to the edge of our consciousness.

I shrugged off the servant uniform and put on a jacket and leather pants that I'd stolen from one of the shops. I inserted Deathsong into the strap on my left boot, climbed out of the window, jumped to the balcony below, then a branch of a tree, and landed in a crouch on the ground.

I darted between the cherry trees and shot out of the backyard of the vampire house, heading northwest, where I felt the faint tug of the Shriekers' foul signature.

They called me. They taunted me. They got used to hunting me and never thought that I'd hunt them back.

I zoomed past the woods, the courtyard, and

BattleStar training field and kept moving north. Under the brilliant sun, I stuck to the shade, avoiding small groups while siphoning a pinch of magic from the students to shield myself from their sight.

Luckily, none of the prince heirs were around to detect my shenanigans.

It'd be bad news for me to bump into any of them, as they were powerful enough to see through my glamour.

Fae called it glamour, as it was part of their natural magic. Mages had to use potions or weave spells from the surrounding elements to cloak themselves. I achieved my kind of glamour by siphoning a tiny drop of magic from supernaturals around me, just enough for everyone to ignore me and not enough to damage them.

This was one hell of a trick I'd taught myself after I came to this realm and watched others do magic in classes.

I bet, since heat steamed from the ground, the princes were napping or fucking. After residing in Mist of Cinder for only a week, I'd found that the supernaturals fucked a lot more than humans ever did. Sy was giddy at the prospect, but our tight schedule had kept her from going out to have fun, and I'd forbidden her from screwing everyone here like it was open season and fucking up our chances of keeping a low profile.

Yet I knew I couldn't keep her locked away for long. She'd need to feed soon.

I bit my lip. We'd brainstorm as to how it should get done later.

After running for nearly two miles, I reached the north edge of the campus. Houses and buildings stretched thinner, with a few uninhabited cabins scattered on the slope. At the far end of the green field, a dark forest and rolling hills loomed.

This part was like the wild west, unclaimed. The region on the other side of the dark forest was the shifters' territory.

As I raced down the slope, foul magic bearing the Shriekers' signature carried in the wind. I sniffed the air in distaste, a battle plan forming in my head. After I'd escaped my father, none of his agents that had encountered me had lived to tell the tale and report back to him about my current magical and fighting ability.

I'd become a monster hunter.

During eight years on the run, I hadn't hidden like a mouse in a hole. I'd used every opportunity to equip myself, to learn, and to better myself in every way. Due to my bloodline, I learned a lot faster than anyone else. I absorbed knowledge like siphoning magic, with a single zealous, desperate purpose—one day, I'd beat and vanquish my father, the ancient evil god.

I paused for a second. I felt only one Shrieker in the dark forest. It was luring me here. It thought that it could trap me. But it offered me no small amount of comfort that there wasn't a horde breaking through the Veil to come after me.

Usually, the scouts ran ahead. But a scout couldn't have penetrated the Veil. My lone stalker was a powerful female, probably the rank of a captain. It had underestimated me because of its power grade, and thus it bore the ambition of capturing "the lost princess" single-handed and dumping me at the feet of my father. The reward would be its alone.

I marched toward the entry of the dark forest; the stench of the Shrieker grew stronger.

A sign whipped against the bark of an enormous black maple in the wind: **Underhill! Enter At Your Own Peril!**

Sounds dangerous, Sy purred.

This was the place where the supernaturals dared the losers of their drinking games to enter. Rumor said that most supernaturals who went in never came out, and those who came out didn't remember a damn thing.

Even standing where I was, I could sense a menacing force within the ancient forest. Yet I wasn't too concerned about the wild, dark, and terrifying magic of Underhill. All magic, dark or light or vicious, always resonated with me.

Feel it, Sy? I asked.

The Shrieker isn't too far in, Sy answered. *It fears the creatures in the forest. But they're watching instead of attacking it, knowing we're coming. The magic told them so, and we shall not hunt any creature of Underhill.*

I hope you stick to your own principles, I said. *You eat everything.*

Not them, she said in displeasure.

A wolf howled in the distance, making me jump out of my skin. The wolf's song rose from the other side of Underhill, which marked the border of the shifter territory.

It was this side that everyone tried to avoid.

As I tried to pinpoint the Shrieker's position with Sy's aid so I could go around it for a sneak attack, I sensed someone else who carried a different magical signature from Underhill's natives. The scent of prey. Bait.

As if on cue, a muffled scream tore out, then a whimper.

I stalked toward the sound.

It's a trap, Sy called.

Of course. The Shrieker probably got a student from the school.

Not our problem, Sy said. *We stick to our plan and kill the enemy. We don't get distracted by any bait. As a rule, we don't risk our neck for anyone.*

Let's see, I said non-committally.

Don't go soft now, she warned.

I cut a path into a copse of ancient trees of all colors, dark magic twirling at my feet and beckoning me forward.

What I hadn't expected was to see Lady America presented as bait.

Tied to a red tree, she whimpered through her gag that looked like her own socks. Sickly fear coated her frosty blue eyes, so thick that I could smell its stench. Another sniff, and I knew that she'd peed herself. When facing fear and death, all men and women were equal. The fae chick didn't turn up her nose at me now.

How had the Shrieker captured her? Had

America wandered to this forbidden zone? She wouldn't be so foolish as to play the game of Truth or Dare and take the dare option to come here, would she? If she had, it only meant that she also had a dirty secret that she wouldn't want anyone else to know about.

Who cares, Sy said. *Just go find our mortal foe and gut it. And I'll sing a song of vanquish and victory.*

Yet unexpected empathy washed over me, despite the fact that I despised this fae. I was going soft, or it was something else. After being in this realm for only a week, I'd grown a sense of protection toward this last magical realm and the living things in it.

"*Princess,*" the Shrieker called. "I feel you. I felt you when I entered this new realm. The magic here is pure and tenfold more potent than in the mortal realm! You must take it all for the master. Daddy will forgive you when you bring him this great gift."

Shriekers were terrible at talking. They mimicked how humans talked and often got it wrong. Daddy? Seriously?

"Have you seen the sacrifice I brought for you— food for your monster?" They always called Sy my monster, as I kept her name from them. "The fae smells sweet. Her meat will taste better than others your monsters ate. Yummy. Yummy!"

America struggled to no avail and whimpered in terror.

Kill the fae girl so we won't be distracted, then we'll deal with that stupid Shrieker, Sy urged. *It called me your monster!*

We do things differently from now on, I said. *We're turning over a new leaf to prove there's hope for us.*

What hope?

We aren't a psychopath anymore, I offered. *Recognize that, and we'll have a future here.*

I darted between the trees, zigzagging until I reached America. Deathsong was out of my boot and in my hand. America stared at me, her eyes white with shock and fear. I shook my head at her to warn her to stay quiet, then I slashed the ropes that tied her with my dagger.

"Run," I said.

She coughed but then covered her mouth quickly and burst into a run without looking back, without sparing me a glance or uttering a thank you.

I shot in the other direction before the Shrieker could lurch at me, luring it deeper into Underhill, so no one would see me battle it should anyone

come   looking.   America   might   bring
reinforcements.

The Shrieker chased me, screeching, not pleased that I'd managed to bypass its trap and free the bait. Its metal scorpion legs stretched to swat at me from several feet away. I ducked behind a tree and veered left. Its claws chipped away the old tree bark, sending it flying everywhere.

A menacing and unforgiving snarl resonated in the forest. My pursuer had just pissed off the dark force here. Even if I didn't finish it, Underhill would turn it inside out. Well, I'd do the honors and earn some points with Underhill.

The wild magic still twirled at my feet, no matter how fast I ran.

Sy's voice nagged in my ear. *We should've killed that snobby fae instead of saving her.*

We can't just kill anyone we don't like, Sy, I said.

You want to kill that vampire captain, she said.

Yeah, he annoyed me, but I won't kill him unless he strikes to maim or murder us first, I said. *There's a difference.*

I don't see the difference. But your bleeding heart will inconvenience us. I bet all my money that fae is going to rat us out.

You don't have a penny, I said. *And even if you*

had money, I wouldn't let you bet on anything since you have no sense. Anyway, things are different now, Sy, and we must adapt.

It got dimmer as I ventured deeper into the forest.

There was barely any visibility under the vast trees. Thick groves of undergrowth extended for miles, blocking my path. I ran my lips between my teeth, pondering my options, as the Shrieker let out an excited shrill, in hot pursuit.

Then, a path parted for me, lined with thorny shrubs on either side.

Shit! My eyes widened in awe. The forest could shift!

The wild magic purred like a pleased kitten that had just had its first sip of milk.

Suddenly, I understood why Underhill had allowed the Shrieker to get so far. It'd sensed me in the realm and taken an interest in me. Underhill wanted me here so it could check me out, as it'd never encountered my kind. Well, I hated to disappoint, but I was one of a kind; I was a singularity.

The forest was now all shivering shadows and unnatural wind. No light sifted through to the ground, yet I could see aspens, cedars, pines, and rare trees and plants that did not grow in the mortal realm vying for space. The air smelled of sweet honeysuckle, bitter oranges, dense pine, and dark magic.

A blur of shadows traveled amid the trees—the predators of Underhill. They'd followed me, stalking and watching.

My every nerve was on high alert; a rush of adrenaline pulsed in my veins.

This will be fun, Sy said, perking up.

She liked monsters.

We've got a pursuer and stalkers, I said. *This isn't a trek into the woods or a stroll in the park!*

The story of our life, Little Bob, she sighed in glee. *Ready for a fight!*

Sure, she said. *I'll do the fighting.*

I didn't have Sy's physical strength and speed. If I was overpowered, I'd take Underhill's magic to overcome the Shrieker, a temptation and outcome I didn't desire.

Blue light streamed through the air ahead, revealing a gem-like lake by two entwined red trees that looked like eternal lovers, making the forest resemble a fairy dream.

I knew that Underhill didn't want me to go further.

Here it is, I told Sy.

Peachy. She nodded.

The Shrieker screamed giddily, closing in on me. I leapt up to a lower branch of Dar Hedge right before its claws grabbed my ankle and swung up to a higher branch.

The Shrieker dug its claws into the trunk to lift itself. I pulled myself higher and faster and perched on a branch twenty feet from the Shrieker.

Here, Sy would take over. We were vulnerable during transformation, but we had time before the Shrieker reached us.

An icy blue ray flashed; pain rushed through my bones, and my skin stretched. Three blinks, and Sy was there, dominating our form. She inhaled the forest scent deeply, soaking in its wild, dark magic, before flexing her shoulders and training her golden eyes below.

The predators in their dark shapes and different sizes growled, reacting to Sy, welcoming her to their ranks as a monster in her own right. Sy threw her head back, her pointed ears pricking in the dark wind, and howled with bloodlust.

Underhill's beasts howled with her.

Sy's skin turned blue, with scales forming on her shoulders, breasts, forearms, and thighs. She was a chameleon with the ability to change her color and physique to blend into the environment.

"Here I come, Houston!" she shouted, borrowing my phrase, and jumped from the branch.

Her fangs elongated, her claws stretched out, and she slashed at the Shrieker.

It was very fast. It gave up on climbing and jumped several feet away from Sy on the forest floor. Two monsters, one ugly and one beautiful, faced each other.

The Shrieker hissed, towering over Sy, its claws rotating like vast hooks. It answered Sy's challenge, ready to charge toward her.

"Halt!" I commanded through Sy's mouth. I had a couple of questions before I let her have fun. And I was better at interrogating.

"How did you get in? How did you track me?" I demanded.

The Shrieker grinned grotesquely. This female was more powerful than other Shriekers and thus more ambitious.

"Master upgraded us with your precious blood," it revealed. "I have your blood in me now, Princess, so we're related."

Chills sank into my bones, and repulsion crawled over my skin.

My father had had my blood stored in his vault before I'd fled him.

So, the upgraded Shriekers could breach the Veil into Mist of Cinder. I'd have to find a way to amend it and stop the abominations from getting into the realm.

"How many of you have been upgraded? How many of Ruin's agents are inside the realm now?"

"A dozen are waiting outside, Princess," it said. "I'm clever, so I got ahead of them. I want the reward! Master needs you now more than ever, and my brethren need more of your blood to become better and superior. Come with me and you won't need to suffer, Princess. The others won't be as gentle as I. Master won't stop until he has you home. You're his most precious, the apple of his eye."

For a second, we froze in fear as the dark memory of my father feeding upon me swirled back. This abomination was right. He and his agents would keep coming now that his agents had caught up with me.

Want me to shut it up? Sy asked.

We can never be caught, I told her.

I won't leave you with him, ever, Sy said fiercely.

She'd taken most of the blunt hits for me in those terrible years, shoving me into the background and trying to endure the agony alone. But I'd always been there, too, shielding her and taking the inhuman pain into myself so she could survive instead of being broken.

I'd never leave Sy alone with him either.

If worst comes to worst, we'll find a way to burn ourselves to ashes and erase our souls so he can't bring us back as his vessel again and again.

Letting out a warrior's roar, Sy charged.

The Shrieker moved like a blur toward her as well. This Shrieker was superior to the others in speed and strength, even more so than the ones we'd fought last week. Sy sidestepped at the last second, her claws extending and slashing toward the Shrieker's heart, but it twisted away like a slippery eel.

Baring her fangs to flash a vicious smile, Sy leapt high, thrusting her claws toward the Shrieker's neck sideways. The Shrieker rolled away, its machine parts squeaking. But Sy had already altered her course, her claws slicing off the Shrieker's left arm in one sweep.

Our foe screamed in pain.

"Shut up and take it like a motherfucker!" Sy barked as her claws opened another gash on the Shrieker's hide from the side.

The Shrieker charged, and Sy retreated, then charged again, cleaving a chunk off our enemy. Sy was going to bleed the Shrieker dry and weaken it before going for the fatal strike.

But the Shrieker started regenerating.

Sy split-kicked it before leaping and landing on its back. Just as we started wondering why this Shrieker didn't have lethal tentacles, a pair of ragged bat wings burst out of its back.

Shit! That was why it could breach the Veil! It had flown in with a drop of my blood in its dirty veins. And that was why this Shrieker was more powerful than the others.

Furious, Sy slashed at the Shrieker's wing with the brutal force of her claws. The Shrieker flapped and thrust its other wing at Sy, the talons digging into her ribcage. Sy gasped in pain, and I dove in to absorb most of it so she could keep fighting.

While I curled into a ball, fighting my tears as a jumble of pain burned in my head, Sy bellowed, hacking and ripping the Shrieker's cervical spine. The Shrieker fell to the dirt and rolled onto Sy, pinning her under its weight.

Ragged breaths wheezed out of Sy. She was much bigger and more muscular than me. Pinned down by the Shrieker's crushing weight, she was immobilized. The Shrieker screamed victoriously even though Sy had weakened it, its claws grabbing

Sy's wrists while its other hand's claws produced a magical chain that emitted my father's foul magic.

Once it succeeded in chaining us, it'd be game over. Ruin's minion would drag us all the way back to him.

Icy fear and terror choked me, closing the air passage to my lungs.

Never! Sy snarled. *We'll fight to the bitter end!*

Or die trying. I signaled her that I was going to take control of our form.

In mid-shift, Sy's size shrank as I took over, which gave us room to maneuver. When I surfaced, I always had the same outfit and gear that I wore previously. My knees bending, I pulled Deathsong from the sheath on my boot and jammed it into the Shrieker's gut with all the strength I had. I didn't stop there. I dragged it up the Shrieker's flesh and machine parts until it pierced my foe's heart.

It felt like forever, but the Shrieker finally shuddered and let out one last bone-chilling shriek.

I wiggled out from under the dead Shrieker, its blood and gore soaking me from head to toe. I gagged at the stench and retched before I rolled onto my back and just lay there to catch my breath.

The job wasn't done. We needed to erase the

evidence of the Shrieker. Forcing myself to get to my feet, I stared at the Shrieker's large corpse.

I shook my head. I wouldn't take magic from Underhill to burn the body.

Let's dump it in the lake, Sy suggested.

I gave the lake a look. Blue light and mist hovered over it, the light coming from the depths of the water. It was so pure and clear that all I wanted was to guard it.

I shook my head. "No, I might swim there. And if things don't work out for us in the school, we might have to live by the lake for a while. We'll just take care of the body the old-fashioned way, like digging a grave. Feel free to take over anytime."

I'd rather she dealt with the blood and gore.

Sure, I'm the grave digger, and handling a murder scene is my specialty, Sy said.

"Of course. I tip my hat to you."

Didn't you hear the sarcasm in my tone? You're not only getting softer, you're also getting slow, little chubby cherub Bob.

"I'm not that chubby."

I haven't fed for a while, so I can't do any heavy lifting. You'll have to clean up the mess yourself. I'm taking a much-needed nap now to regenerate.

And she checked out.

I shook my head in disgust. I couldn't believe that she'd bail just like that. These days, even my other half wasn't reliable.

The wind stirred in the forest. Wild magic danced, delighting in the battle that I'd fought. The predators loomed in closer, not lurking anymore. They wouldn't hurt me, as I didn't smell like prey.

An idea hit me.

"All yours, my kin! Feast!" I called, kicking the corpse of the Shrieker, and Underhill's shadow beasts descended upon my offering.

I sprang toward the lake and jumped into it. The pure, icy water shot energy into me, my fatigue receding. Thoughts and plans ran wild in my mind. I needed to tip off the prince heirs, the most powerful supernaturals in the realm, and get them to patch up the Veil.

And there was another issue to worry about. America had seen the Shrieker and me, and the Shrieker had called me "princess." Even though everyone thought I was a boy, the fae chick could still bring me trouble.

America might've told the authorities who ranked higher than her, someone like the princes or the headmaster or headmistress, whoever it may be. I needed to get out of Underhill soon, but my current state—bruised, wounded, my clothes shredded and ruined—would make it difficult to sneak back to my room in the vampire house. One small mercy was that the prince was away.

I dozed off in the lake until pounding lust jerked me awake.

Chapter Thirteen

My eyes flashed open. I was no longer floating on the crystal-clear lake in Underhill.

Sy had taken over, fucking, judging from the moans she made.

I peeked out of her golden eyes, still disoriented, as I took in our surroundings. The ivory tower, Skyward, shone in the moonlight in the north. It appeared that I must've passed out for hours in Underhill.

Panning forty-five degrees, a violet building of steel and glass that belonged to the House of Chaos stood tall. Drawing back to where we were now, Sy's back was pressed against the wall of a lime-colored, curved brick building with a tiled roof.

I stared at the giant male whom Sy was riding.

He carried her like she weighed as much as a naked ear of corn, his large hands grabbing her butt cheeks to support her while propelling his powerful hips toward her. His hard cock filled her. His power, nearly as strong as Killian's, was a beacon in the vast ocean of darkness.

Sy wasn't even slightly concerned about how powerful and dangerous her random fuck buddy was. She drank it in as if she hadn't had a good meal until now. Sy was super toned and taller than most females. She matched the male's physique perfectly, and they both had the same type of savage beauty.

For the first time in front of a sexual partner, Sy didn't hide her lethalness. And she was damn deadly; even her hair was a weapon. She'd once used it to wrap around a rapist's neck and squeeze out the last inch of his life while watching with a fascinated smile.

Sex was her best energy drink, but she had boundaries—consent was one of them. She wouldn't break that rule and wouldn't allow her mark to break it either. And that was the main difference between sex predators and Sy.

Sy threw her head back and laughed, enjoying it too much, her clawed hands sinking into his broad shoulders, and he growled in approval. They were two peas in a pod.

She fucked him back just as fiercely, thrusting her ass toward him, riding his steel-hard length, and moaned like this was the best fuck she'd ever had.

That was a little disturbing.

As I drank in the scene, I realized that they were fucking against the wall of Clockwork, the academy's Public Studies building. It had to be past midnight, yet a few windows still had lights on.

What the fuck, Sy? I cursed. *You should know better than fucking a stranger here. You'll endanger us!*

And how had she even come across this powerful male? I felt betrayed that she'd taken over while I was napping in the lake. But then, it wasn't the first time she'd done that.

In fact, more than a few times, I'd woken up in the middle of consuming a corpse that Sy had just slaughtered. Every time, I'd freaked out and retched while she watched me in wicked delight. She knew that I did not consume raw meat and could never get used to it. And that was her terrible sense of humor,

if she had any.

It was also a power play to say "fuck you" to me now and then since despite my smaller, weaker form,

I was the primary, dominant one. When it came to blows, I always won.

You know my nature. I'm a sex worker, Sy purred while not missing a beat riding that male.

Now she thought she was a sex worker?

Do you even know what a sex worker actually does? I sneered. I didn't think she could tell the difference between a sex worker and a miracle worker.

No more slut shaming, she warned, her legs tightening around the male's hips as he pounded into her relentlessly. *I finally met a male who can take me and match me. He's giving me double—no, triple the energy that anyone else could offer.*

She had to feed. Even though I wanted to deny it, I also needed her to feed to sustain me. No matter how innocent and harmless I looked most of the time, I was a predator in every fiber of my being. Consuming regular food could never sate the vast void in me, where my core magic still slumbered.

So, I either let her do her and go on a sex binge or watched her go around eating intelligent beings, which would haunt my nightmares.

I should just shut the fuck up, close my eyes, let her ride the big dick, and pray that it'd be over soon.

But I didn't close my eyes.

While they pounded each other vehemently, my

heart was in my throat, my eyes darting around wildly as my worries of getting caught on the academy grounds tied knots in my stomach.

Luckily, no one strolled past, not even the creatures of the night. But when I squinted and resumed my study of the male she was screwing, I was furious again. Sy was too reckless and out of control.

During my stay at the academy and accompanying Louis everywhere, I'd never met this male who was obviously a force of nature. His radiant silver hair framed his strong face and cruel lips. His silver eyes flashed in pleasure as he pounded into Sy, his gaze never leaving Sy's face unless it darted to her gorgeous breasts. The way he looked at her was indulgent, fascinated, and possessive, as if he'd found a hidden gem, as if he'd never met his equal until her.

He was a fae. And Sy looked very close to a fae as well.

Shit! This was bad. If Sy developed an attachment...

I hissed a warning from my parched throat, and Sy hissed in incredible pleasure, exposing her fangs. The male growled, showing her his fangs.

Double fuck! Sy had already made a mistake by feeding so close to home. If she got even more stupid and thought that she'd found her perfect match, she'd do us in! My father didn't even need to come and finish us off. After this, I'd make her avoid this male, just like I'd run from the prince of the House of Chaos.

You think I'm going to be a problem? I've kept you safe all these years! she grated while riding a fae cock with abandon, as if that would punish me. *Must you be so judgmental when I finally have a good fuck? Stop thinking you're my conscience!*

I sulked. I didn't want to get into a fight with Sy. A rift between us did no one any good, but Sy was going too far this time.

Wait until the day you fuck the chaos prince, then you'll get me, she added.

I huffed in anger and disbelief. *Are you insane, Sy? I'd never do such a thing! He's unfuckable; forbidden fruit!*

Not to us. We always challenge every rule under the sun and moon, she said. *Now back off and let me enjoy this mighty cock. You're welcome to stay and watch though. You can even offer me notes later.*

I bit my nails before I shouted, *Remember, this is just a fuck. It means nothing!*

Before I zoned out, the fae male dropped her to the ground and spun her around. Sy obliged and planted her palms on the wall, arching her back and thrusting her ass toward the fae to urge him on while giving him better access.

She'd never shown her back to anyone else before. She'd always insisted on riding the males on top, so she could be in control during sex. She had never allowed anyone to cage her beneath them or to fuck her from behind.

She'd been the one fucking.

I was shocked at her sudden switching of the rules.

You're letting him fuck you, Sy! I shouted.

Chill. It's time to explore, she said. *I'm tired of one position all the time.*

The fae male thrust into her hard, so deliciously that even I arched my back. Sy moaned and moaned. The fae groaned. He embedded himself deeply in her before drawing out a couple inches and thrusting back in, harder and faster. The sound of flesh slapping flesh beat in a rapid rhythm, disturbing the night, yet neither of them gave a shit. Sy's heavy breasts bounced up and down. The male cupped her left breast from behind, kneading her taut tit as if it was gold he had found. His other hand gripped her hip to pin her against him and maneuver their movements.

She slammed her ass back into his groin, fast and

furious, granting them the joy of fucking like two wild beasts. Together, they built waves, higher and higher, the leftovers crashing into me through Sy, and the tide kept rising, the pressure painful and euphoric all at once.

Sy was going to come soon. I could feel it. Despite its intensity for her, I experienced it through a glass door. I was thankful for that, as I didn't want to feel the full impact of being fucked by the powerful fae.

No one had fucked her like this fae male.

When he drove into her next, long and hard and deep, Sy reached the final point and climaxed. The waves of pleasure rippled and spread through Sy, and the fae tensed behind her, tightening his grip on her, pulling her against him.

And Sy let him while relishing and riding her prolonged, intense orgasm.

Are you done? I checked in impatiently.

Sy didn't do long orgasms. In the past, she'd always had a quick one, sucked in the energy she needed, gotten off her mark, and run off in a blur, often leaving them writhing and unfinished.

She wasn't exactly the sentimental type.

Yet with this dangerous fae, Sy tossed all our rules out of the window. She didn't even disguise herself by putting a veil over her face or a pair of sunglasses over her eyes. She'd let him see her true form and even showed him her fangs proudly. He showed her his as well.

Two fucking psychos!

I widened my eyes incredulously as the fae male groaned roughly and emptied himself in her! Sy had never let anyone spill their seed in her. Right in front of my eyes, the unthinkable thing happened—he started feeding on her while she did the same.

The fae was like her, and Sy knew!

I screamed at her.

Too bad, I didn't want to take over in this situation while she had a cock in her.

Sy turned over her shoulder to gaze up at the fae male through her lush eyelashes while he smiled back at her.

It's wonderful, she sighed, sated.

Fuck wonderful! I grated in a panic. I was about to lose her. *Fuck it!*

No worries, tight-butt, she purred. *You still have me. I just wanted to experience this one time, and I got what I needed. I know what's at stake, and emotions are for fools.*

She pulled away from the fae before he pulled out of her and scrambled to pick up the two pieces she sometimes wore when she didn't shift to her naked form—a cuirass breastplate with a short skirt that barely covered the tops of her thighs.

She slapped the two pieces on, gave the fae a sultry glance, and took off in a spring. I blew out a relieved breath. In the end, she'd stuck to her routine—no cuddle. Fuck and run.

"Wait, tell me your name!" the fae demanded.

Don't tell him, I warned.

"Sy," she offered in delight.

It was the first time she'd ever said her name to anyone besides me.

"Where can I find you?" he said, about to give chase.

I hissed at Sy in a serious warning.

"I'll find you." Sy laughed and picked up speed. "California, here I come!"

You think this is a fucking game? I yelled at her furiously.

Sy cut across the training field of BattleStar, where no one was exercising at this hour, and darted into the woods from their west entry point. The vampire house was close to the end of the north side.

A figure moved toward us under the moonlight sifting through the leaves.

Shit.

Sy dashed behind a thick shrub at my urging. I took the reins and staggered up in my form. And then I was looking up at Killian, his handsome face harsh, backlit by the dim moonlight, his eyes as cold as midnight ice.

I blinked. What was he doing in this neck of the woods so deep into the night?

My heart thundered in my ribcage. It was bad to bump into anyone while I was disheveled, let alone running into the prince of the House of Chaos, whom I'd tried my best to avoid.

A dark, surprised look flashed in his eyes as he darted his gaze from my face to my tattered clothes. I instantly folded my arms across my chest.

"You!" His voice was rough. "What are you doing here?"

I'd been fast. Even if he'd caught a glimpse of Sy and my transformation, he'd think that his eyes were playing tricks on him in the dark woods.

I just needed to swagger and give him some attitude.

"Taking a leak, sir," I said.

He sniffed, a sheen of molten gold rolling over his storm-blue eyes. He knew that I was lying, and he probably smelled sex on me. I cursed Sy again under my breath.

Before he could reach to grab me or stop me, I shot in the opposite direction like a bat out of hell, fleeing as fast as I could.

"I'm sorry, high sir. It won't happen again! Goodnight!" I let the wind carry my rushed words to him.

My racing heart was still pounding in the back of my throat after I collapsed in my bed on the top floor of the House of Vampires.

I'd nearly been compromised because of Sy, and she didn't feel one bit of guilt. She was still high from fucking the powerful fae, and I was mentally too exhausted to think further.

Yet I had the presence of mind to take care of what I needed to. I tossed my tattered outfit into the trash can, found a Sarahi binding from the bottom drawer to flatten my breasts, and shrugged on a new shirt and a pair of trousers.

My head hit the pillow, but before I let myself pass out, an ominous feeling latched on in the pit of my belly.

Something bad was coming, and I couldn't stop it.

Chapter Fourteen

I hadn't gotten more than an hour's sleep when my door was kicked open with a loud bang. At the force, the hinge popped out and fell to the floor. The door slammed into the wall, its top half tilting at an odd angle.

I rolled to a sitting position in the bed, dark fog still clouding my head. Judging from the weak gray light coming through the window, dawn wasn't here yet.

I tried to rub the sleep from my eyelids as I realized it was Louis who had barged into my room. He'd returned from the vampire kingdom then, but I had no idea why his eyes were full of fury, his face puffy with drunkenness, which wasn't too attractive.

Well, things might not have gone well for him in

the vampire court. Drusilla had had a slip of the tongue and mentioned that the vampire king wasn't too happy with his heir's progress in the academy. The old king had expected his son to gain more advantage over other heirs. Disappointing the vampire king too much might cause Louis's status as the heir to be stripped.

Constant pressure and high expectations from his daddy drove Louis to indulge in vampire orgies. That was why he fucked a lot, even compared to other supernaturals. In general, supernaturals were way more sexual than humans, and they didn't even need to watch porn to spice up their libido.

Anyway, his pain wasn't mine, and I had my own demons to deal with—lately, it was mostly Sy. So, the prince needed to cool his vampire man tits in his own room where he could also jerk off in his private time and space.

"Excuse me, sir, but your room is on the other end of the floor," I offered, trying not to sound irritated. But I must be firm.

"Excuse you?" He sniffed, his nostrils flaring, and crimson rings appeared around his pale blue irises.

"This is my room, Your Highness. I just want to humbly and respectfully remind you." I softened my tone.

"Remind me? Everything here is *mine*, including you!" he spat, his blond hair flowing down to his broad shoulders. I'd read some vampire romance novels, but Louis was nothing like the stereotypical vampire. His skin wasn't even pale or milk white but very much tanned. "Yet you betrayed me, little Bob. Who did you fuck when I was away for only one day?"

Shit!

I ceased rubbing my eyelids and stared at him. "What? You say crazy things, sir."

I should've taken a bath after Sy's fucking, which was different than any of her sexual feeding in the past.

"Who?! Where is your lover?" Louis demanded, jealous fire searing his eyes.

He'd detected another male's scent on me. A shot of unreasonable jealousy confused him and made him even madder since he loathed to be attracted to a servant boy. He wouldn't let anyone else have me, even though he wouldn't touch me. Unbeknownst to him, while his mind was telling him that I was a boy, his body recognized me as a woman.

And Sy constantly emitted her pheromones to entice and disarm her prey. Even when she lurked within me, her sexual appeal and scent still leaked through me when I had my guard down.

She'd got me in a pickle this time.

"I've got no lover, sir," I insisted. "But you need to go back to your own room, sir!"

"You're a fucking liar, little Bob!" he snarled, baring his fangs. "Your lover's stench is all over you, and it has replaced my mark on you!"

"Your imprint didn't stick," I said. "It never does because no one can mark me."

It was the truth. I ate magic, curses, spells, and ownership claims like candies and asked for seconds, but he wouldn't understand my ability and nature.

"I won't allow anyone to poach you!" he spat. "I dare them! I saved you, and you belong to me and my house. Time to learn to be loyal, little Bob! Your days of shenanigans are over. I won't tolerate your stupidity and insolence anymore!"

He lunged before I could jump off the bed. Faster than a flash, his fangs sank into the main vein in my neck as he drank, fast and furious. He didn't even savor it like before. He took my blood into him as if it were a fountain of a god's nectar.

I felt my strength fading, an alarm blaring in my head.

"Stop, sir," I called.

He wouldn't stop.

He pinned me down with his brutal vampire strength and drank faster from my vein, his power increasing rapidly as he took that much blood. The vampire prince was now drunk on my power.

I knew the feeling. He felt invincible.

He wouldn't stop. He couldn't, as he was lost to his bloodlust. No one else's blood could offer him that kind of high. My blood was more addictive than any drugs.

It was almost like Ruin was feeding on me again, except instead of pain, pleasure rippled through me from his potent venom, and thus I was in worse danger.

"Fuck off!" I yelled.

He couldn't hear me anymore, lost to bloodlust and the power trip he got from my blood. He was going to drain me. I shoved him away, but he clung to me with his vise-grip. I elbowed him and punched him to no avail. He was like an unmovable rock. With his power reaching its pinnacle, boosted by my blood, and me weakened from losing blood, I couldn't shake him off me.

Sy roared, trying to surface, but Louis's venom prevented her from breaking out of my skin. Even if she could take over, at this point, she was no match for the vampire prince. I could try and suck the magic of the house into me to stop him, but once I did, I was afraid that I wouldn't be able to stop.

I reached for my pillow, my fingers curving around the hilt of Deathsong. He didn't like my struggling, so he yanked me against him roughly, his fangs sinking even deeper into my vein, as if he'd found eternal sunshine within.

His nostrils flared at my scent. His fangs started to tear my flesh.

It was the last straw.

I rammed the dagger into his chest, then twisted the blade to inflict more pain, so his bloodlust-muddled mind would register.

Louis howled. His fangs dropped from my neck. I shoved him, and he went down.

It all happened so fast.

The vampire prince stared up at me from the floor by the bed, shock on his face, his hand clutching the hilt of the dagger buried in his chest. The haze of bloodlust cleared slowly from his pale blue eyes.

"You stabbed me," he murmured weakly. "I kept thinking of you even when I was away."

Even now, he was disgusted with himself at being drawn to me, a servant boy. He'd had this dark, possessive lust toward me the moment he'd tasted a drop of my blood, and that had been his downfall right from the beginning.

Dark blood oozed out of his chest. I hadn't aimed for his heart.

I breathed laboriously, my head dizzy, my vision dancing gold from losing too much blood.

"You'll live, prince," I said. "The blood you took from me will make sure of it, but I won't be here when you wake up. I'll send Drusilla for you."

"Don't go, little Bob," he pleaded. "I won't retaliate. I—I wasn't myself."

"We're done," I told him. "Don't ever come for me."

I shot out of the door and left him on the floor.

Chapter Fifteen

I sprang out of the House of Vampires in a black mood, after I'd told Drusilla where she could find the wounded prince.

I didn't know where to go.

As soon as Prince Louis recovered, or even before he came to, the vampires would hunt me down. Maybe it was best that I escaped the realm and returned to the human world. But I knew that Shriekers would be waiting for me outside. They were getting better and faster at tracking me, which showed how desperate my father was.

At least where I was, the Veil would still halt the majority of the Shrieker army. They couldn't sense me unless they came through the Veil.

There was no place like Mist of Cinder. I felt like

I belonged here with the wild magic. Its pulse ran through my veins. The realm nourished me, and I didn't even need to eat magic.

I turned away from the direction of the Veil. I didn't want to leave. I detoured to avoid my haunts, like the campus woods and Jubilee Haven, knowing the vampires would flood those areas to hunt me. I shot northeast toward the library, then cut through the broad terrain between the House of Chaos and the House of Shifters, heading west toward Underhill, where the temperamental wild magic dwelled and no supernaturals dared to enter, let alone venture deeper.

I stopped cold. The west entry of Underhill was blocked.

Two females in academy uniforms emerged from behind an ancient angel oak tree and stepped into my path. The taller one had broad shoulders like a dude. If she only showed me her rear, I'd mistake her for a dude, especially with her buzzed hair dyed silver. She also had a tiny pink diamond stud on her nose.

She crossed her muscled arms over her chest, her dark blue eyes regarding me and her long eyebrows quirking. I wasn't what she expected.

She was a wolf. The shorter girl beside her was a honey badger. This one had honey-brown eyes, wide lips, and big boobs. Honey badgers were always vicious, but the wolf chick was the dominant one.

The House of Shifters had five tribes. Though bears and large cats like tigers and lions were more powerful, wolves dominated the house with their sheer numbers. And their prince was the largest wolf in the house.

I'd bumped into a small pack at the most inconvenient time, and I knew these two weren't the only ones.

They should not be here. From what I'd heard, even the meanest shifters avoided this area and stuck to their neck of the woods on the other side of Underhill.

They were so quiet that I hadn't registered their presence earlier, but then my senses had dulled after the vampire prince had taken too much blood from me. It was a wonder that I hadn't fallen on my face yet. Sy was in no better shape. The juice she'd gotten from fucking the fae had been spent on getting me here.

I shrugged and turned away without a word, not planning to engage. I just didn't have the energy for this shit, so I'd get the fuck out of here. The shifters could have this territory, but Underhill would bite their asses.

A panther slinked out from somewhere and blocked my path, its ink-black eyes fixing on me with cruel glee. It felt familiar, but I didn't care to find out why.

Sy and I were in no shape to fight, even though we were pissed at the ambush. I'd set a rule that I wouldn't take from this realm and drain it unless I was on the brink of death. I'd also learned not to say, "I want no trouble," when facing bullies. You'd only invite more shit.

"What the fuck?" I said roughly. "This isn't your shifter territory." I nodded in the other direction. "Your house is that way. I already stepped back to let you pee to mark the tree, and you still got a mean, small-eyed panther to stall me? By the way, is it a boy or a girl?" I shrugged. "Well, don't tell me. I don't care. Just let me pass. If you fight me, you won't like the outcome. I can assure you that it won't be pretty. I might look small, but I'm vicious."

The two girls laughed, and the panther peeled its lips back, not as amused as its pack members. The way it regarded me, it was marking me as a dish.

I bared my teeth. "I'm damn serious! I won't issue a second warning. Most people don't deserve a second chance. Better not to test me!"

"This is the notorious Little Bob? Seriously?" the honey badger said, and the wolf chick giggled more.

"Relax, Little Bob, we aren't going to eat you," the wolf said, flashing her white teeth as if that was friendly. "You know Bea, the witch from the House of Mages?"

"Yeah? You got beef with her?" I challenged, throwing my politeness out of the window, since no matter what I said or did, they wouldn't leave me alone. "Come at me then! Pick on someone your own size, bitches!"

"Call us bitches again, boy, and I'll knock out all your front teeth and you won't ever get to kiss a girl," the wolf said without heat.

The honey badger nodded. "The boy is all prickly, huffing and puffing like a chihuahua. It's a wonder he lasted so long in the vampire house."

They knew about me, but I knew nothing about them.

"Stop being annoying, Little Bob," the wolf said, drawing a full circle without closing it in the air with her index finger; I missed out on the meaning. "Today is your lucky day. Bea said you'd be here, and I owe her a favor."

Bea sent them? Had she seen this coming in her tealeaves?

I had positioned myself sideways, in case any one of the trios jumped me. I left my back exposed to no one.

"Really? No fight?" I asked.

"It sucks, I know." The wolf sniffed and nodded at my blood-stained clothes. "But time is of the essence, as you're being hunted."

There was no need to lie. Soon, the news about me stabbing the vampire prince would spread to every corner of the academy. The vampires wouldn't be the only creatures to hunt me. There were campus sentinels.

I was lucky that it was the shifters who blocked me, as they had no love for vampires.

"Good women and good cat!" I waved at them. "Now, will you step aside and let me pass? And you won't tell a soul that I'm hiding in Underhill for a day or two?"

It might be longer than that, but they didn't need to know that. I trusted and shared secrets with no one, and Sy agreed. She'd been solemn and quiet after getting us in this shit, but I was already over it. Who didn't make mistakes? She was now watching the shifters like a hawk through my eyes, even though she was exhausted.

"You can't hide here," the honey badger snorted. "You're as senseless as they say, Little Bob."

I bristled. "Which fuckers badmouthed me?"

The panther chirped like an angry bird.

"Underhill is the last place you should go to hide," the wolf chick said warily.

"I can deal," I said impatiently. "Just let me pass. I need to bathe inside, so no one will sneak up on me."

And then I needed to find a place to crash and recuperate.

"You'll be dead before you even finish the bath in that forbidden forest," said the honey badger. "We're the baddest in the realm, and even we don't go in."

So, they resided on the other side of Underhill to show how badass they were.

"You need some meat and bread first, boy." The wolf softened her tone. "I can feel your hunger a mile away, which is disturbing. So, I'll tell you why you should go with us since you're as wound up and distrusting and paranoid as a baby crocodile. Bea told us to wait for you here. She saw this coming in a tealeaf reading." She spread her arms at my look. "Don't ask me how, but she's getting better at tapping into her seer gift, and her readings have been mostly accurate. So, stop barking aggressively and annoyingly, Little Bob. We aren't here to waylay you but to rescue you, lending you a hand that you very much need. Say, what about we bring you to our house and give you food and a place to sleep for the rest of the night?"

It sounded too good to be true.

I regarded them, uncertainty and temptation warring in my head.

I'm Dixie," the wolf chick said while jerking a thumb toward the honey badger. "She's Luna. The panther to your left is Javier."

"So, no strings attached?" I asked.

Dixie tilted her head. "What strings?"

"I've just escaped the House of Vampires due to irreconcilable differences," I said. "I won't let myself be used as a pawn in a dispute between the two houses since I'm sure that I'd be the collateral damage or the sacrificial lamb. I don't do house politics. I stand for myself only, and I owe no houses my fealty."

"Woo, Little Bob isn't as dumb as my source said," Luna said.

"You overpaid your source then," I offered in sympathy.

She laughed. "The boy can be fun."

Dixie nodded. "You'll change your mind about

fealty, Little Bob, since you're a shifter after all."

Sy perked up, intrigued. We could shift back and forth, but we weren't exactly a shifter.

I shook my head. I didn't want to reveal what we were. Nor did I want to mislead the shifters.

"Your animal is dormant," Dixie concluded, and Luna nodded her agreement. "Stay with us, and you'll shift."

Yeah, right. They'd freak out when Sy came out with a mouthful of fangs.

Sy seethed.

"The vampires will flood the area soon," Dixie said, looking around, a bit urgent now. "Let's go."

I was still running on adrenaline, but I would collapse as soon as it departed. I urgently needed a temporary, safe place to stay before I could think clearly and sort things out.

However—

"Are you sure?" I asked, hesitation in my eyes. I had to come clean a little. "I—stabbed Prince Louis."

All three shifters trained their eyes on my bloody clothes. Shocked silence stretched for three and a half seconds before Luna whistled, and the panther snorted softly, no longer looking like it wanted to eat me for a midnight snack.

"How?" Luna asked, and the panther moved in closer, wanting to hear this juicy gossip.

"He was going to—" I said sulkily. "I don't want to talk more about it."

"The vampires should never have held you captive in their house in the first place," Dixie said, her face turning hard. "We should've known and come to get you earlier. You're one of our own."

My chest warmed. I'd never been considered part of a pack.

"Louis would never let me go." I shook my head. "I don't want to bring you and your house trouble. I might just take refuge in Underhill for a while. It'll be kind to me. You should go before the vampires come."

I didn't want to insult her, but I understood shifters' strict hierarchy. She wasn't the shifter prince, so she couldn't really decide for her house. But I'd remember her kindness. I never forgot anyone who showed me a drop of kindness.

"Underhill isn't kind to anyone," Dixie said. "Hasn't been for a millennium. Our house is the only one near its border, not because we're the scariest predators in the realm but because we have a truce with Underhill. We don't hunt in the dark forest, and we guard it, and its beasts don't hunt in the academy grounds. But if you go in, Little Bob, we can't protect you. And you won't come out."

Every monster thought it was the scariest. Yet I could be scarier than the scariest monsters, except for my father. Every breathing thing should fear him if they knew what he was—the true eater of the worlds.

"Dixie will get you into our house," Luna said, then turned to gaze up at the wolf chick. These two were fucking. "She's the beta and Prince Silas's favorite cousin."

That was why Bea sent them. Dixie could really help me.

"We have to go," Dixie urged. "I bet the vampires are on the move, and we've overstayed Underhill's welcome."

Yet I felt differently than the shifters. Underhill was calling me. The wild magic wanted me to go in. It'd shield me.

Dixie turned and sprang east toward the shifters' territory, Luna catching up with her. They were looking back, expecting me to follow. The panther would herd me. So, I ran after them, a few paces behind, with the panther bringing up the rear. When the pack picked up speed, I had no problem following suit, even in my depleted condition.

"Told you that you're a shifter." Dixie gave me a

glance over her shoulder. "You might be a little wolf."

I felt it the moment we reached the shifters' territory and were enveloped by their water magic.

An olive-colored wood-and-stone building came into view, vast fountains surrounding it.

Shifters patrolled the perimeter, some in their animal forms. Most were wolves of all colors, although gray was most common. They pricked their ears and turned in our direction.

Dixie slowed to a jog, and I slowed down as well, ignoring the shifters' suspicious stares training on me. Sy almost wanted to come out and show them that their intimidation game was child's play.

A few of them howled.

"Wait here, Little Bob," Dixie ordered as she paused in front of the stairs of a three-story building. "You'll need to be initiated by Prince Silas to enter the House of Shifters."

Chapter Sixteen

I waited on the lawn of violet grass outside the House of Shifters as Dixie entered through the door. Luna followed her in. Javier, the panther, crouched, his hostile eyes on me. I retreated a few paces and bent my knees, ready to hit the dirt and kick him with both feet should he lunge at me.

A faint puff of smoke swirled, then where the panther had been, a dark-skinned, small-eyed teenage boy took its place, butt naked. My jaw dropped. My gaze automatically darted to his lame dick.

"What are you looking at, boy?" he snarled.

I pulled my gaze up.

Shit, I remembered him. He was the shifter I'd kicked in the nuts.

"I wasn't checking out your balls, dude." I

shrugged. "It's not like I've never seen balls before. I got a pair myself, and yours aren't any more impressive."

The shifters around laughed. Those in their animal forms made a long "rowwoo" sound, their version of laughter.

Javier growled. I growled back. The shifters laughed harder.

I dropped our growling match first, as a dark sense of danger shot into me. A heartbeat later, the shifters' laughter turned to snarls.

The vampires were approaching fast. They'd tracked me down here. I wasn't going to wait for them to swarm me then drag me back to Louis by my ear. There was a chance that they might try to kill me on sight, depending on their prince's orders and his mood, if he'd already revived. I bet his mood was black and murderous.

I was on the brink of breaking. If the vamps sent me into an utter panic, I'd lose control and bring disaster to everyone. I had no doubt that the shifters would intervene, since I was in their territory, and I didn't want to be the one to cause a house war or the bone two species were fighting over.

If I was out of sight, there should be less or hopefully no conflict.

Running my lips between my teeth as I made up my mind, I sprang up the stairs toward the main door that Dixie had just entered, not giving two shits about shifter etiquette or hierarchy anymore. The door swung open for me, the house magic flowing out, then escorting me in.

I made it.

I halted my steps in the foyer. A sheet of water rushed down a glass screen, and water poured from the mouths of animal sculptures in the center of the hall. The animals represented a variety of shifters.

The house magic, unlike the wild magic from Underhill, urged me on, as if afraid that I'd chicken out. It rippled around me and licked me like a wolf pup with its wet tongue. The vampires' house magic was also welcoming toward me, but it had boundaries. It was partly shaped by the most powerful vampire, so it wasn't exactly cuddly.

Just then a giant man with hard muscles strolled down the stairs with staggering arrogance. I was sure he owned every inch of this place, but he thought he owned the air as well.

Silas, the prince of the House of Shifters, didn't own the magic in the house either, because I could easily take it from him. He'd try to kill me if he knew that.

He was shirtless, a gleam of sweat dotting his broad chest. He smelled of sex. Sy peeked out at him longingly. From the scowl on his face, the prince was obviously in the middle of banging when Dixie went to get him. She was right behind him on the stairs.

The annoyance and imperiousness in his amber eyes flickered as he noticed me admiring the water sculptures. I'd entered his house without being invited or initiated. His brows lowered in menace after his initial surprise. His predatory gaze homed in on me.

Dixie also halted, staring at me, shock evident on her face. Her nose ring fluttered. She wasn't going to attack me, but her prince was ready to pounce on me.

The heirs all had a brutal reputation, and I heard that Prince Silas was even less forgiving if anyone crossed him.

He shook away the hair flopping into his face and resumed his purposeful gait, coming toward me. His sharp gaze never left me. Dixie rushed down the stairs after him.

I was bone tired, so I traipsed to the enormous sofa a few paces away and perched on the edge. I didn't have blood on my pants, so I wouldn't dirty the sofa, which was the color of gray clouds. There were large cushions all around. I wanted to take a nap more than anything. Then I realized those cushions were dog beds—well, they were for shifters in their animal forms. They wouldn't be happy if I curled up on their cots. Shifters were territorial.

"How did you get in, boy?" Silas's demanding voice boomed in my ear.

I snapped my eyes open, not knowing when I'd shut them. It was like one second, he'd been on the stairs, then next, he was here, growling and glaring down at me, not caring about personal space.

"I walked in, sir. The door was open," I answered meekly and dutifully, rubbing my eyelids. "I was with Dixie, who's behind you." I craned my neck to peer at Dixie while she frowned at me in puzzlement and worry. "I thought it would be better to wait for her inside rather than outside. It's getting hot, and I don't do too well in heat."

Silas turned to Dixie, his voice cutting. "Did you initiate him?"

She stepped out from behind her cousin and shook her head. "Only you can initiate a pack member, Highness. I wouldn't be so foolish as to even try as your beta." She looked down at me. "You shouldn't be able to get into our house without being properly marked by Prince Silas. The house shouldn't have admitted you!"

"But the house admitted me," I protested, then softened my tone a notch. "If you want, I can go out again and wait for you outside after the vampires leave. They're at the perimeter, and they're hunting me."

Silas and Dixie traded a look, and Silas growled.

"Check the ward and see if it's down," he ordered.

With a nod, Dixie sprang toward the door while the prince pinned me down with his alpha stare as if I were a harmful fly. Dixie returned with a brisk gait and shook her head.

"The ward is still up. No one tampered with it," she said. "Everything is normal."

Silas still scowled at me. I didn't know what his deal was.

"The house let Little Bob in," Dixie offered. "It means he belongs to our house, cousin. It's unprecedented, but the house has decided to accept him. Little Bob is a shifter, though his animal is dormant. He might be a wolf pup."

Silas sniffed, his nostrils flaring. Lust rolled off him with a heady scent, and heat fogged his eyes that glowed violent amber now.

A growl and a grunt tore out of his throat.

Shit!

Sy was emitting pheromones to lure the prince and manipulate him into letting us stay in his house. *That* was her version of a sex worker! She understood a male's primal need and knew how to use it against him, but this was the wrong place, and she was targeting the wrong dude!

The shifter prince, who was said to be the most ambitious heir, wouldn't appreciate being seen having the hots for a servant boy. He might even think that I'd bespelled him. He was already a little paranoid since I'd gotten into his house without being initiated by him, and he parked atop the pyramid of power.

Drop it, Sy, I hissed inwardly. *We aren't in the wilderness. This is a civilized magical world!*

If you say so. But men are all the same. They're beasts. She pouted and retreated.

A magical wind flitted across the room, thinning the scent of lust in the air. The house magic somehow diluted the sexual tension in the hall.

"I didn't mean to intrude, sir," I offered. "I didn't mess up your ward either. If you don't want me here, I can leave now. No hard feelings."

I rose from the sofa on my wobbly legs.

"Cousin!" Dixie called. "The vampires are after the boy! He's one of us. We can't just throw him out."

"I'm not throwing out this damned boy!" Silas snarled, but his amber eyes no longer glowed aggressively. "I was trying to find out how he snuck into my house!"

"But I didn't sneak in," I said.

The shifters bristled. Right, as a low servant boy, I shouldn't speak unless spoken to. Academy rules.

These shifters were sticklers for rules and hierarchy. I wasn't supposed to hold the prince's stare, so I cast my eyes downward, even though I could hold his alpha stare as long as I wanted.

But there was no need to get into a pissing match. I didn't even have a cock.

Silas narrowed his eyes on me. "Stay here, Little Bob. When I return, I'll get to the bottom of this!"

I widened my eyes. "You aren't going to give me back to the vampires?"

Both Silas and Dixie hissed. "No!"

Speaking of which, commotion had broken out outside. The vampires had arrived at the scene.

"They're here," I called. "They won't leave until they have me."

Silas nodded at Dixie. "Get me only if the vamp prince comes."

"Yes, Your Highness." Dixie jogged out of the door.

Silas strolled closer to the door to monitor the situation, and I followed him at a safe distance, peeking out through the side window.

Gunnar was in the lead, arguing with the shifters. Prince Louis wasn't here. Even though I'd wounded him, the powerful vampire prince would have recovered, especially with the perk of having taken a large amount of my blood. But as a prince, he wouldn't come to the shifters' house in person to demand the return of a servant. Then again, I wasn't just any servant. I was *the* servant.

"We tracked Prince Louis's squire here," Gunnar said. "We're sure that Little Bob is hiding in your house. He's a criminal. Give him to us, and we'll walk away without any trouble. And you'll have Prince Louis's gratitude."

"Little Bob is a shifter," Dixie said, taking up the position as a beta and a main negotiator. "Your house had no business taking him hostage in the first place. Now he's finally returned to his rightful house after all the abuse. Your prince no longer has jurisdiction over Little Bob, now that he's under the protection of Prince Silas."

"If Little Bob is a shifter, the sun will shine out of my ass," Gunner sneered. "Call him out. If he shifts, we'll apologize, and we'll never come after him again."

"He's a late bloomer, but I don't need to explain it to you, bloodsucker!" Dixie said. "You don't come to my backyard and poke into my house's affairs!"

"If you don't want a war, return what's Prince Louis's," Gunnar demanded.

"You came to our territory to demand a shifter boy when you have no right," Dixie said coldly. "You're the offender. If you want a war, it's a war you'll get! The council of Mist of Cinder will rule in our favor, and all supernaturals will go to war with your house."

"You're naïve," Gunnar said. "None of the houses will fight your war. At least, Prince Killian won't back up your house."

I blinked. I didn't know that. I had been in the realm too briefly to grasp house politics.

"Then start the war and see how far you bloodsuckers can go," Dixie said. "We don't need the other houses to fight our war. We can take your house!"

"Try, she-wolf," Gunnar snorted.

The two opposing forces were about to collide. The last thing I wanted was a civil war breaking out while we had a much bigger threat coming. But none of them could see the real issues. I needed to intervene to send the vampires away or lead them away before hell broke loose.

I shot past Silas as he started to swagger toward the door. He lunged to grab me, but I was faster. He snarled, but I had already flung open the door and charged out.

"Hello, hello, dude," I greeted Gunnar, halting beside Dixie.

Two dozen vampires flanked Gunnar, and three dozen shifters, some in their animal forms, orbited around Dixie.

Gunnar glared at me, venom in his gray eyes, and I smirked at him.

Dixie also glared down at me. "I told you to stay put!"

I shifted my grin to her. "And miss the fireworks?"

"You need to come with me, Little Bob!" Gunnar said.

"You don't want me to come with you," I said. "I'm a free agent now. Just go back and tell the high sir to forget about me. I'm done with him and his house."

"You aren't done!" Gunnar bared his fangs at me. "You signed the contract!"

"Yeah? Show me the contract with my signature," I said.

"Oral agreement is binding in this realm," Gunnar said. "You're the property of our house. The prince marked you."

"Then where's his mark on me?" I asked.

No one could mark me, not even the God of Ruin, my father.

Dixie sniffed and smiled. "Little Bob doesn't carry anyone's scent. He doesn't bear your prince's mark because he's shifter through and through."

Gunnar sniffed, and his eyes widened in disbelief before he narrowed them in menace again. "Prove that you're a shifter, Little Bob. You probably aren't even supernatural, so anyone in the realm can claim you. It's one of the rules of Mist of Cinder, chihuahua!"

"Not a supernatural?" I smirked. "Gunnar, Gunnar, you can't see what's right in front of you. You're rusty in your old age."

I'd need to have a little demonstration to end this charade while showing the shifter prince that I could be useful to his house. I inhaled and sucked in a drop of magic from all the vamps and a few mean-looking shifters here, weaving each drop into a mini-rainbow between my palms.

The shifters gasped or growled in approval. The vampires stared at me with hunger in their eyes. Thirst glinted in Gunnar's hazel eyes as well before he suppressed it.

"A party trick!" Gunnar sneered dismissively after he collected himself. "You can't shift, can you? You're no shifter!" He turned to look around at the shifters. "This Little Bob is only good at pretending. We're done with his shenanigans here. We're taking him back to our house, and if he truly belongs to another house, then the house head can come to claim him from us after he's punished for his crime against Prince Louis and the House of Vampires!"

"You aren't taking our new shifter anywhere, bloodsucker!" Dixie snarled.

The shifters around her bared their teeth. Those in their animal forms snarled, closing ranks, bracing for a battle.

Just then, Prince Silas strolled out, darting a glance at the tiny rainbow swirling between my hands before focusing on the vampire captain.

Gunnar bowed slightly. "Your Highness, we—"

"Get the fuck out of my territory. Now!" Silas said coldly. "You'll only get this one fucking warning."

Gunnar's face hardened, his hateful gaze that promised retaliation shifting to me, but he turned on his heels.

"Kiss, kiss," I called.

I flung my rainbow at Gunnar's face, faster than a flash, before he could dodge. The rainbow danced on his head, turning him bald instantly. His eyebrows were gone as well. Then the rainbow vanished.

The shifters couldn't help but roar with laughter since Gunnar now looked ridiculous. He shot into the shadows, his team with him.

"Will you remember me fondly, Gunnar, pretty please?" I shouted after his figure faded into the night. He said I had no manners, so I showed him manners by saying please.

"No wonder the vampires hate you, Little Bob," Dixie sighed.

"It's more like a dark, twisted love." I grinned. "There's a thin line between love and hate. They just haven't realized it yet."

Prince Silas turned to look down at me with a

frown. "Now that you're in my house, you'll be my new squire."

What was this damn thing about having a squire? It was like every prince in this realm desired an honorable burial. But I could do it. I'd make sure to find Silas a good burial ground when he was slain.

"Get Little Bob settled, Dixie," Silas ordered. "Keep him out of trouble."

The prince turned to stroll back into the building, most likely returning to fucking.

"Are you hungry, Little Bob?" Dixie asked, and that sounded like music to my ears.

Chapter Seventeen

They gave me a small room near Dixie's on the fourth floor, and I lay low as she ordered. As long as I hid in the House of Shifters, Louis and his goons wouldn't risk starting a house war by coming in to drag me out. They wouldn't be able to breach the shifters' magical house either.

I'd have to wait for his wrath to subside. He couldn't be angry forever, right? Negative emotions consumed energy and wouldn't be good for his mental health.

But a small band of vindictive vampires still patrolled outside the shifter territory, waiting to pop me. Dixie had warned me a dozen times that if I ventured out, no one could guarantee my safety.

When I roamed within the confines of the building, many shifters openly stared at me wherever I went. It was rare that two princes from different houses fought over a servant boy. And the word spread that I entered the house without being initiated.

Addicted to my blood, Louis wanted me back. Silas kept me to annoy the vampire prince. It was more of a power play to him. The two houses had been at each other's throats since the beginning. Only a century-old truce was holding them back from slaughtering each other again. The realm didn't want another house war, so the council had decided whoever started a war would face war with all the other houses.

After holing up in the shifter house for four long days and listening to Dixie repeating the rules, the orders of the five houses in the realm, and the mating rituals of the Brides Selection into my overheated brain, I decided I was bored and done.

I especially didn't give two shits about the mating, since I'd seen enough of Sy fucking. I would never mate; Sy might just eat whomever I mated with afterwards.

I'm not amused by your sick sense of humor, Sy

bristled. *When you find your true mate, he'll be a mate to both of us! I'd never eat our true mate!*

Like there's some true mate for monsters like us, I snorted, yet my mind drifted to Killian for a long second. I could never have him, even if he wasn't spoken for. And regardless of the heat in his storm-blue eyes, there was no fucking way he truly desired me.

And they said his fiancée was a great beauty, a powerful queen who aimed to be the High Queen of Mist of Cinder.

I was a fool to even waste time thinking of him. I shook off the image of how he smirked and winked at me and focused on what kept gnawing at me inside: what if more Shriekers had gotten into the realm?

I stood in the west corner of the pentagon courtyard before a lime-and-gold building. Elaborate spells crawled over every brick, glass, and stone of its seven floors like vines. Even the crimson dwarf burning bushes that fenced in the entirety of the House of Mages were warded.

All five houses in Mist of Cinder were paranoid,

their security ass-tight, as if they were ready to go to war in a blink, even in this school. But then, it wasn't exactly a normal school. The classes mostly taught offensive magic, combat, defense, and war strategies.

Bea's dormitory was on the third floor. Her small window had a painting of two butterflies chasing each other.

She was like a geek witch. It was a surprise that she had befriended Dixie. Maybe the shifter beta bought some spells from Bea.

I took a tiny rock from the pocket of my light jacket and threw it at Bea's window; it hit the frame. I waited for two seconds, and when she didn't show up, I threw another one that hit the center of the glass.

The window flew open before I could throw a third rock. Bea poked her blue head out and gazed down at me.

I grinned at her and waved for her to come down.

"It's dangerous for you to roam the campus!" she whispered loudly.

"Don't worry, little Bea," I said. "It's high noon." I squinted at the sun in the sky. "The vampires are slumbering like babies. Anyway, didn't you see me coming in your tealeaves?"

She sighed, withdrew her head, her blue hair flapping in the wind, and closed the window.

I edged toward the crimson dwarf burning shrubs and studied the spells coating them while waiting for Bea. The plants and flowers breathed heavily, weighed down by the spells. I nodded at the magic twirling around me. I had to free the bushes, as I didn't like them being enslaved.

I placed a hand on the bushes and sucked in a breath. A flux of red mist flowed toward me, sinking into me. As my body started to absorb the spells, the dwarf burning bushes turned brighter.

"There, better," I purred, my smile dropping quickly as I sensed a powerful presence stalking toward me. I'd been so absorbed in eating the repulsion spells latching onto the bushes that I hadn't detected the prince heir of the House of Mages earlier.

"What are you doing here?" Cade demanded.

"Waiting for a friend, sir." I wheeled toward him. "And you?"

"This is my house!"

"Of course. Congratulations, sir!"

He glared at me. "How the hell did you get past the wards set up by my top mages?"

"Maybe they're getting lazy and sloppy?" I suggested. "It happens to the best of us."

He stalked closer, a calculating light glinting in his turquoise eyes. At least he didn't emit menacing vibes like the other princes, but it didn't mean I should let my guard down. I hunched to make myself even smaller and to show him that I wasn't much of a threat, ready to duck or charge him if he decided to pounce on me.

He frowned at me. "Why are you so tense, Little Bob?"

"Uh, toothache," I said, pressing my left cheek.

"So, you understand advanced spells," he asked.

"A little, sir," I said humbly.

"Where did you learn to master the spells? You aren't even a student here."

"I'm self-taught, sir. I don't have money for school."

He studied me. "Your techniques are quite unusual, unlike anything I've seen."

"I ate it." I winced. "The repulsion spell didn't taste good, but that was the sacrifice I was willing to make for the sake of healthy bushes. Plants just don't like spells on them, especially offensive spell. Perhaps your mages can install wooden fences and latch spells onto them instead?"

"That'll be an extra cost! Do you know how much raw materials cost these days?"

"But they say you're loaded," I said.

"Who said it? Who dares to stick their nose into my finances?" He waved a hand to express his ire. "Now, you'd better come clean if you want to get out of here in one piece."

I blinked. "What do you mean come clean, sir? I'm not doing drugs, but I heard fae students are doing it plenty."

"I'm talking about your magic! What do you have?"

Just then, I spotted Bea standing amid the other mages on the sideline, face paling, eyes wide. The other mages gaped at me, their hands raised, palms facing me, ready to throw spells at me at their prince's nod. I flicked my fingers toward Bea, gesturing for her to return to her dorm, as I didn't want to drag her into another mess.

"I didn't have a lot growing up, sir," I said humbly, utter sincerity in my eyes. "I was a drifter before I came here. I had a job in the House of Vampires, but it didn't work out. I'm a squire to Prince Silas now."

"You turned down my offer, then you jumped

ship to kiss Silas's ass? Think the mage house isn't good enough for you?"

"What? No! I kissed no one's ass, sir! Never!" I said. "Your humble servant is more of a victim of the houses' politics."

He knew that I was hunted, and it wouldn't benefit him to bring me into his fold currently. The princes and all their games.

"Everyone loves to use a victim card," he snorted.

Bea sidled up to my side and bowed deeply to her prince. "Your Highness, Little Bob is an Echo, a natural who can neutralize magic. That's how he entered the House of Mages. I don't think he understands his rare magic either. As he said, he wasn't schooled. He just has a raw talent."

Professor Longweed had pronounced me an Echo, so it wasn't exactly a secret. It was probably the best explanation for my magic in their book.

Cade glanced at Bea, not noticing her pale face turning red, before fixing his piercing gaze on me again. "Echoes are a myth. Aren't you full of surprises, Little Bob?"

Even though he berated me, he was easy to talk to. An idea sparked in my mind.

Originally, I'd wanted Bea's help to strengthen the Veil to prevent any more Shriekers from getting into the realm. Now that Cade was here, he'd be a much better option since he was the most powerful mage here.

He was also less violent and more open minded than the other princes. I hadn't met the fae prince, but I had a bad feeling about him, considering Sy had fucked a powerful fae and left a hot mess for me to deal with.

Sy fumed at my constructive criticism, and I ignored her.

If I needed help, Prince Cade was the safest bet. I just needed to convince him to go along with my plan.

"I respect you a lot more than the other princes, sir," I said. "It's the reason I came here. I believe only you can handle the situation, since it pretty much falls into your specialty."

He narrowed his eyes at me.

"I'm concerned about the weakened Veil on the south side of the campus," I said. "Any good citizen of Mist of Cinder should be concerned. I came through that portal effortlessly. Any being that has a drop of magic can pass through now, and we don't want anyone who's up to no good to come into the realm, sir!"

"The ward of the Veil is above your pay grade."

"But not above yours, high sir. That's why I came to you instead of reporting it to the other princes, including my new boss," I said, and the mage prince gave an almost unnoticeable nod. Flattery never fails. It's the number one rule in the book. "I hope it's not a hype when they say the prince heir of the House of Mages is most qualified at patching up and strengthening the Veil."

"How dare you have doubts, ye of little faith?" He scowled at me before allowing a smile to tug his curvy lips. "Are you sure you can see the spells warding the Veil?"

"Yes, sir," I said. I had to give him something more. Power called to power. "Wards and spells don't stop me unless they're woven by the gods."

My father, God of Ruin, was the only one who could bind me with his commands and runes, though they'd always faded in time. When I was his captive, he'd have to renew his power words, spells, and runes that he'd implanted in me once a week in order to control me.

"The gods are dead," said the mage prince.

He'd be in the valley of tears just like the rest of the world when Ruin came calling, raining down wrath and destruction. I shuddered at the thought of facing my father again. I was the only one who understood that no one and no realms were safe from him, and I had to prepare for Armageddon.

"I can sense magic and spells. I can see their colors and shapes and foundation. I can feel the pulses of their strength. The magic in the realm is fading, and it saddens me."

Wars between the houses would be so disastrous. It was one of the reasons the houses were willing to cooperate to a degree in order to preserve, or more accurately, to slow down the fading of the magic. The supernaturals' future and their survival were at stake.

The wild magic in Underhill, the strongest and purest element in all the worlds, would be most vulnerable if Ruin came.

No one could tame or harvest the wild magic except me.

I'd never harm it.

"I feel the wild magic in Underhill as well," I revealed more.

Cade's eyes sharpened, homing in on me. "How did you get to know the wild magic in Underhill? It doesn't welcome anyone. Even Killian can't venture into the depths of Underhill."

"I can be a friend to all magic." I shrugged. "Anyway, we should focus on the urgent matter, which is to strengthen the Veil."

Disapproving murmurs spread across the courtyard. I shouldn't have talked to a prince that way.

"I might not have manners, as I wasn't schooled and taught in society, high sir," I said, bowing my head a little to appease the prince and the crowd. "I'm merely a wild boy who has found a home here. I want to be of use. In a century or two, when corruption from the human realm keeps leaking into our realm, the wild magic might be our only defense to keep Mist of Cinder from fading. So, sir, please, we need to fix and strengthen the Veil. I'll be at your disposal if you're up to the challenge."

"Your Highness, forgive me for speaking out of turn," Bea chimed in. "Detecting a security breach and amending the Veil will earn our house points, so all will see that mages' spells are superior to the fae glamour. Your Highness will be the hero again by protecting the realm."

"Of course," Cade said as he lifted his gorgeous chin. "We mages are masters of spells and wards, and no house can beat the House of Mages at laying wards."

Cheers erupted, and a band of high mages stepped out of the crowd, spells twirling around their palms. A few of them rolled up their sleeves, eager to prove their prowess.

Cade snapped his fingers at his people. "Let's go take a look at the broken Veil. It's long overdue anyway." He shook his reddish head in disgust while Bea and I beamed at each other. "Our house has to do everything for the benefit of the rest of the realm, don't we?"

Cade strolled toward the open fence of the dwarf burning bushes, which now flourished bright crimson, spell free.

The mages rallied around their prince.

"Hurry up, Little Bob," Cade snapped. "We don't have the whole day."

I sprang after him, a bit dazed that my plan had worked. But I stayed a few paces in his shadow, just in case any vampire suddenly came out at me, even at noon.

We cut across the less traveled path at the back end of the shops and wandered through a cluster of shacks and a theater. This was the edge of the campus grounds, where those who didn't belong to any house dwelled. They had more freedom, but they weren't granted any house's protection.

As the mage prince led us through a shortcut to the Veil, we didn't meet many students; while steam rose from the ground and the breeze blew hot like an oven at high noon, most students chose to stay indoors.

We strode through the fields of long grass until there were only hills between us and the Veil. Even from this distance, I could feel corruption leaking into the realm from the bottom of the portal like a trail of oily smoke. A dark web crawled over the Veil, turning its shimmering to black veins. A Shrieker had breached the Veil a week ago.

"What the bloody hell?" Cade growled.

The mages gasped and cursed. Then all at once, they abandoned their stroll, raced to climb the hill, and charged down toward the Veil.

I was right behind the prince, who led the race.

The magic, weaker than last time I was here, whimpered.

Uneasiness surged into me as I felt the nearness of the Shriekers. Then, like a nightmare coming true, long claws pushed through the Veil. A Shrieker was coming through, and it would expose me!

My heart pounded. Cold sweat grew slick under my armpits.

I acted instinctively and shot past Cade. Sy pumped her strength and speed into me.

Faster! she urged.

She could get there sooner than I, but I was fast enough, running on fear, rage, and adrenaline.

"Little Bob! Come back!" Cade yelled.

I pumped my legs faster, Deathsong tight in my grip.

The Shrieker poked its hideous head out of the Veil before the rest of its body followed. It was a male. The creature saw me and grinned grotesquely and delightedly.

"Prin—" it started.

I leapt a dozen feet in one jump and thrust my dagger into the space between its eyes, which was a Shrieker's Achilles heel. When my father made the abominations, he stored his magic in their third eye.

Shriekers always protected their faces, and with their height, they usually didn't need to worry about being stabbed in their third eye. This Shrieker was caught by surprise, and I'd moved more swiftly than it'd anticipated.

Remember rule number three in a battle: talk less.

I held Deathsong and slashed all the way down until my blade split open the Shrieker's face. The Veil suddenly reacted and cut the rest of the Shrieker's body in half. Black blood shot out of the foul abomination, soaking the soil as the Shrieker fell to the ground in two large heaps.

It all happened in seconds. Then Cade was in my face, furious.

"What the bloody hell, Little Bob?" the mage prince yelled.

"The creature caused the corrosion of the Veil!" I cried out, pointing at the hole in the bottom of the Veil. A trail of sooty smoke came through the gap and drifted into the air. "It dug a hole beneath. Look, the corruption from the mortal world is leaking through. The creature must be stopped. We must redo the ward and patch up the hole, sir!"

Bea and the other mages approached, panting from running. They cursed, then everyone shouted their opinions as they saw smoke trickling to this side from the crack.

Bea's eyes widened like two big peas, shocked at seeing how violently I slew the Shrieker. My witch friend, though she had been bullied in this magical school, hadn't seen real violence.

The mages shouted their outraged questions, demanding answers. I ignored them. I even ignored the prince's weighty stare on me. I was on edge, as I sensed more Shriekers on the other side of the unsteady Veil.

"I'd like to go check if there are more abominations on the other side, Your Highness," I volunteered in my husky voice.

"You don't charge blindly again unless I give an order," Prince Cade snapped. "Am I clear?"

I snapped to attention with a salute. "Yes, high sir."

But he didn't need to know that I never was good at following rules and orders.

Cade placed a hand on the Veil, and a tongue of fire streamed out of his palm into the ward. The mages behind him watched in awe. Their prince was a natural. He didn't need any premade spells to make his elemental magic known.

Bea also stared at the prince, drooling along with the other witches and mages at the back of the row. They dragged their gazes from his fire to his taut ass.

The ward on the Veil flickered with a sick, pale light, allowing me to see through the other side.

Two Shriekers, a male and a female, crouched by the Veil, their vast claws digging a tunnel beneath. They were new models with the appearance of giant lizards walking on two legs.

As I stared at them, they raised their heads, sensing me through the Veil, which was made possible by the open window Cade had created.

"Princess!" the male shrieked. "Bring her back to Master!"

It was a small comfort that they spoke Ruin's original tongue this time.

Cade released his hand from the ward, fury twisting his handsome face. He also saw the problem.

It took great effort for me to stand my ground and wait for the mage prince to give his order instead of darting through the Veil to finish off the Shriekers. If I appeared too eager again, I'd bring suspicion upon myself, and Cade would interrogate me. But I was determined to be the first out of the Veil as soon as the mage prince said the word. I would end Ruin's agents before they uttered another unholy sound.

"Two abominations are on the other side, digging to get into our realm," Cade snarled, turning to his mage subjects, his eyes on fire. "Kill one and capture the other. We must find out who sent them!"

A wand sixteen inches long with a peacock-blue tip materialized in his hand. The mage prince directed it toward the Veil. "Go get them, mages!"

He stepped through the Veil in the lead, the mages shouting and charging after him. I'd darted out before the prince. For a second, it felt like being blown away by the wind and freefalling before I found my footing.

The false impression of a ruin of shattered columns and piles of skulls had been stripped, revealing an expanse of blackened grass. No magic existed here. The air smelled of blight.

A quarter mile away, where the forest used to be, it'd been burned to blackened stumps. The Shriekers had torched the forest to find me. My eyes landed on the two Shriekers as they rose to their feet and stood over eight feet tall. Yellow scales covered their grotesque heads and lethal bodies.

They opened their beastly mouths, ancient words pouring out. *"Come home, Princess."*

I charged. Cade caught me, expecting my move this time, and yanked me back.

"What did I say, boy?" he growled. "Stay put!"

My heart thundered.

The mage prince strolled toward the male Shrieker. The female had four scaled breasts. Everyone always assumed that males were more of a threat. How wrong they were.

"Kill the male and capture the female alive," the prince ordered.

Good luck catching the female. I'd wait for the mages to kill the male Shrieker if they could, but no way would I allow the female to live. I'd make my move when chaos resumed, so no one would know it was me.

Cade flung a stream of orange fire toward the male Shrieker. It raised its armguard to block the fire, and the mage fire fizzled out.

Cade snarled, and two large fireballs popped out of his palms. He hurled both at his target. His aim was true, but the potent mage fire winked out against the Shrieker's half-machine, half scaled lizard chest.

The mages' fire, even from the strongest of them, couldn't burn a Shrieker!

Then every mage lurched toward the Shriekers and tossed spells and fire at them. The fire dissipated as soon as it touched the monsters. The spells sank into the creatures but couldn't do much. The abominations came from Ruin's magic. Now I was sure only my father and I could kill Shriekers.

Unless the mages used a weapon like Deathsong, the dagger in my hand.

The Shriekers pushed through the torrent of spells toward me, shrieking in glee. Sy snarled, wanting to fight, but I reined her in.

Cade shook his wand. As it vibrated, wind and fire surged toward the Shriekers. They staggered for a second or two before advancing toward me again.

"They're immune to our magic and spells!" a mage called frantically.

"Cut them! Cut them down!" Cade called, and he yanked out a sword strapped to his thigh and lunged at the male Shrieker.

He swung his blade up at the Shrieker, aiming to behead it, but the Shrieker proved to be too tall. Cade changed his aim, going low at the last second, and thrust his sword at its chest. The creature raised its claws to fend off the strike. The mage prince's blade bounced off, as if it was hitting impenetrable metal.

Even a supernatural's weapon couldn't cut into Ruin's creatures, but I wouldn't lend the prince Deathsong to drag myself into shit.

The war mages surrounded the female Shrieker, battering it with their blades to no avail. That kind of attack could cut any other being to ribbons but had no effect on a Shrieker.

"How do we kill these things?" Two mages echoed their shouts while stabbing the Shrieker to keep it at bay.

The prince and the male Shrieker dueled back and forth. Though the prince, an excellent swords-man, ducked the Shrieker's claws and scored while getting a few scratches, his blade couldn't bleed his opponent.

Bea darted forward and directed her wand at the male Shrieker to aid her prince. Her spells complemented his, yet they couldn't take down the creature. More mages joined the siege.

The female Shrieker wheeled like a black wind, its claws sending several mages flying into the air then crashing into the ground. A tall mage was sent flying back through the Veil. The sound of bones cracking made me wince.

Then a mage and a witch fell at the feet of the female Shrieker, one set of its claws cutting into a mage's neck while its other set thrust into a witch's chest as she screamed.

The Shriekers had sped up their attacks, eager to end the fight and come for me. More wounded mages littered the blackened field between the Shriekers and me.

"Throw spells and fireballs at them again! They've been weakened," I screamed a lie, my words beating with power.

The mages obeyed. They let their spells and fireballs sail at the Shriekers, chanting collectively. That was when I made my move while no one was watching me. I turned the spells mine by absorbing them then releasing and directing them toward the Shriekers before anyone could notice how the spells had transformed after having changed ownership.

The spells and fireballs tainted with my power sank into both Shriekers and detonated.

The prince and the mages jumped back as the Shriekers were blown apart.

"What a bloody show! Too bad we couldn't capture the female alive," Cade said, staring at the chunks of the Shriekers and the blackened land. "The threat that the oracle foretold to come to Mist of Cinder is finally here. We must warn the councils of the abominations and the blight!"

His words struck a chord in me. So, Mist of Cinder had heard about Ruin after all, or at least, their oracle wasn't so blind. I hoped they truly realized what kind of threat Ruin would pose. Even without me leading him here, he'd eventually have found this last realm of magic that he'd been seeking. It was only a matter of time, even though I'd led him here earlier. The guilt and burden were mine alone, but I'd defend this realm with my life.

Cade turned to me. "You discovered this threat first, Little Bob. I don't think you're what they say you are."

Ice coursed in my veins. Had he discovered me? Should I flee right now?

"What—what do you mean?" I asked defensively as I shifted my weight from foot to foot, ready to bolt.

"You're not a shifter, Little Bob," he said, the wind ruffling his reddish hair, "unless you prove me wrong and shift to a chihuahua, or a small bulldog if you prefer."

He was half-teasing. While I was relieved that I hadn't been made, both Sy and I bristled at the insult.

"You have a mage's fire," Cade continued. "I'll have to settle this with Silas, since you're obviously in the wrong house."

I wasn't a mage either. If any of the princes knew what I really was, they wouldn't let me continue to breathe.

The Veil rippled. Instantly, I felt the presence of powerful beings on the other side. Two of the power signatures were familiar, and the third was also kind of familiar.

Prince Silas and Prince Killian stepped through.

Everyone looked on. Then the fae male Sy had fucked emerged. He was the third power.

Shit!

Warriors from different houses poured out as well, rallying around their princes.

I shrank back, ducking behind Cade, since he was closest to me and the biggest, but he stalked off toward the other princes, exposing me.

All three powerful men snagged their sharp gazes on me, as if power called power, especially after I'd just used my siphon ability.

A half-snarl appeared on Silas's face. He was not pleased with my presence.

The fae sniffed in my direction, recognition flickering in his silvery eyes before a confused look dominated his strong, gorgeous face. He scented Sy in me, but his mind was telling him that no way could I be that female who fucked him into oblivion.

Sy perked up, peeking out at the fae through my eyes. *Yummy, look at my man. I want to take him to the ground again.*

Like hell you will, I snarled inwardly.

My heart thundering, my throat parched, I shoved Sy down harder than usual.

Surprise flitted by Killian's storm-blue eyes at the sight of me before dark amusement tugged up his sensual lips. Heat pooled at my core, just like it did any time I was in his presence.

"Prince Rowan, how kind of you to finally join

us mortals," Cade purred, a smug smirk on his lips and a deep dimple on his cheek.

Double shit! This couldn't be happening! The fae whom Sy fucked was the prince heir of the House of Fae. The only small mercy was that Prince Louis wasn't here.

Cade flung his wand in the direction of the remains of the Shriekers. "And who else do we have here? Prince Killian and Prince Silas, you're late! I've taken care of the problem for the realm. Again."

"What is all this?" Silas demanded. "What the hell is going on?"

"We've got intruders," Cade said grimly. "We need to sweep the entire realm and see if any more abominations got through the Veil. They'll be killing supernaturals. I lost two members in the battle."

Killian growled, dark lightning sparking at his fingertips. My eyes widened. He had power not of this realm. I wondered how strong his lightning was and if it could work on the Shriekers and reduce them to ashes.

"I've been hunting them outside the realm," the chaos prince said, his gaze darting to me again before regarding the dead Shriekers.

"As have I and my men," Prince Rowan said.

"The abominations are here now. If they're what I think they are, our realm is under the worst threat."

I swallowed hard at his words, my heart racing. What else did the princes know? But at least they were finally aware of the threat posed by Ruin.

I can go to the fae prince tonight and find out, Sy offered.

Not a chance! I told her coldly. *You'll stay away from him.*

"So, you two have been holding back crucial information that concerns the realm's safety," Cade drawled.

"Why am I not surprised?" Silas snorted bitterly, glaring at Killian.

"I don't entertain children." Killian flashed a cold smile.

"We're all kids, since none of us have graduated from Shades Academy," Cade said. "It's time for you two to share what you know. But first, we need to see to the Veil, *children.*"

Chapter Eighteen

I stood to attention in Silas's outer suite, peering down at the profile of a howling black wolf on the Persian rug as the prince lectured me from behind his desk, his voice harsh, his tone impatient. I let his words pass from my left ear out through the right.

He should just let me take a nap. The afternoon sunlight splashed generously through the hexagon windows and made me incredibly sleepy.

Behind Silas, a large dog bed nestled against the wall. A strand of wolf fur stuck to the curve of the cot.

Dixie parked herself by the desk, facing the window that overlooked the forest of Underhill. She frowned at me, but concern sparked in her eyes. She was a hard chick, but she had a soft spot for me.

"I now doubt if it was a good idea to take you in, Little Bob," Silas grated. "Within a week, you turned the vampire house upside down. It was a delight to watch while you were a wrecking ball in Louis's house, but if you try your shit here, you'll wish you never came to my house."

"He can be useful, Your Highness," Dixie said. "He'll learn our way of life."

"His usefulness is limited to shifting to a chihuahua if he finally does," Silas sneered. "But do we need a house pet who's more a pest?"

Anger rose in me, yet I said nothing. My face remained impassive.

"Everyone in this house must contribute, even a street urchin," Silas said. "You don't work, you don't eat."

"It's a mutual feeling that it might be a mistake for me to be in your house, sir," I said sweetly. "I probably belong to the House of Mages. Would you dismiss me, high sir? No hard feelings—"

Before I could finish, the prince was suddenly in my face, backhanding me in the jaw and sending me flying across the room.

I didn't crash into the wall, though, as I twisted

in the air and landed in a crouch. The prince looked surprised, as he'd expected me to sprawl on the floor then crawl toward him to beg for forgiveness.

I rose to my feet and hissed, as I felt the sting of the blow on my face.

Supernatural magic had no effect on me, but I could suffer physical harm from beatings, and I always felt intense pain inflicted by every blow.

"You'll learn loyalty in my court, boy!" Silas snarled. "You're under my authority, and you don't belong to any other house! Get that through your skull!"

"Prince Louis lost control one time, but even he never laid a hand on me," I said.

"He's a pussy, and I'm not him," Silas said, using his alpha stare on me.

I held my chin up and stared back, unblinking. Alpha stares were a real thing. It was all about power and domination. No other shifter could stand the weight of the alpha stare, but I could brush it off like an annoying fly. I might have a careless, clueless look with my round cheeks and small frame, but I was a born monster and apex predator, much more so than the shifter prick in front of me.

Dixie let out an audible gasp, shock slamming

into her face. Right, I wasn't just some powerless servant boy.

"Look down, Little Bob," she said.

I liked Dixie, but her alpha was now one of my least favorite people. Sy could hold a grudge forever. She didn't tolerate anyone hurting me, and I had to put extra effort into reining her in to prevent her from erupting out to shred Silas.

Chill, I told her. *We won't be in the shifters' house for long.*

"Why?" I said defiantly, looking at the promise of death in Silas's eyes, ready to turn on my kind of alpha stare and bend his fucking knees.

Silas growled, his eyes turning golden. Was he going to shift and tear into me? Well, then, I'd tear away his magic and essence and see how he liked it. He'd never be able to shift again. If he knew that I could be that kind of threat, he'd try to kill me. I could defeat him, but then I'd have no future in this realm. I'd be hunted by every supernatural.

I might be powerful, but they had the numbers.

We'll deal with it, Sy urged me on. *Let me out. Let me beat the shit out of him and he'll never lay his uncouth hand on us again.*

"Foolish boy. He's your alpha!" Dixie said as she moved to step between her prince and me, taking a knee. "Your Highness, Little Bob doesn't understand any rules. He has no education or any training. Even his grammar is terrible at times. His accent also tells me that he came from the streets in the slum. He's incredibly and stupidly rude, but he's that way with everyone. He might be an insufferable, insolent urchin, but he's our urchin."

Wow, should I stay here and continue to listen to more insults? I thought that the shifter house could provide me with temporary shelter, but I was getting abused again.

"I'm not a shifter," I said, turning with a shrug. "I don't belong to your house, sir. Sorry for the bother. I'll see myself out."

"You're a shifter, boy," the prince said. "I scented the animal in you; whether it's a mouse or a chihuahua is anyone's guess though."

He flicked two fingers, and the wind shut the door.

Interesting. All supernaturals possessed one elemental magic, but all the prince heirs were gifted with two or possibly more.

"You're going nowhere, Little Bob," Silas said. "You'll learn to behave in record time as my new squire. If there's any issue in the future, you'll report to me right away instead of seeking out heirs from other houses."

That was what this was all about. I'd overstepped my boundaries by asking for help from the mage prince.

"Should you look wrong or step wrong, I won't just punish you; I'll punish Dixie. So think twice before you act. And this time, you'll still get your share of punishment for stepping out of line."

My heart sank. I didn't want shit to drop on Dixie. I clenched my jaw and looked down at the ground, showing my submissiveness.

"Are you going to whip me for punishment, sir?" I asked. "Just keep Dixie out of this. She has nothing to do with my shit."

"I'm not a barbarian, unlike your former master," he growled.

Well, hadn't the fucker backhanded me a minute ago?

"You'll join the construction team and do manual labor work for a month when you aren't attending to me as my squire," he said.

Maybe it was time I built up some muscles. I could always use Sy's strength to handle the heavy lifting. Sy rolled her eyes at my scheming.

"Now beat it," Silas said, wrinkling his nose. "You stink, Little Bob. You need to take a bath."

"Before carrying the rocks or after carrying the rocks, sir?" I deadpanned and sniffed my armpit noisily for show.

"Quit it, boy," Dixie warned, but she muffled a chortle and dragged me toward the door before Silas could come to punch me. "Let's get you to the bath chamber and wash off the odor of your sweat."

"It's not that bad," I protested. "You're exaggerating. I could go a week or two without a bath in the past."

"You need to learn to keep your big mouth shut and your eyes down in front of your betters if you know what's good for you, boy!" Dixie barked at me as she towed me down the corridor with her hand on my elbow, away from Silas's suite.

"They might have more money than me and be in a powerful position," I said, smirking at her, "but they aren't my betters."

"I'll have to drill more rules into your thick knucklehead on a daily basis then," she sighed. "I'm determined to turn you into a proper shifter. At least

you won't run your mouth like there're no consequences."

We approached the shifters' bath chamber that
was like a large chicken coop. It didn't even have
stalls.

Truth be told, I'd never taken a bath here.

Lower-ranking shifters didn't have their own
bathrooms, but no one seemed to care about being
nude in public, except me. Well, they were shifters.
They were used to being naked since they were little.

I'd bathed in the icy lake in Underhill once.
Other times, I'd snuck into Dixie and other higher
ranking shifters' private bathrooms to have a quick
shower when they went for a run or were in a class. I
watched everyone's schedules closely.

No wards or spells could stop me, and neither
could their locks. A lot of shifters didn't even lock
their doors.

"Off you go." Dixie pushed me ahead. "Scrub
yourself good and hard. I don't want to hear the
prince complaining about your smell again.
Understand?"

"Yes, ma'am," I said, my shoulders slouched.

"After your bath, come find me," she said.

"Why? You've drilled so many rules into me, my
ears are bleeding."

She slapped the back of my head fondly. "You'll get a break tonight. We'll go to a bar."

My eyes lit up. "For drinks, like booze?"

She smiled. "Why else would you go to a bar, silly boy?"

To steal. All the drunkards in the bar made it easier.

"I don't have money yet, Dixie," I confessed. "Prince Louis hasn't paid me a penny for my hard work, and it's not the best time to chase his vamp ass at the moment."

"You haven't told Prince Silas or me what exactly happened with the vampire prince," Dixie said.

"My memories are a bit blurry," I said. "It's the PTSD."

She didn't look convinced.

I didn't want to badmouth Louis, and not just because he was dangerous. I knew he hadn't intended to hurt me. He'd lost his shit, as my blood was too powerful for anyone to handle, and he'd been in a jealous rage when he came to me.

"May I borrow some money from you?" I asked. "Prince Silas hasn't talked to me about my pay either. I won't work for free, but he seems to be in a constant bad mood."

"The prince is under a lot of stress," Dixie said,

her brows pinched in worry. "His ambitious sister, a year younger than him, has been gunning for his position as the heir. She's been gathering power around her for a few months now, yet she refuses to challenge him." Then she blinked and shook her head, her nose ring making a faint sound. "Why am I telling you this? Anyway, forget what I said. And don't worry about your stomach. No shifters go hungry in the house."

"I still want to get paid though." I pouted. "I'm a boy, and I have needs."

"You'll start with the minimum wage in the House of Shifters, squire," she said and walked away before I could protest or curse.

Chapter Nineteen

I snuck into Luna's two-bedroom, one-bath apartment she shared with Javier, that panther prick. They'd both gone out on an errand for the prince. It wasn't the first time I'd helped myself to their place. Even though they were shifters, they wouldn't be able to smell me if I covered up my scent well.

I quickly checked out the apartment. Javier's room was as messy as usual, and Luna's was a lot tidier and cleaner. Luna was secretly dating Dixie, and she mostly went to Dixie's place to get laid.

I went to their small kitchen first, finishing a slice of cold pizza, then strode to their bathroom.

If I had more leisure time, I'd bathe in the lake in Underhill, the most dangerous place for everyone but the safest place for me. Luna's shared bathroom would do for now. She'd think the panther showered earlier if the bathtub remained wet when she returned, and Javier would assume the same. They wouldn't ask about each other's hygiene habits, and it'd never cross their puny minds that someone else had been using their bathroom.

Shifters might be paranoid, but they weren't the think-outside-the-box kind. That was why I came in and boldly consumed a slice of pizza. Sometimes, I took a cookie. No one would miss a cookie. The key was not to be too greedy, even though I'd been tempted to take the whole cookie jar with me, since I really liked almond chocolate cookies.

I was no stranger here, so here I came.

Houston! Sy added.

I shut the bathroom door, stripped, piled my clothes on the counter, and stepped into the tub.

A stream of water poured onto me from the showerhead, and I sighed happily. One of the reasons I liked to shower here was that the water was strong. Shifters' house magic was water element, so that was a perk.

I grabbed a lavender-scented soap, lathered myself up nicely, and hummed a song I'd once heard from an old record, 'Cry Me A River.'

As I swept the soap across my perky tits, I suddenly felt a large, powerful hand cupping my left breast, then kneading my nipple, gentle at first, then hard and possessive. The soap slipped from my fingers and hit my toes, but I had no time and no desire to pick it up.

My back arched as unholy pleasure glided over my skin like hot waves wrapped in a tongue of fire, humming and caressing. I wanted more. I needed more.

I gasped at the sensation, but I wasn't fool enough to just let anyone touch me, no matter how pleasurable it was.

Sy surged to the edge of my skin, thrilled and alarmed as well.

I grabbed the hand that came around to fondle my breast from behind while a hard body pressed against my back. I bent his hand backward at the wrist to inflict pain with my strength and twisted my body to face the invader.

Like a rug being pulled away from under me, suddenly, I was no longer in the bathtub. Well, I was still in a tub, but a different one. It seemed that I'd been teleported to a round gold and marble bathtub that could fit an entire squad.

"What the fuck?" I yipped. "You'll regret this, asshole!"

"Will I?" A rich, sensual male voice tangled with the wind. "I wonder what else that filthy mouth of yours can do."

The hand that had been playing with my tit spun me around, and I found myself pressing against a hard body as I came face to face with the man who had haunted my waking hours ever since I'd come to this realm.

The prince of the House of Chaos gazed down at me, laughter and heat in his storm-blue eyes, as the water in the tub lapped at his waist and my lower chest. He wore only a pair of white swimming trunks, which only gave him more sex appeal. My gaze roamed from his muscled chest and dipped lower and lower. He had golden skin like mine, but more tanned.

There wasn't an ounce of fat on any inch of his hard, perfect body. His stomach was an eight pack of hard muscles, his thighs large and powerful, and his muscles tight like silky steel. His every line exuded incredible power, sexuality, and masculine beauty.

Our man is built to fuck, Sy said in approval.

Shove it, I said.

I didn't want her to come out to fuck him. I

didn't want her to touch him. And I didn't want him to see her and either choose her or freak out.

"Have an eyeful?" Killian crooned, his voice wrapping around me with heat and seduction.

By sheer will, I forced my wanton gaze from the bulge in his groin to focus on his god-like face. If he were in the mortal world, his incredible beauty and carnal looks would cause a chain of accidents and riots. No man should be this sexy.

"You look like spoiled honey that traps all the flies," I blurted out.

He arched an eyebrow, and my pussy throbbed with burning need. Damn this man beast!

"This must be some kind of dream, a most ridiculous one," I said, more to myself than to him. Or had my mere thoughts and desires summoned him? My mind hadn't had that kind of power before. Or had I developed a new power? I shook my head. This was all so confusing. "I'm going to pinch my tit and wake the fuck up!"

"Or I can pinch your tit, little dagger," he offered with a smirk. "Actually, I can do more than that if you let me."

Let him. Sy gave me bad advice again.

I stared at him, lust pounding in my flesh. I couldn't wrap my mind around all this. They said he was the coldest and most ruthless power in the realm, but with me in this place, he was different.

"You can call this the dreamland that exists parallel to our world, little dagger," he added softly. He didn't want me to leave.

A lock of his hair dropped over his storm-blue eyes that heated my naked flesh as they traced my body inch by inch. My breath hitched, my mind picturing having him sucking my nipple, having his wicked way with me, then burying his cock deep within my aching flesh. I wanted to know how it felt, not that kind of feeling I got when Sy fucked, like I was peering through thick glass.

I licked my lips. "Why am I here?"

I should get away from the sexy, golden, and dangerous man, but I couldn't move. I didn't want to move. I wanted to be trapped by his darkness and burned by his starlight.

"Here, you can be with me," he said. "I don't think either of us can deny this thing between us."

"But you aren't real, and I'm not going to fool myself," I said defiantly while soaking in his intoxicating scent of spring rain and pine and powerful male.

Men were liars. Women were liars too. And I was a liar.

"Say that again." He laughed, his hand sliding between my thighs and palming my pussy hard. The force pulled me to him.

Liquid flame tongued my needy sex, and I moaned in pleasure. His heat radiated to me in waves. I rested my hands on his shoulders, my fingernails sinking into his skin.

"Your flesh craves me as much as mine craves you," he said, his palm, warm and strong, rubbing my sex, "so I forged this dreamland for us, little dagger."

"You'll fuck me and give me the kind of pleasure I need?" I asked in my husky voice, my tone demanding. "I'm not like any woman you've fucked before." I didn't spell out for him that I was more than immortal though. "I'm insatiable once I start. Can you keep up? Be careful of what you're getting into."

He chuckled, his eyes searing with desire, as my challenge turned him on even more.

"Keep challenging me, my little dagger. I might just find my match," he growled, then his mouth slanted onto mine.

It was the first time I had been kissed. Sy fucked and fed, but she never kissed.

Instantly, my body was on fire. My body arched like a tensed bow ready to release.

His breath mingled with mine, the taste of him delicious, the feel of him dangerous, unpredictable, yet utterly addictive.

I moaned, and then I bit the tip of his tongue, tasting his rich blood and formidable power as he pushed it into my mouth. He let out a rough groan as our tongues started to dance, tangle, and play a game of dominance.

He thrust two fingers into my tightness. I nearly screamed in pleasure.

I kissed him with lips, teeth, and tongue, tasted him, and bit him like a starved wild wind. A chuckle vibrated from the depths of his throat, but he liked it just fine.

My fingers threaded into his thick hair, twisted a few locks, and pulled his head further down to me, as I didn't want him to get away. My entire body hummed, in tune with his; my hips propelled toward him to push his fingers deeper into my molten heat.

He pulled away, his lips leaving mine, when our lungs were long overdue a breath of air.

"Aren't you a greedy little thing?" he crooned, his fingers driving in and out of my pussy vehemently.

"You knew I wasn't a boy?" I asked breathlessly. "How?"

"I'm not a fool like the others," he purred. "I

wanted to fuck you the first time I laid eyes on you." He groaned, his fingers turning in my narrow passage. "This is the cunt for me, tight, hot, and demanding. It's made for me to fuck."

I arched my back, clinging to him. It also felt like he was made to fuck me. Then something else flashed in my head.

"But aren't you spoken for, prince?" I asked tensely.

"It doesn't matter," he said dismissively. "With you, nothing else matters. I can get to you and fuck you here."

I didn't understand how he had made this happen. Was this one of his powers? Legend said that only Hades' bloodline could dream walk. And rumor said that Prince Killian had a bit of every supernatural in him. That was why he was the chaos prince.

I couldn't mark him out as I did others, especially not now, while intense lust muddled my mind, reducing me to a wild beast that only needed and hungered.

Heat radiated into me from his powerful body, and then my heat reciprocated, trapping him as well. I slid my hand into his swimming trunks and seized his erection mercilessly.

Fuck, it was huge and rock hard. I'd need two

hands to wrap around it. I pumped my fist up and down his length, my thumb playing with the thick ring of his crown, flicking it, brushing it, rubbing it, and pinching it. He hissed in pleasure, his eyes turning molten sapphire.

"You're playing with fire, little dagger," he said.

"You came to me first," I countered. "You asked for it."

"Did I? It's always my fault, isn't it?"

I wasn't a fan of his attitude, though my blood strummed for him and my body burned for him, so I dragged down his trunks and let them drop.

"Fierce, my little dagger, but I can do better." He smirked and flicked a finger, and his trunks vanished.

My gaze snagged on the tattoo of an emerald dragon sprawled from his left hip to his powerful thigh. Rumor also said that Killian was the last dragon, though no one had seen his dragon form.

I'd overheard the vampire prince challenging him. *Is it true that your dragon will come out only when he recognizes his fated mate? Are you even a dragon?*

Before I could inspect the dragon tattoo further, he spun me and bent me, my back to him. My hands planted on the marble bank of the enormous tub with a hard cock brushing across my butt cheeks.

Shit, this was hot!

My desire burning, I wiggled my ass to urge him to get it going.

His granite-hard cock nudged at my slick entrance.

"Like it rough, little dagger?"

"Do you always talk so much?"

"No one's ever complained about my dirty talk before." He chuckled. "I don't even do talk, but I haven't been rough for a very long time. Now, little dagger, I need to be rough with you and fuck you however I want." His voice turned to a dark whisper, and I wouldn't even have heard him if I hadn't had superior hearing. "You're made for me, and I wonder if a man like me can still hope, as you're probably the only one who can free me. Then I can have you sit on my cock day and night without care."

I didn't understand. What did he mean that I could free him? From whom or what? Yet his erotic promise of having me sitting on his cock day and night heated my blood.

And I should probably tell him that this form of mine was a virgin, so I wasn't sure if being very rough was a good idea. Before I could voice either my questions or concern, he thrust into my depths with one powerful move.

Fireworks of pleasure hit my nerve endings, and I cried out as he thrust in and out of me with abandon. The sound of flesh slapping against flesh mixed with the lapping sound of water in the tub.

"So fucking tight!" he hissed, sheathing himself deep in me, one hand fondling my breast hard, his other hand grabbing my hip to anchor me while he thrust and thrust.

My pussy gloved him tightly, needing and wanting. I breathed hard, my mouth open like a fish, not sure if I wanted oxygen or water. A couple more brutal thrusts and I would climax. It'd be my first. I threw my head back, waiting for the waves to hit, and I'd roar my orgasm.

An angry bellow broke out, pumping dismay and apprehension into me while lust still strummed in my every fiber.

"Who the fuck is there?!"

Chapter Twenty

A blink, and I was no longer bent over, being fucked in the golden tub. Instead, I stood in a stupor in Luna's bathtub. Strong water from the showerhead plummeted onto my face, my curled golden hair lathered with shampoo.

The prince of the House of Chaos was gone. It was like the force of reality had just torn apart the fabric of our private world and snatched me back.

A panicked realization hit my head like a brick.

Fuck! The panther shifter had returned. He wasn't supposed to be back so soon.

But I didn't know how much time had passed since I had become entangled with Killian in his dream walk. I had put myself in danger with both my guard and my pants down.

I turned off the shower and grabbed a large towel from the rack in a rush. I had barely wrapped it around myself when the door was kicked open. Luckily, the towel covered most of my small form from my shoulders to my knees. Unluckily, Javier charged in, Luna at his heels.

They stared at me, more shocked than I.

"Hey guys, how're you doing?" I greeted, smiling at them as I pulled the towel tighter around myself. "Good to see you."

"What the fuck are you doing here?!" Javier yelled, his nasty small eyes on fire.

"Taking a shower?" I offered.

"Do you know whose place this is?" Luna drawled in a hard voice.

"Yours, Luna," I said humbly. "The door was open, so I invited myself in."

"You didn't close the door, Javier?" Luna chided. "You left after me. You gotta close the door next time. I'm a high-profile shifter in the house now. The last thing I want is to provide convenience for anyone to invade my privacy."

She thought she was high profile because she was fucking the prince's royal cousin.

Javier narrowed his eyes on me, making them

even smaller. I squinted at him while waving a hand, wondering if he could still see me.

"I closed the fucking door," Javier cursed in fury before he sniffed.

Shit, the scent of my arousal from a moment ago lingered in the air.

"Did you jerk off in my bathtub, Little Bob?" Javier demanded.

Heat rose in the slits of his eyes. He couldn't help it, and he hated that he was now aroused too and that I was the source.

"What, dude?" I flushed. "How could you even say things so gross and insane?"

With a snarl, he stepped toward me with malicious intent.

Fear shot straight into my belly, and I staggered back, but there was no more room in the tub. I'd pressed my back against the shower wall.

My hand clutched the towel tighter to prevent it from dropping and exposing myself. My right knee bent a little, ready for a quick, brutal kick to his throat or groin, depending on the situation.

My goal was clear: I wouldn't let him tear the towel from me and expose me as a girl. I had made it so far that I wouldn't allow anyone to sabotage my stay in this realm. My mind worked fast, several plans running through it at once.

Option one: jump kick the panther in the throat or groin when he came at me, decapacitate him, jump out of the tub, shove Luna away, then run like a bat out of hell while the panther bent to hold his groin in pain.

Option two: apologize and beg for mercy, appealing to their good sides.

Option three: play it by ear and restrain myself from attacking them first.

If I had to resort to violence in the end, I'd make sure to kick him to the ground with one strike. Hopefully, neither of them would see my "cock" or the lack of it in the blur.

Fingers crossed and hope for the best.

Sy made a gesture of crossing fingers while looking out in intrigue. She loved to see me in a pickle like this.

Luna pulled Javier back just in time. "C'mon, let's give Little Bob a chance to explain first. You made the poor boy shake like a cornered chihuahua." She chuckled. "He bites too when he's pushed too hard."

Sy bristled. She'd rather get into a battle than be belittled.

Javier still bared his teeth, but he seemed to forget the idea of lunging at me without issuing more threats. That was better.

"So you think it was a fucking good idea to invite yourself in and take a shower in my tub?" the panther hissed.

"Technically, it isn't merely yours," I said. "Luna owns half of it. So technically, I can say that I'm using the half of the tub she owns." The panther looked like he wanted to lunge and strike me again, so I added in a hurry, "Sorry, man, this is a big misunderstanding. I was looking for Luna, since Dixie mentioned that we'd all go out for a drink to a shifter bar!"

They didn't seem to share my excitement but still glared at me like two mean judges.

"When I didn't find Luna," I continued, "I remembered what the prince said."

"What did His Highness say?" Luna asked.

"He said that I needed to take a bath," I confessed. "That's what I was doing before it was disrupted."

Both Javier and Luna stared at me incredulously, and I nodded, staring back at them with a meaningful look. "Dixie heard it as well. You can check with either the prince or Dixie if you want."

"What the hell is going on?" Dixie's voice sounded at the door.

Worry and hope warred in my belly, then Dixie appeared in the doorway of the bathroom behind Luna. Now instead of two pairs of eyes, three pairs stared at me, as if I needed that kind of pressure.

"Dixie, so glad you're here," I called, a bit cheerfully and a bit ruefully. "Luna and Javier returned before I finished my shower."

Javier bared his teeth fully now.

Dixie frowned at me. "I left you for two minutes and you already got yourself into some shit again. Didn't I escort you to the bath chamber?"

"But there were too many people there," I said.

"That's where you should bathe with the other shifters!" Dixie snapped. "You aren't ranked high enough to have your own private bath. Be grateful that I didn't assign you to the bunk quarters! And you can't just go to other people's places to take a shower whenever you feel like it. You gotta respect other people's privacy! Learn boundaries."

"I have boundaries," I said. "I've never taken a dump here. It isn't the right thing to do to another supernatural."

"Fuck!" Javier cursed. "This wasn't the first time Little Bob took a shower here and defiled our space."

Luna nodded. "All those times, I thought you made a mess."

"And I thought you did," Javier confessed.

"Not my finest moments," I admitted, biting my lower lip in regret. "I could do better."

"And he did something to cover up his fucking scent!" Javier said.

"No more showering in anyone's places," Dixie hissed at me before a dark realization sparked in her eyes. "Did you ever shower in my place, Little Bob? Don't you dare lie to me!"

I lowered my head and said sheepishly, "Only once. I like lavender soap, Dixie. Did you gift Luna a lavender soap? That's why she always smells good."

As I said, flattery never got old, and I needed to gain favor in this tricky situation.

"That lavender soap is mine!" Javier growled.

"No shit, man," I said. "You might need to get a new one then, since I kind of used it all this time."

"I'm going to beat the shit out of this little shit!" Javier said, but Luna held his arm as she started laughing.

"And I thought it was the vampires' issue that they despised Little Bob," she said.

"Rules are set for a reason, Little Bob," Dixie sighed. "You cross the wrong people and you might not get to live to tomorrow. Next time, just stick to the public bath chamber!"

"But I'm shy," I said in a low voice.

"You're a shifter." Dixie started to lose patience. "Act like it!"

Javier's gaze roved over me, then a spark of realization came alive in his narrow eyes, and he tittered.

"Little Bob has a tiny dick," he revealed, "and he's afraid of anyone finding out."

My face burned red, anger and embarrassment rising in my eyes, which only made the panther shifter giggle delightedly at my expense.

"You're still a virgin, aren't you, Little Bob?" he crooned.

"It's none of your business!" I hissed.

Dixie and Luna started laughing, too, which only encouraged Javier.

"Javier, don't be an ass," Luna chided him while giggling more.

I grabbed my towel tighter, glaring at them. If he came to check me out to confirm his theory, I'd make him regret that he was ever born.

"Little Bob might be short, but he could have a big dick," Dixie said. "Don't judge books by the cover."

"Oh, I judge a book by the cover," Luna said, flashing her lover a flirtatious glance, her lips tilting up in good humor. "Not to belittle our Little Bob here, but the size of a guy's hand shows the size of his dick. I fucked enough men to know this before I quit fucking men."

Everyone stared at my hands, and I stared at them too while they gripped the two ends of the towel to make sure my small frame remained covered.

Shit! I had small hands. I had a tiny dick! The socks I put inside my underwear every morning to make me look like I had a bulge there weren't fooling anyone.

The three of them looked at my hands, darted their eyes to my groin covered by the towel, then looked at the expression on my face and roared with laughter. The glass in the living room shook a little. In fact, they all doubled over, they were laughing so hard. Javier even wiped tears out of his small eyes.

"Don't worry, Little Bob." Luna tried to straighten up before falling apart in Dixie's arms. "You're still growing, right? And tiny dick or not, you'll find a girl who wants you just as you are. Besides, you're prettier than a girl. Any girl would kill to have your long, thick lashes and dreamy eyes."

"Stop it!" Dixie called, laughing harder.

"I don't like dick jokes!" I said. "I'm not going to finish this shower since I'm no longer in the mood. Could you excuse me and let me dress? I gotta get the fuck out of here."

"If you ever come back here, you're dead!" Javier warned before swaggering out of the bathroom. The talk of my tiny dick had really boosted his ego.

"We're still going to that shifter bar, right?" I asked hopefully before Dixie made an exit with Luna.

She wiggled a finger at me chidingly. "You're canceled and grounded, Little Bob. I'll drill the rules and boundaries into your knucklehead until you get them, so you'll live to adulthood."

Then she slammed the bathroom door shut.

I jumped out of the bathtub, grabbed my pile of clothes and leaned my ass against the door to prevent someone from kicking open the door to check out the size of my junk.

I quickly dressed myself.

Lucky for me, none of them had seen the breast binder at the bottom of the pile.

When I was done, I picked a new lavender soap bar and put it in my pocket, then I opened the door and shot out like a puppy that had got kicked with its tail between its legs.

My whole body still strummed with deep frustration from not being sated—I'd been so close to my first orgasm.

Chapter Twenty-One

Instead of letting myself be grounded, I snuck out of the shifters' house, stuck to the shadows, and shot toward Underhill. The place called me like the home I'd never had.

My hands in my pants pocket, I jogged toward the dark forest, streaming moonlight illuminating the sign of **Underhill! Enter At Your Own Peril!**

"Hello, hello," I greeted.

"Hello," a voice answered, and I leapt back, my heart pounding in my throat.

A dark figure stepped out from behind a vast tree and into my path, his pale blue eyes shining.

Somehow, the wild magic had covered his presence. It'd allowed the Shrieker, and now the vampire, to get into its territory because it wanted to see me play. Underhill had its own mischievous mind. It wanted to learn more about me.

Prince Louis stood tall and still in the night wind, like a pale god, not bothered by the sinister air around here. He was a creature of the night anyway.

The wind flapped his trench coat and rustled his blond hair. Power rippled off him.

He'd recovered fully, so now he'd come to ambush me, lurking in the shadows and waiting for me to leave the House of Shifters. I knew he would come for me eventually and that I couldn't avoid him forever, but I hadn't expected today would be the day.

At least he didn't bring his cronies with him. I sensed that we were alone. A few plans rushed through my mind: scream and run, or knee him in the crotch and run.

He'd just chase me and get more excited.

I stared back at him silently. He studied me a few moments longer and opened his mouth.

"I see you're still looking for trouble everywhere, little Bob."

"That's not true, sir," I said. "I've been trying to fly under the radar."

"Yet here you are, coming to the place no other supernatural dares to linger."

"That's the thing, sir," I sighed. "What's considered dangerous to others isn't a danger to me. What everyone thinks is safe often hurts me."

"Now who thinks he's clever?"

"Cleverness can't outrun death. I just want to live a little longer."

He gave me a long look again, but his eyes softened a little.

"Then come back with me and rejoin my house, and I'll make sure of it."

"No, thanks, sir," I said, sucking in a breath. "I have to address the elephant in the room now. We both know that if I hadn't stabbed you last time, you'd have drained me."

"My bad, I admit it. But I won't lose control again," he said, licking his lips before he forced himself to dart his hungry gaze from the veins in my neck to my face. "I promise. Now it's time to name your price, and I'll grant all your demands."

"I'm doing you a favor by staying away, sir," I said. "Or you'll only be addicted to my blood until one day you won't be able to function without thinking of drinking from me every second. It'll fuck you up, and I won't be safe."

He knew that my blood boosted his power, so he wanted me even more. My words wouldn't persuade him to back off, and it was easier to shame a slut than shame a thirsty vampire.

"Don't be dramatic, little Bob," he snorted. "We can work this out. Now, come with me back to my house."

"No means no," I said firmly. "No one sinks his fucking teeth into my neck anymore. Get out of my way, please."

"I've asked nicely, boy," he said. "You're more insolent than ever, and you leave me with no choice but to persuade you the hard way."

"You'll regret it."

"Will I?" He chuckled darkly. "I can hear how fast your heart is racing, which only makes your blood smell more delicious." He licked his lips shamelessly, hunger burning in his eyes. "Your blood always tasted like nectar from a god's veins. I've missed it. I won't be denied my drink anymore!"

He lunged, and I darted sideways just as fast, or faster. A flicker of surprise flitted by his eyes, and the muscles under them twitched in anger.

"Run, little Bob, run!" he half-purred and half-snarled. "I'll give you a head start."

Vampires loved to hunt as much as shifters. His prey would taste better when the vampire prince caught it after a thrilling hunt. But I was no prey, and it was his mistake to assume so.

He'd once caught me and fed upon me, but the good old days were gone for him.

The strong and powerful did not defend the weak. They took whatever they wanted, insisting it was their right. Louis had no fucking idea that I was stronger, and that Underhill was not his friend but mine.

"Suck my tiny dick!" I shouted in a high-pitched voice in French before dashing into the dark forest.

I bet no one had told him to suck a dick. He was so shocked at my taunt that he didn't have a come-back, so he growled viciously, promising to make me pay once he seized me.

Wild magic twirled at my feet eagerly as the vampire prince stalked in, all swaggering, passing the threshold of Underhill.

Let's give the vamp a taste to remember, I told Underhill.

Wild magic hummed, and the dark forest shifted in front of the wild-eyed vampire prince.

Thorny vines broke out on the ground, seizing Louis by the ankles before he could take one more step into Underhill. Several branches shot out from the ancient sentinel trees at the entrance, grabbed his arms and neck, and yanked him into the air.

Suspended in the air, Louis kicked and snarled, slashing at the branches and vines with his wind, but Underhill wouldn't let him go. The vampire prince managed to get his arm free, a dagger appearing in his hand. But as soon as he chopped off a branch, more replaced it.

Underhill was playing, the wild magic humming a vicious song.

The thorny vines sank into Louis's flesh, his blood dripping to the forest floor. The branches holding him started to pull him in different directions, ready to rip him apart.

Fear coating his eyes, Louis cursed, struggling harder in vain. A new branch appeared like a stake, aiming toward his heart.

"Don't take his life," I ordered. "At least, not yet. Just throw him out."

You're no fun, the wild magic purred.

Fun hurts these days, I said. *And I don't want to tip the balance of the houses and realm.*

Who cares, said the wild magic.

You don't want all the vampires coming here, gathering outside with shouts and banners and going on strike, do you?

Will they do that? the wild magic whimpered.

They might've joined the union, I said. *It's better to just throw him out. That's humiliating enough. Trust me.*

After I have a little more fun with the pretty vampire, the wild magic promised.

A twist of darkness formed into a shadow beast, roaring into Louis's face, all terrible claws and fangs and nightmares. The vampire prince froze, his eyes widening. I bet he hadn't known fear before.

"Go back to your house, Prince Louis," I purred. "Next time, Underhill won't be so merciful."

"Who are you?" Louis whispered; despite his fear, he remained vicious.

"When you stare at the darkness, it stares back," I quoted.

The shadow beast struck, slashing its claws along Louis's chest and legs before tossing him out of the entrance.

"Don't seek me out again, Highness." I stood over him as I raised a hand to sort out my messy golden curls.

Chapter Twenty-Two

Vampires no longer patrolled the border of the shifters' territory since my confrontation with Louis. For the next couple of days, life was peachy. Everyone, especially Silas, was worrying about their own shit, so no one came to bother me. Dixie and her team were busy with a new task that she didn't tell me about, and with no one hovering over me, I spent my days roaming the school grounds, watching students practicing magic from a distance and picking a thing or two up for my future use.

I also enjoyed hanging out with Bea at breakfast. She always got to Jubilee Hall earlier than anyone else to avoid those bullies. When those douches arrived, she'd already finished her plate.

"Little Bea!" I grinned at her, joining her at a corner table and putting down a tray weighted down by dishes and three large milkshakes. "I have a question for you."

My witch friend was a walking Wikipedia of magic and houses.

She eyed me and the food. "Where does that food go?"

"Do you really want to know?" I asked.

"No, but I know that you're not eating for two," she teased, in reference to those days when I had to let Louis drink my blood.

I pulled out a chair and sat to her left.

"Did you see lightning fizzing at Prince Killian's fingertips last time when he came through the Veil?" I asked in a low voice, even though no one else was within earshot.

She nodded and leaned closer to me. "It's not often that anyone gets to see his display of true power. The rumors say that he's bonded with a storm dragon. No one sees the dragon though. All we know is that dragons went extinct after their last war."

I pondered, remembering how I responded to his power alone and that I couldn't siphon his magic. Maybe it had something to do with his dragon, or his questionable origin.

"Maybe he bonded with the last dragon," I suggested. "Maybe we should call out his dragon to take a look for ourselves."

My father hated dragons. Perhaps one of the two original gods who joined forces to defeat him was a half-dragon.

She gasped. "I know you're crazy, Little Bob, but you aren't that crazy, right? Tell me that you aren't really going to poke the bear."

"In this case, it would be poking the dragon."

"Some say that the prince heir of the House of Chaos also has high demon blood, but it's dangerous talk," Bea whispered. "He has never explained his origin to anyone, and no one dares to challenge him. That's why his house is called the House of Chaos, and his house accepts any hybrids or supernaturals of unknown origin. He's the most powerful prince in the realm, which is probably one of the reasons that Queen Lilith chose him as her future consort. She's been campaigning to be the High Queen of all the realm and make the House of the Underworld a legit house in the realm as well.

My heart skipped a beat then pumped rapidly at hearing about Killian's woman, and bile suddenly rose to the back of my parched throat. I had no idea why I had this cold and terrible reaction every time I heard the name Queen Lilith. I was also baffled and angry at my possessiveness toward the chaos prince, especially since my cold logic kept telling me that I might have a stupid crush on him, but Killian wasn't mine and never would be.

My mind chose this moment to replay the bizarre, scandalous sex scene that involved both Killian and me. It'd felt more real than anything. When he was balls deep in me, he had whispered, *"You're made for me, and I wonder if a man like me can still hope, as you're probably the only one who can free me."*

I hadn't understood, and I still didn't get it. Free from whom or what?

"Who is this Queen Lilith again?" I tried my best to keep the snarl out of my husky voice.

"The myth says that she's a direct descendant of one of the brightest fallen stars," Bea said, "before they fell to Earth. Better not to talk about her, especially not to mention her name and draw her attention to us." Her eyes suddenly turned eerily milky white. *"Magic fades; Mist reveals, and Ruin comes. The chosen one—the cursed and the blessed—comes before him to bring tides. She's the darkness in light and light in massive darkness. Find the buried living flame and hope kindles. Turn the wheels of the Fates and the vicious cycle stops. Time is running out. Beware of the hanged. Join the Brides Selection and be the BRIDE!"*

My heart rammed into my ribcage. Was my witch friend speaking prophecy or just talking shit? Luckily, no one was near us. I dared not disturb her but stared at her, especially after I heard my father's name spat out of her mouth.

A blink, and Bea gasped, returning to normal. The whiteness cleared from her eyes.

"What happened?"

"You said to beware of the hanged and something about the bride," I said, still a little freaked out. "Wtf?"

"I don't know what those mean," she said, face paling and worry knotting her eyebrows. "I've been having episodes like this, and I don't remember what I said afterwards."

"We'll figure it out," I said, putting my hand on top of hers to ease her anxiety. "I'm here for you."

She nodded, her eyes glowing a little before they dulled. "I saw you again in my tealeaves last night. I think there'll be power plays in the realm, and you'll be a key player, despite your current low position. Be careful, Little Bob. Don't trust anyone."

I smirked to lighten the mood. "Including you."

"Yes, including me," she offered, her voice a little rough. "Things change. People change. Alliances change as well. No friends are forever, and no enemies are forever."

"We'll be friends forever. I know it."

"Could you tell me what else I said when I wasn't myself?" she asked.

"You said—" I started.

"Here you are, you little shit!" Javier stalked across the dining hall toward our table; more students filed in for coffee and breakfast.

"Shit," I said, swallowing a buttered bun without chewing much. "That big shit is coming our way. You'd better move along."

"I'll stand by you," Bea said, pulling out her wand. "If he hurts you, I'll turn my wand on him."

Javier stopped by my table, his small eyes narrowing on me.

"You're summoned to attend to His Highness at the ice skating rink. Right now!" he barked.

"What for?" I asked, swallowing a big mouthful of milkshake, and Javier growled at the burp I made. "I don't know how to skate."

"Little asshole, not everything is about you!" Javier grated.

"I need to finish my breakfast first. I don't like to work on an empty stomach." I gave him a slanted look. "Why didn't Luna come to fetch me? She likes me, and she smells better."

"No one likes you!"

"You wound me, man. And that's not true! Even you like me in secret. Anyway, where's Luna?"

"No one has seen her since yesterday morning. I'm going to help Dixie track her down after the princes' hockey sport." He then shook his head in disgust. "Why did I tell you that, you little shit?" He didn't know, of course, that I could compel people to answer my questions. It was just part of who I was.

"I know where the ice rink is, man," I said. "I'll head there as soon as I finish my second milkshake. Deal?"

"Get your ass up. You aren't going to finish your shit," he snarled and raised his hand to backhand me.

I ducked, tore the plastic lid off the milkshake cup, and tossed the contents at his groin.

Several bystanders laughed.

I broke into a run.

A hair-raising snarl sounded from behind me. A panther spilled out of Javier, his ruined trousers in shreds, pink milkshake dripping from his rear legs.

I called for Sy to give me speed and pumped my

legs faster. It was only several blocks between Jubilee Haven and BattleStar stadium. I covered the campus grounds like the wind, then shot across the training field, where students carried heavy equipment into the oval-shaped stadium.

When I looked over my shoulder, it seemed Javier was nowhere in sight. He'd probably given up chasing me. It wouldn't look good on him that he couldn't catch up with a servant boy. I slowed down to catch my breath, smiled, and jogged through the door of the stadium as if I belonged.

The stadium was like a vast beast composed of three areas: a general training field with full facilities, an advanced training field, and a raised ice rink fifty feet above the ground with thousands of spectator seats on three sides.

Ice hockey was one of the most popular sports in Mist of Cinder. It was a little different than human hockey, with less inhibitions and more violence, plus it was magical.

I stepped out of the lift fueled by magic and gasped.

In front of me, a spectacular ice skating rink floated in the air. Early morning sun shone on the expanse of ice and made it look like a vast sparkling diamond.

The princes were on the ice, looking absurdly hot. None of them wore protective gear; no helmets, shoulder or elbow pads, or mouthguards. They were showcasing their muscled chests and six-packs with only hockey trousers hanging on their hips.

My blood heated.

Who wouldn't? Sy chimed in, her gaze homing in on the princes with great interest, desire rising in her. *There he is! I want to lick every drop of sweat from the fae prince. I can try the others as well, since they're all too delicious to resist, sugar.*

Not wanting Sy to make more lewd comments, I dropped my gaze to the princes' skates, only for my jaw to drop in envy.

Every prince had gems adorning the rims of their skates. Louis had black opals, Silas had emeralds, Cade had sapphires, Rowan had rubies, and blue diamonds lined Killian's skates.

Those gemstones represented their houses.

A squire from each house dropped to one knee to double check their prince's skates and laces while the princes bantered, snickering, or growling at one another's comments. From their arrogant, entitled looks, they knew the whole stadium was watching them and took their effect on everyone for granted.

But they did have the best chests and eight-packs in the realm.

The audience cheered from their seats; male students stared at them with envy, wanting to be them, and female students ogled them openly, whispering to their friends and giggling with lust.

I took my time drinking in the scene, my hands in my pockets. Then suddenly, all the princes turned their heads and snapped their intense gazes on me, as if they couldn't help it, as if they were drawn to me like moths to the biggest flame, heat searing their eyes.

A second later, their anger pushed through, anchoring in the cold, logical part of their brains as they realized their unusual reactions toward me.

Their bodies wanted me, but their minds were telling them that as the heirs at the peak of power, it was stupid for them to be attracted to a servant boy.

Despite their resistance, their powers flirted with me, then wrestled with mine. Power called power. Then, like a wildfire stoked by a gust of wind, the locked magic in the princes roared to come out at my call—or not exactly my call. A strand of the wild magic from Underhill had followed me here, prancing on my skin, taunting and flirting with the princes' power and their deepest need.

With wild magic boosting me and all the powers on the ice, Sy giddily broadcast her pheromones. She'd need to feed soon, and now everyone was her target. All the powerful alphas gathered here tempted her to drink in their powers as they started to drink in mine and the wild magic.

I felt the undercurrent of the princes' heat and fury. Louis licked his lips, craving my blood more than anything while staring at me murderously. Confusion and arousal flashed in Silas's amber eyes, only to be replaced by more confusion and anger.

Prince Rowan homed in on me like an icy predator, struggling to figure me out, as he sensed the connection between Sy and me, but only a genius would link Sy and me, as we appeared to have nothing in common.

My gaze skipped the other princes and centered on Killian. I couldn't help it; my eyes were always drawn to him. A dark, knowing smirk ghosted his sensual lips as he locked gazes with me, which unnerved me more.

The memory of him fucking me in the dream-land burned in my head. Flames leapt up, fueling my lust, and my pussy grew slick with hot wetness.

Shit! They'd smell my arousal.

Quit it, Sy, I snarled inwardly as she kept

pumping her pheromones into the air. *Or I'll shut you down!*

I wasn't kidding.

Don't you just love to blame me for everything? she crooned in vicious delight. *But it isn't me this time. Look who's leaking magic wildly, little cherub Bob.*

Chapter Twenty-Three

"Your new squire is something, Silas," Cade said as every prince pinned me with their gaze.

I jogged toward the ice rink, a little defensive, a little protective of myself. My forearms folded across my chest, pressing my breasts hard as I noticed Killian darting his gaze toward them. While his look heated my blood, an alarm blared in my head. Had he really discovered that I was a girl, or was it just a suspicion?

It was bad enough to draw attention from any prince, but when all of their eyes were fixed on me? My stomach flipped a couple of times, and my gaits faltered a little. If I didn't find a way to divert their attention from me, the day would turn sour.

Why couldn't Silas leave me alone? Why must he summon me? I thought that he'd forgotten about me.

"He's unschooled," Silas snarled. "I don't know why I even assigned him to be my squire. The boy is a wild little beast waiting to be tamed."

"Good luck taming him," Louis snorted. "He was the worst squire in history. There isn't a single service bone in his body. All he worried about was filling his belly and going wherever he wanted." He shook his head. "He's the most self-interested being I've ever met. His tiny mind can't think any further than that."

I pretended not to hear them badmouthing me, though my superior hearing had caught every word. Anxiety buzzing in my ears, I only prayed for the princes to shift their attention somewhere or to someone else. There were knockout noble ladies in the spectator seats, ogling the princes, screaming their names, and wanting a piece of their taut asses.

Don't look at me. I'm a boring servant boy. Nothing to see here.

Yet I couldn't take my eyes off the princes either, until I realized what I was looking at. I was staring at the princes' hands, moving from one hand to the other as my mind automatically evaluated and compared their sizes. Damn Luna for saying that the size of a man's hand indicated the size of his junk. Now I couldn't unlearn the secret knowledge. I wasn't even sure if it was true.

It's true, Sy offered smugly. *I never made the connection until that honey badger pointed it out.*

His stern alpha gaze alighting on me, Silas crooked two fingers, beckoning me to approach. Why did he even want me here? I was useless as a squire, as he frequently complained. The prince was all about hierarchy and status. I was the lowest shifter in his pack, and I hadn't even shifted, not the way they would expect.

I studied the petty viciousness glinting in the shifter prince's amber eyes, a realization striking me. He brought me here to parade in front of Louis to irk his nemesis before the game in the hopes of messing with the vampire prince's head.

The heir of the House of Vampires would hate me even more. I'd be the one to suffer the fallout while the princes played their games.

I spread my arms, then pointed a finger at my foot, then spread my arms again to inquire silently how I was supposed to cross the ice to get to him without skates. He glared at me, and I widened my two-toned eyes with my signature innocent look while making another gesture that I was afraid of falling on my ass on the ice and thus embarrassing him as his squire.

Cade laughed, Killian smirked in amusement, Louis snickered, liking the show, and Rowan tilted his head to the side to study me some more. Damn it, I really hoped that the fae prince didn't see through me. A dose of healthy fear flooding me, I urged Sy to stay put.

"Little Bob always strikes back," Louis said. "He'll make you a laughingstock, Silas. If you're as smart as you try to show everyone, you should kick him out of your house now, before the little hellion brings chaos under your nose."

"Nice try, Louis. He sprinted away from your house to mine, didn't he?" Silas snorted. "You might have failed to rein him in, but I'll make a model shifter out of him."

Silas snapped his fingers and nodded toward a bulky shifter. The shifter sped toward me, a pair of new skates dangling from his hand. They were for me.

Why didn't that prick prince just dismiss me?

"He isn't a shifter," Cade said.

"I second Cade," Louis said. "No way is my former squire a shifter. My men made a mistake by joking about the boy being a chihuahua, so Silas took advantage of a bad joke and stole my squire. I won't let this matter slide. He'll be returned to my house eventually."

"I didn't steal him, Louis," Silas snapped coldly. "And you aren't taking him back. He might be an omega my house has been looking for."

"No bloody way is he an omega." Cade chuckled derisively. "Little Bob is the last person who will calm your wolves down." He gave Louis a look. "Neither should you claim him back and drink from a supernatural like him. The boy looks meek and clueless to hide his rebellion. He can be dangerous. That squire has some powerful weird-ass magic. He understands advanced spells and wards. I have no doubt that he's a mage, so he should be transferred to my house where he truly belongs."

"Why are you all fighting over a servant boy?" Rowan said, but then his frown deepened. "On another note, though, I sense fae in him," he mused. "Speaking of which, I believe that he should have his trials in my house and see if he fits in with other fae."

Fuck, he could feel Sy's essence in me, though he wasn't entirely sure. So he also wanted to recruit me into his house to figure me out. Sy had left an impression on the fae prince.

A dark thought occurred to me.

Did you mark the fae? I asked Sy as I finished putting on the skates the shifter had brought me. Now I must go to Silas and serve the prick.

I left my scent on him, if you must know. Sy shrugged.

You don't play with fire or food, Sy, I said furiously. *The fae prince heir is one of the most powerful, dangerous beings in Mist of Cinder!*

You think I don't know that?

Then why did you do it?!

A spur-of-the moment lapse? she consulted me. *Or something like a power struggle?*

Sy was reckless and remorseless. She was primal and never understood my moral compass, not that it was very strong. She was forever drawn to power. Now that she'd finally met a powerful supernatural like her kind, she couldn't help herself. Among the princes, she was most interested in Killian and the fae heir. Killian was forbidden fruit, spoken for already, and Sy was pragmatic. So, while she might drool over Killian, she'd definitely go for the fae prince.

I didn't do it intentionally, if that makes you feel better, Sy added. *It just happened.*

Now he's watching me like a hawk, I said irritably.

We can handle a hawk. We can handle all of the

delicious princes. She smacked her lips. *Do your pretense of innocence. You're good at it.*

Fuck off, I said. *Just try not to stir more shit!*

"Since no one can place his origin," Louis drawled, "I propose to have Little Bob take turns serving each house for a week. He can rotate being a squire to Cade, Rowan, me, and Silas."

Killian arched an eyebrow. "Have you forgotten a house, Louis?"

"You don't seem interested in that squire, so why waste him on you?" Louis said. "But if you want him to be in your house as well, sure, why not. But mark my words, he's trouble."

"Yet you're desperate to get him into your house."

So the fucker could drink his fill of me during that week.

"Well, he has his moments." Louis shrugged, staring at me in hunger. "And I'm the only one who knows how to handle him."

Cade and Rowan murmured their agreement about having me serve each house for a week, like I was some kind of highend whore for them to pass around.

Rage enveloped me. Sy seethed as well.

"No fucking way," Silas retorted. "He's a shifter,

and he'll serve as my exclusive squire."

"On what basis, Silas? None of us believe that this Little Bob is a shifter," Killian said.

What? My heart skipped a beat. This Killian was bad news.

The other heirs all chimed in, backing up the chaos heir.

"He entered my house even without being initiated," Silas said.

He'd wanted to kick me out at some point, fed up with me, and now he was fighting tooth and nail to keep me because the other princes wanted to poach me.

"Do you know he got into my house the same way?" Louis chuckled without mirth. "He just walked through the door as if he was born in my house. You don't have a claim on him based on that, Silas."

Cade nodded. "That little squire snuck into the courtyard of my house as well, playing with the wards before I caught him. That's how I'm sure that he's a mage."

A dark, brooding look coated Rowan's silver eyes, and he drawled, "Are you saying he entered all of your houses without being invited or initiated?"

"He's immune to magic, wards, and spells,"

Louis offered. "Professor Longweed deemed him an Echo, a null. The rarest magic type, she said."

All the princes turned their stares to Louis like birds of prey.

"And you didn't inform us or the council that we have the first Echo in the realm?" Rowan demanded, suspicion and fury whirling in his eyes.

Shit! If the council got involved, more unwanted attention would shoot my way. Then shit was going to hit the fan.

The fae prince turned to glare at Cade. "You knew it too, since you're a high mage. You can tell the squire's magical grade. That's why you're desperately trying to enroll him in your house. Are you planning to use him as your spy since he can get into any house?"

"Fuck off, Rowan. You're as paranoid as Killian." Cade spread his arms. "And why the fuck am I under fire?"

"Way to try to poach my squire, assholes," Silas hissed at the vampire prince.

"I'm releasing this information so the other heirs won't be fooled by you," Louis said. "You can't hoard the squire. The sooner you release him from your grip, the better for every house."

"This changes everything," Rowan said. "No

house should hoard an Echo, and the council must be informed while we investigate Little Bob's true origin."

I set my skates apart, stopping a few feet from the princes.

"Your Highness!" I shouted to interrupt the fae prince. "I'm reporting for duty, though no one has told me what my duty is! If you want, I can go fetch more drinks and cakes for you."

"Don't ever let him go near the kitchen," Louis said. "You probably won't see him again before the game is over. He'll be busy feeding himself, and then he'll find excuses for not doing his job. He always finds many excuses. Last time, he snuck out while attending to me. When I caught him, he was eating a whole table of food, and he said he was eating for two because he had to donate a pint of blood."

Cade chuckled, Rowan shook his head in disapproval, and Silas scowled as if I was an embarrassment. Killian stared hard at Louis, his stormy-blue eyes on fire.

"You shall not drink from your squire," he growled.

"You didn't protest last time I told you." Louis rolled his eyes. "And why do you care? He isn't your squire."

Killian stood up, his fist balled, as if he wanted to punch the vampire prince.

Just then, a war horn blared across the entire stadium, and the audience stood up and bellowed.

The game was about to start.

A magical billboard materialized, the words **Saints vs Sinners** streaming in the air.

All the princes rose from their comfy chairs, and the audience roared their cheers.

"Stay here, Little Bob. Don't fuck it up!" Silas snapped at me unnecessarily.

That was a bad order, since it was too vague. He didn't exactly give me an outline, so how was I going to know how not to fuck it up? But there was no time to ask him to clarify, since he'd followed Cade and shot toward the center of the ice rink.

The rink had no boards around the borders, unlike human ice rinks. For supernaturals, it was never about protecting the weak. The strong ruled, and if anyone got hurt, it'd be their own fault.

Like a media whore, Louis executed a twirl on the ice to draw attention, and his house bellowed their support. Those vampires knew how to scream. The shifters howled for their prince, trying to drown out the vampires' deafening sound, as Silas raised a fist in the air like a pompous fool. The fae whistled and clapped as Rowan skated along the edge, faster and faster, beyond lithe. Cade tap-danced to introduce himself. In the section where the mages and witches sat, a riot of colors surged above them like fireworks. They were showing off their spectacular spells.

I applauded and laughed. After this, I'd conspire with Cade and request to join his house. Among all the princes, I liked him the most. He wouldn't drink from me or hit me.

All the princes were on the ice now, competing for attention, except Killian.

I wheeled around, then nearly fell on my butt, as the prince of the House of Chaos was suddenly in my face. He stabilized me, his strong hands clasping my shoulders as he towered over me. His heat radiated into me, his intoxicating male scent muddling my mind. My whole body strummed with desire. It took everything I had not to throw myself at him.

"Watch yourself," I said in a low, husky voice. All I wanted was to climb onto him.

He arched an eyebrow, his eyes laughing at me with dark humor.

"Little Bob, isn't it?" he asked. "My bad if I startled you."

"Shouldn't you race to the center of the ice rink

to receive cheers like the other princes, high sir?" I grunted as I tried to get a hold of myself.

He grinned, flashing his perfect white teeth. He didn't have fangs like Louis or Rowan, but I could tell he was more dangerous than them. "You see, I'm not like the others. Let them enjoy the limelight."

His intense gaze set my heart beating frantically and my pulse spiking. I was also sweating, which was not to my liking. His hands were still on my shoulders. Pleasure hummed on my skin, even though I wore a long-sleeved tunic.

I wondered what it would feel like if his hands were on my bare skin instead. The image of how he'd fucked me in that gold and marble tub from the dreamland flashed in front of me, and my face burned with raw need. My breath hitched, my mouth parched, and my desire kept rising until I feared that I might combust in front of the prince of the House of Chaos.

Pure male need turned his storm-blue eyes to midnight sapphire; the tangible sexual tension between us grew unbearable.

Maybe this insane attraction was all in my head? I lusted after him, so I thought he desired me too.

I flushed in embarrassment, anger, and heat, cursing my body's reaction at such an inappropriate moment. I hoped that the spectators were focusing on the other flashy princes instead of looking in our direction. But then, no one would put the chaos prince and me, a low servant boy, together, would they?

"You've gotten all the princes fighting over you," Killian purred, his lips tilting up in amusement. "I don't recall any of them ever fighting this hard over a woman. Are you sure you're a boy?"

Just like that, I felt a bucket of icy water dropping on my head, yet it still couldn't quench the damned desire I harbored for this male.

One thing was for sure: the chaos prince was lingering behind to mess with me.

"Keep your big mouth shut and mind your own business!" I hissed in a low voice.

I wasn't a fool. I knew if anyone dared to challenge any of the princes like that, they wouldn't live to tell the tale. He'd put me on edge since the first time he'd spotted me, and I couldn't even null his magic. And whenever he was around, I just wanted to fuck him so badly. As I didn't know how to react around him, I did the only thing that made sense to me—I lashed out.

He grinned innocently. "Defensive much? What set you off?"

I'd had enough of his games. My face burned in humiliation and frustration.

"Don't play dumb!" I hissed more. "Don't think I didn't hear you give bad advice to Prince Louis about sending his women to suck my little cock!"

He raised his eyebrows, amusement sparking in his eyes. "Did I hear little?"

"That was what you said! Don't deny it!"

"Were you eavesdropping?" He widened his eyes mockingly. "Maybe you shouldn't have mentioned little, especially since you're petite, even for a girl. But you're a boy, so I assumed—" He gestured at my front, where I'd put a sock in my undergarment.

My face flamed redder, and my gaze darted to his hand. Damn, that man had a large and powerful hand, like his cock that pounded into me in that unholy dreamland.

"Hmm, you disagree, I see," he purred sensually. "I apologize if I was mistaken."

My jaw clenched so hard that it hurt. While I glared at the chaos prince in defiance, my body strummed with a song of desire, wanting to be stroked by him like a guitar. My pussy was aching with need. Killian sniffed, his eyes darkening as deep as midnight.

I bit my inner cheek until it bled. Every moment

around him spelled danger for me. I needed to get out of here if I wanted to stay in one piece.

Before I could shoot away from the ice rink, he stopped me, his voice a caress. "Tell me, who was the lucky one who sucked your little cock?"

My face burned, but my eyes burned hotter. "Fuck off, asshole! You know nothing about me!"

I'd blurted out the curse. A few squires and elite guards nearby stared at me and gasped. They'd been darting sneaky glances between the prince and me, wondering what the prince of the House of Chaos could want from a lowly squire from another house. Rumor had it that the chaos prince didn't even bother talking to nobles on his best days.

If one so much as looked at the princes wrong, they'd snuff you out, just as Louis had declared. And now I'd offended the deadliest prince in public. Killian could cut me down, and no one would lift a finger to help me; they would probably spit on my corpse.

Gunnar dashed toward me like a black widow on steroids. He was wearing a blond wig now since I'd turned him bald last time. Still holding a grudge, he'd been waiting to get to me, and I'd presented him with this perfect opportunity. Not even Silas could fault him for striking me, and he didn't care for me much, and then Louis was all for "if I couldn't have you, then no one else should have you."

"How dare you offend His Highness!" Gunnar scolded, his claws out to swipe at my face.

I ducked lower like a white flash, ready to retaliate and kick the vampire in the nuts, but Killian shot forward, faster than a blink, and gripped Gunnar's wrist.

"Don't. Ever. Fucking. Touch. This squire!" Killian said icily. "This one is *mine*."

Gunnar blinked, shock, fear, and confusion slamming into his face. I was a little shocked too, since the chaos prince should know that I wasn't his. I wasn't even in his house.

"Beat it," Killian ordered.

Gunnar cowered, bowed, and fled after he shot me a hateful glare.

"But I'm not yours, sir," I said. "I'm not the kind of bo—person who needs anyone to fight my battles. I can handle Gunnar. I was about to kick him between his legs really hard, and you shouldn't have saved him the pleasure of being kicked in the nuts by an ice skate!"

"Aren't you fierce, little dagger." He chuckled, his hooded eyes falling on my lips. "Better watch that mouth of yours."

The blood drained from my face and pounded furiously in my ears. When he'd thrust deep into my heated channel, he'd called me little dagger. I had thought what happened in the dreamland hadn't been real.

A sequence of drumbeats rose from the spectator seats where the members of the House of Chaos assembled, shouting their prince's name.

The other princes had gathered in the center of the ice rink, the opposing teams facing each other. They turned to look at Killian, waiting for him to join them.

The prince of the House of Chaos took his time skating toward them, smooth and fast and powerful like a war god, his chest bare, his muscles flexed, his smirk devastating.

The audience, especially the girls from all the houses, jumped up and down, waving their hands and screaming his fucking name, and the drumbeats rose to a fever pitch.

The drumbeats pounded into my bones like a war song, or a song of lust, as heat infused my bloodstream. I was afraid that the song would never fade.

My body went hot, then cold, then hot again, and the chaos prince's pet name "little dagger" haunted my restless mind.

Chapter Twenty-Four

No sport on Earth could compare to the supernatural hockey game. The supernaturals were playing in a bigger league. Human hockey players might be tough, but they were still mortals, susceptible to injuries. Supernaturals were more ruthless since every one of them could regenerate fast.

The sport was also a contest of dick size for the princes, serving as the prelude of a mating game—the biggest predator with the biggest cock would draw more females to his breeding pool and have his pick.

That was what the Brides Selection was all about, wasn't it? Bea had told me about the Selection a few times. She was also one of the thousands of candidates.

I watched the Saints (Silas, Rowan, and Cade, with Dixie as their goaltender) and Sinners (Killian, Louis, a dark-haired girl whom I'd never met, and a man whom I saw hanging out with Killian as a goaltender) fight to take control of the puck with their hockey sticks.

One second, the Saints were driving the puck toward the Sinners' gate. Then next, Killian shoulder-slammed into Silas and seized the puck.

Judging from the action on the ice, I could tell a bit about the relationship between the prince heirs. Both Killian and Louis didn't like Silas, and vice-versa. Cade got along with everyone. I wasn't sure about Rowan though.

Silas spun to the other end of the rink, but he managed to stop the motion by crouching on the ice, planting a hand in front of him. A less powerful being would've fallen on his ass. Snarling, Silas rose and sped toward Killian.

"To me, Killian!" Louis realized Silas's intention and shouted at the chaos prince.

Killian passed the puck to Louis, who was the chaos prince's left winger. Louis took over the puck and drove it forward, invading the Saints' territory. Human players were quick on their feet, but these supernaturals were on another level. Their figures blurred on the ice, and it was getting harder to track their movements.

"Slow down, assholes," I murmured.

Instead of going after the puck as he was supposed to, Silas charged Killian, rage darkening the shifter prince's face as he swung his stick at the chaos prince. Killian wheeled away, smiling coldly, before he brought his stick up and struck back.

The sticks slammed into each other, emitting sparks.

Things are going to get ugly, I told Sy.

Woohoo! she cheered, her gaze mostly following Rowan as she licked her lips.

"Little Bob!" I heard Bea calling my name and turned my head.

My witch friend waved at me. I grinned and skated toward her to the edge of the ice. No one would lecture me on how to be a proper squire, since every eye was on the princes and their game.

"Little Bea!" I greeted. "Shouldn't you be in the stands cheering for your prince?"

"I don't like crowds," she said.

"You and me both."

"I saw Prince Killian laughing with you," she whispered, her eyes wide.

At the reminder of my humiliation, my face reddened in anger. "He was fucking with me!"

I didn't even want to dwell on the fact that he'd called me "little dagger" or what it meant. All I knew was that nothing good would come of it.

"You don't get it," Bea said. "You made him laugh. It's rare that Prince Killian ever laughs. What did you say to him?"

I frowned at her after a blink. "I told him to go fuck himself."

She smiled at me. She didn't believe me. "There's a connection between you and the prince heir of the House of Chaos. Maybe you belong to his house. I don't think you're a shifter. You aren't a mage either."

A shot of guilt washed over me. I'd been keeping dangerous secrets from my friend, but then my secrets could drag her down with me if I was discovered. It was best that she was kept in the dark as well.

The audience's roars brought my attention back to the game on the ice.

The Saints and the Sinners were bodychecking each other. The players fell in a pile with Killian at the bottom, ice cracking.

"Isn't that a dirty hit?" I asked, a bit worried for the chaos prince, and looked around. "Where is the referee?"

"This isn't a mortal ice hockey game," Bea said. "It's a way for the heirs to work out their aggression toward each other while showing their subjects their powers."

"So there're no rules except not to kill each other?"

"There're a few technique restrictions, like the players may not forward pass the puck to their team-mates with their hands. Don't worry, the game will escalate as soon as a goal is scored." Bea smiled as if she was looking forward to it. "You'll see the princes' true powers at play. They'll compete with magic."

Killian roared, throwing the Saints team off him. Louis rolled away, cursing. The dark-haired Sinners girl was the only one who didn't join the brawl. She waited to the side. Killian shot the puck from under his opponents. The girl came alive instantly, brought it around at high speed, and shot it toward the Saints' gate while the other players were still untangling themselves from one another.

Dixie lunged from the semicircle, plucked the puck, and tossed it out before it could reach the goal. But Killian had shot forward. He swung his stick, striking the puck in the air with force and precision. It flew in an arc into the net before Dixie could rescue it a second time.

The audience rooting for the Sinners stood up and roared their cheers, but the Saints' supporters booed in equal measure. The drumbeats pounded, trying to drown out the jeers.

A strong current of water shot toward Killian, but the chaos prince erected his darkness as a shield, starlight twirling around him. Silas shifted to an enormous half-wolf, half-human form. Just as he lunged at Killian with a snarl, Louis tossed wind at Silas and threw him off track. Cade laughed, flinging spells and fire at Killian's darkness, trying to crack it and find a way in. Rowan clasped his hands together, sending thorned vines surging toward Killian.

Chapter Twenty-Five

An ominous sense of danger gripped me, my shoulder blades tingling, chills slithering up from the base of my spine. It didn't come from the ice rink where the princes fought with magic. The puck spun in the air as they fought to take control of it. I snapped my head to the source of my uneasiness just as a lift slid open, spitting out an armed force, led by a tall noble fae lady, with America by her side.

That was Mistress Ethel, the headmistress, in an impeccable pantsuit. She had made a speech at the Jubilee Haven a couple of days ago and bored me to tears. In her middle age, she still looked stunningly beautiful, though her beauty was on the stern and icy side with light gray eyes as sharp as broken glass.

A druid in a white robe and a squad of academy sentinels rallied around her. They were heading toward me. My heart leapt erratically, and I prayed that they didn't come for me. I was nobody.

But America's shouts shattered my hope.

"That's Little Bob!" She pointed her rude finger at me. "He let in the abominations!"

I'd been made.

I told you that we should've eaten that fae female, Sy said. *You saved her, and now she's betrayed you.*

America flashed me a smug and disdainful smile, forgetting that she'd been that petrified fae chick who'd peed her pants before I'd freed her from the Shrieker. She wore a fancy red gown, which was overkill for a sports event, but then she was aiming to get all eyes on her, especially the princes'.

She'd schemed and timed this so she could be seen as the hero who caught the bad boy and saved the day.

Fear seared my throat, and icy dread filled my chest. I was now hunted not only by Shriekers but also supernaturals.

"Seize Little Bob!" Mistress Ethel barked her order.

Bea stared at me, her eyes wide. "What's going on? What did you do this time?"

"Save yourself, Bea," I hissed. "Leave me!"

The academy sentinels, seven of them, drew their weapons. The druid held two bottles of nasty-looking potions in his hands, ready to toss at me.

I zoomed toward the lift, but then more sentinels poured out of it.

Shit!

I braked and glanced around, the blades of my skates cutting into the ice. They'd blocked every entrance and exit except the north border of the ice rink near the princes.

The audience quieted down. All eyes were on the headmistress, her henchmen, and me. The princes stopped throwing magic at each other, homing in on me as well in confusion and irritation.

"What the fuck is going on?" Silas shouted, starting to skate toward me. "Why the heck are you after my new squire? What did he do?"

The other princes started to come for me as well, narrowing their eyes in displeasure at the interruption.

An idea hit me. I had to shoot in the direction of the princes, get past them, reach the edge, then let Sy take control. I'd break an arm or twist an ankle jumping down from the ice rink, but Sy would survive. We'd then escape from the ground floor.

This was the end of our journey in Mist of Cinder. There'd be no haven for us anymore. But it couldn't be helped.

Shit happens. No need to mope about it.

Mapping out my escape route, I steadied the blades of my skates and shot across the ice like a golden arrow, away from Mistress Ethel and her sentinels. Silas and Louis both headed toward me to intervene. I ducked to the side at the last second and swung my arm at Silas, who was closer to me, and sent him spinning toward Louis. I was lightning fast in my survival mode. The shifter prince collided with the vampire prince with a profanity. Louis dropped to one knee, his hand on the ice to break the fall. Silas grabbed his shoulders to steady himself, and Louis shrugged him off with a growl.

Fuck, I'd struck a prince while sending the other reeling. They'd make sure that I was a dead boy walking. But I no longer cared as one purposed burned in my head—flee.

The entire stadium was shocked to silence for several beats, as no one had expected a low servant boy like me to pull a stunt like that and have the strength to counter a prince. Amid the silence, Silas snarled, and Louis hissed. Both promised retaliation.

"Apologies, Highnesses," I shouted, remembering my manners. "I'm in a hurry!"

Two twists of elemental magic hurled toward me, but they fizzled off me then dropped like sheets of tissue paper at my feet.

"Nice try!" I shouted my compliment to appease their anger, but more snarls responded.

A thick wall of fire shooting out of the ice in front of me made me do a double take. As I braked for a second and broke my pace, I slipped on a whirlpool on the ice. Before I could gather myself and keep going, thick threads of thorny vines emerged out of the blue and gripped the blades of my skates.

That was a clever move. Magic didn't work on me, but the skates weren't a part of me. How did that fae prince figure it out? Or was it a lucky shot? Magic wouldn't turn against me, but it could still create distractions and roadblocks for me if my opponents knew my weakness.

I rolled on the ice, faster than a thought, before the vines could string me up. My hands grabbed the vines conjured by powerful magic. As soon as I touched them, they withdrew. I got to my feet in a heartbeat, but that beat had already cost me.

I wasn't dealing with humans. I was facing off

with the most powerful immortals. The princes fenced me in from three sides, a united front now, impenetrable walls of steel and muscles. Dixie and all the Sinners joined as reinforcement. Killian blocked my direct path, a lazy smile on his cruel, sensual lips. Mistress Ethel, the druid, America, and their sentinels blocked the fourth side.

My heart pumped like a wild animal wanting to escape its cage, fear infusing my bloodstream. I'd learned to never give my back to my enemies, but right now, whichever way I turned, my back was to many adversaries.

A variety of scenes composed of possible actions and consequences rushed through my mind. If I pulled out Deathsong, it would only make things worse, as supernaturals didn't take any threat kindly.

And I was one against thousands. The audience had all stood up, ready to swarm me like a mob of vultures.

If I resorted to my second choice, I would drop to the ice, cry my lungs out, and beg for mercy.

But that was too pathetic, and supernaturals hated weakness more than anything. They wouldn't show mercy since they didn't have an ounce of empathy in their bones. They'd put me down like I was a weak-ass rabid dog.

We can take them, Sy hissed. She wasn't the kind who would back off from any situation, and I had to be the strategic one. *Let's suck up every drop of magic in this realm and leave them with nothing! Fuck them all to hell!*

I won't, I said, my jaw clenched. *I promised us that we wouldn't be like our father.*

I halted on the ice, my pose casual and disarming, my hands shooting up in a gesture of surrender. My eyes went wide as I put on an innocent look, my lips parting in slightly faked shock.

If worst came to worst and I couldn't talk my way out of this, I needed to roll with the punches. I'd even let them cuff me. I'd spotted a pair of magical handcuffs in the hand of the druid. It'd work to my benefit if they took me off the ice. I'd then escape on the way to their prison. I had to bet on their intent of imprisoning and torturing me to get some answers before they decided to kill me.

"Hello, guys." I licked my dry lips, blood still pounding in my ears even though I tried to get this cold panic under control. "What's up?"

"What the fuck did you do this time, Little Bob?" Silas snarled. "You'll regret it if you embarrass my house."

Louis chuckled in vicious delight.

"But I didn't do anything," I said, my eyes wide. "It's a nice day, so I don't know why they even came after me."

I held Silas's potent alpha stare even as it pressed into my chest like a loaded truck. I no longer held back and showed him my belly, since I wouldn't be in his house after this. I wouldn't even bother sending him a written notice of my resignation.

He wasn't a protector. All he cared about was his reputation and ambition. I didn't respect a man like that, and neither did Sy.

Whispered murmurs spread across the ice as everyone witnessed my boldness and strength at holding the shifter prince's alpha stare. The other princes watched with mute interest.

Silas's amber eyes were on fire, as were Mistress Ethel's.

"You led a shrieking abomination into the grounds of Shades Academy," Mistress Ethel accused scathingly. "Two students were slaughtered; one was a honey badger shifter called Luna."

I blinked?

What? Luna was dead? It couldn't be! But then Javier had said that she'd been missing since yesterday morning.

A wave of grief for Luna, fear for myself, and hate for the Shriekers hit me like icy hail.

"If you had anything to do with Luna's death, Little Bob," Dixie snarled, her face drained of blood and dark, vengeful fire burning in her eyes, "I'll tear you apart with my bare hands."

"You'll have to get in line, wolf," Gunnar chimed in. "He owes the House of Vampires a debt first."

Louis looked at him hard, and the vampire captain shut up.

"Edward, a noble fae student, was also slain!" Mistress Ethel hissed, her silver eyes burning like cold steel.

"I don't know where you got this dumb idea that I led in a Shri—a monster," I protested.

The sentinels growled at me threateningly for being disrespectful. Well, manners wouldn't get me out of this mess.

"My niece saw you!" Mistress Ethel hissed.

America thrust her chest out for all to admire. Her push-up bra and low-necked red gown did a good job highlighting her cleavage. She knew how to advertise her assets, free for all.

"I saw you talking to an abomination at the entrance of Underhill," she said. "It called you *prince!*"

"Do I look like a fucking prince to you, fae chick?" I asked.

"Watch your mouth, servant boy!" Mistress Ethel hissed. "You will address a noble lady as 'my lady.' I could have you whipped for such an offense!"

I shuddered. "That's intense, man—sorry, it's ma'am."

The headmistress's eyes spat fire, but I was immune to her kind of fire.

"My lady America, as a noble fae lady, what were you doing near Underhill, since it's a forbidden region?" I asked loudly for all to hear. "Isn't it?"

"I followed you there!" America shouted, fireballs popping out of her palms as she conjured them. "And you don't get to question me, servant boy!"

"My bad, my lady America," I offered. "I apologize sincerely and immensely. But may I ask humbly what made you follow a low servant boy, my lady America?"

Someone chuckled. It sounded like Killian and Cade.

"You dare to talk back to your better?" Mistress Ethel growled, pointing a long, elegant finger at me. "Take him!"

"My Lady Headmistress, it'd be an unlawful

arrest," I shouted. "I want my attorney, and you haven't read me my rights!"

Outraged shouts and curses came at me from every direction, especially from the mob. If they had eggs or stones, they'd throw them at me.

Facing me, Mistress Ethel looked hot and murderous. The druid appeared cold and cruel. America lifted her chin high and glanced at the princes to see if their eyes were on her. Unfortunately for both of us, every eye was on me. Bea stood at the edge of the ice rink, her eyes wide with shock and dread.

I wheeled slowly in order to find the weakest link where I could break out. There was none.

As my gaze skimmed the princes, Cade arched his long dark brows, not concerned. Silas glared at me, the promise of punishment in his dark amber eyes. Louis regarded me, calculation whirling in his pale blue eyes. Rowan sniffed again as he scented Sy, confusion and intrigue coating his silver eyes.

Killian smiled at me cruelly, like he had something really bad in store for me.

The druid led two sentinels toward me. They didn't need to wear skates, since their magic allowed them to traverse the ice. I would make them fall on their faces before I let them cuff me and take me away.

Before I could strip their magic, Killian moved like a flash, standing between me, the druid, and the sentinels.

"You aren't removing Little Bob merely based on your niece's unfounded accusation, Lady Ethel," said the prince of the House of Chaos.

"Leave it be, Prince Killian," Mistress Ethel sighed exasperatedly. "The servant boy doesn't concern you. It's an academy matter and I'm taking care of it."

"Oh, he concerns me," Killian said. "There're proper procedures when convicting any supernatural. Any supernatural, even a servant boy, has certain rights. And I'm not done with this interview. In fact, I haven't started yet. I want to get to the bottom of this and sort it out if our Little Bob indeed associates with the creatures that got into the realm and killed two of our own."

"Back off, Killian," Silas snapped. "The boy belongs to my house. Only I have the right to interrogate him before I hand him over to Lady Ethel."

"How many times must I say that he isn't a damn shifter?!" Louis sneered. "We're still trying to determine which house little Bob truly belongs to.

And since he was taken from my house illegally, I still hold authority over him, and thus I decide his fate."

"All right, princes. Let's all interrogate him here for the sake of transparency," Killian said. "Why don't you start, Silas, since you insist that he's your subject."

Silas glared at Killian before clearing this throat and shooting daggers at me. "Little Bob, listen very carefully. Here's your alpha asking you, and you must answer truthfully."

I used my middle finger to rub the tip of my nose as if it were itching, and Cade laughed.

"What's your true name?" Silas boomed, his voice carrying across the ice.

"Bobbi," I said. "But everyone here calls me Little Bob. I have no idea why, sir. I'm not exactly little. I'll be twenty in four months. I don't celebrate my birthday, though. I—"

"Which region did you come from?" Silas cut in in a curt tone.

I made a show of cupping my ear to show my confusion at his question. "Pardon? What do you mean, sir? Could you specify, kindly?"

"There're five kingdoms and one neutral zone in Mist of Cinder!" he barked, his angry face turning purple. "Everyone knows it!"

All the shifters around nodded their agreement and glared at me.

Each house had a kingdom, and the sixth region was called CrimsonTide, unclaimed by any house. They'd expect me to be from there, but I decided to surprise them a little with my honesty.

"I come from the mountains in the mortal realm, far from here," I said.

The supernaturals traded surprised, dark looks.

"Then how did you find our realm?" Mistress Ethel demanded sternly.

"By luck, My Lady Headmistress," I said. "I passed by and saw it in front of my eyes."

"Impossible," the druid chimed in. "I was one of the founders who glamoured the Veil."

"This little squire can see through any magic, spells, and glamours," Cade said.

"Even so, no outsiders could get in," Rowan said. "How did he get in?"

"You're asking me, high sir?" I asked.

He nodded, more intrigued than upset.

"One foot after the other," I offered, "and then I stepped in."

A faint smile ghosted Killian's lips.

"In fact, Little Bob came to me first and informed me about the weakening and corruption of the Veil," Cade said. "When I led a team to the Veil to deal with the issue, we confronted three creatures that were a blend of giant scorpions and machines that tried to get into the academy."

That was one of the upgraded versions of the Shriekers. My father had been busy. It also spelled that he was stronger than when I escaped him. But I couldn't tell any of them this. The supernaturals rounding me up might just be a sign that I had to go on the run again.

"We killed the abominations," Cade continued. "Little Bob here finished off the first one, so he couldn't be their associate. It proves he's a mage. It's my right to take him back to my house and investigate further, as it's obviously a house affair."

"No way will you take him!"

Everyone started to shout at one another.

An alarm shot through me, as if something alien had brushed me. My gaze snapped to an egg-sized crystal ball in the druid's hand. The crystal ball pulsed seven shades and colors.

The druid's eyes widened, darting a loaded glance at me then staring at his crystal ball again.

"Can it be?" he whispered.

"What did you see?" Mistress Ethel asked curtly.

The druid leaned over to her in an inaudible

whisper, yet my superior hearing caught it all while everyone was still lashing out at each other, screaming and cursing. "The crystal shows that this boy has godly essence."

"But the gods are dead or left." Mistress Ethel regarded me, cruel and disdainful calculation fogging her icy eyes. "It can't be him, can it? He's but a wild, stupid servant boy."

My heart sank further. There were rumors about Ruin, my father, but no mortal or immortal had learned about him and lived to tell the tale. Had something changed while I was here?

"They say one of the original gods remains," the druid whispered back. "The boy is more than meets the eye. He wears a glamour unlike anything I've seen. If he's the demigod we've been looking for..."

Greed shone in Mistress Ethel's eyes, which snagged on me like a serpents. Now she and the druid wanted me for a different reason, which had nothing to do with the murder case. They'd want to lock me up and experiment on me until they got every drop of the godly power they thought I harbored out of me.

Mist of Cinder was no longer safe for me.

"I'm taking Little Bob into the custody of Shades Academy," Mistress Ethel shouted over the clamor. "This is a serious matter that I won't take lightly. The Veil weakened after he came through it to Mist of Cinder, and that provided a window for the abominations to get into our realm. Outside the Veil, five hundred acres of land were scorched and blackened, the magic drained. The timing also aligns with the servant boy's unlawful entry. If the blight reaches Mist of Cinder, there'll be no realm left for us. We believe, somehow, that Little Bob triggered the blight and brought danger to our realm."

The manipulative fae headmistress pinned all this on me without knowing it was actually true. But I was a bigger liar than her.

"Oh yeah?" I snorted. "You think a low servant boy like me is that mighty, My Lady Headmistress? Am I also responsible for the fading of magic centuries before I was born? Should I be blamed for the rise of human technology that also caused the weakening of magic in all the cities as well?"

Lots of threatening growls came my way, but I shrugged them off.

"I'm not the threat," I said, looking around then focusing on the princes. "But if you're the shit as you try to show everyone, you should prepare for the real threat, because it'll be coming for your realm. Those abominations that tried to get through the Veil?

They're nothing, but it's a sign that you should all pay attention to."

I shouldn't have revealed even that, but it might never be the right time to tell them that Ruin, the ancient evil god, would find this realm and come for them. It was a matter of time. If he got his evil hands on this land, he'd drain the magic here, and supernaturals would go extinct.

There would be nothing left.

I might be a great enemy to the realm, but I was also their best defense. The wild magic knew it, so it was trying to form a kinship with me.

These arrogant supernaturals had no fucking idea that their world was going to burn with all the worlds while they were busy competing to display their powers.

Never, ever be arrogant, I told Sy.

Save your breath, Sy said. *I'm not the one you should lecture.*

"What threat are you talking about, Little Bob?" Rowan asked, narrowing his eyes. He seemed to take me more seriously than the others, even though I was still a servant boy in everyone's eyes.

"This insolent servant hides a dangerous secret," the druid said, "so dark even my crystal can't pierce through it. He has the darkest aura around him."

"Oh, shup up," I said. I grew tired of their interrogation, and I wanted to move on to the next stage, my escape plan in place. "Whatever you came to do, just get it over with. I have somewhere else to go."

"Take him!" Mistress Ethel barked.

Chapter Twenty-Six

A flash of starlight accompanied by blistering, icy wind slammed into the sentinels and tossed them away. They tumbled over each other and rolled on the ice, but they threw out their magic in time to prevent them from falling over the edge of the floating ice rink.

Everyone stepped back as swirling darkness formed around me, encircling me like moving walls and imprisoning me. Not even the other princes could snatch me.

Killian stood between me and Mistress Ethel and her team.

"Prince Killian, please do not interfere further," Mistress Ethel said, her voice hard. "I've indulged your fancy and allowed you to lead the interrogation in front of everyone."

Killian let out a cold chuckle. "Allow? Choose your next words carefully, Lady Ethel."

Mistress Ethel sucked in a breath, wariness and anger flashing in her silver eyes.

"We all have duties to the realm. You should know that better than the rest, Your Grace," she said, her voice growing indignant with a hint of irony that spelled she knew something about Killian the rest of us didn't. "Little Bob is a criminal who hides a deep, dark secret. I intend to use every means at my disposal to extract it to protect the realm. We believe that he's a disguised agent of the dark force the oracle said would be coming."

The bitch meant to torture me, but she had no idea whom she was dealing with. After I'd escaped my father, I'd vowed to allow no one to lay a hand on me. Torture me, and I'd drain her magic and leave her a shriveled shell.

I homed my gaze in on her as Sy marked her as prey.

But we must learn about this oracle, Sy said. *If there's prophecy about Ruin and us, we must find out what it is, even if we'll have to stay in her prison.*

"I'm not done. I haven't got to the best part yet,"

Killian said harshly. "You want to know the dark secret of this squire?" He turned to me, his lips curled up in a cruel smile, his eyes burning with ruthlessness and dark lightning. "Let me show it to you, and then it's for me to decide what to do with Barbie."

I'd said my name was Bobbi, yet he insisted on calling me Barbie.

What was he going to show them?

My pulse raced wildly. Fear bubbled up like lava, closing my airway.

My darkest fear was that Ruin would find me. Next to it was for anyone to uncover that I was Ruin's daughter—the damned princess who could siphon magic, drain the land, and feed all the magic she had no right to take and steal to the eater of worlds. And if my father fully recovered and manifested in his original dark glory, there'd be no more worlds left in the end.

"No!" I uttered as I threw out my hands to rip away the whirling darkness that caged me, to drain it and take it into myself, and then I'd toss it at everyone to clear a path to escape.

Nothing happened.

I widened my eyes, remembering that I'd tried to siphon his power last time and I hadn't been able to, though I hadn't really tried, for fear of exposing myself.

But nothing could hold me back now.

I called my own kind of siphoning dark wind and unleashed it, but Killian's darkness still wheeled around me, sealing me inside. It dawned on me that I'd finally met my kryptonite.

The chaos prince stepped closer, his intense gaze pinning me. I glared at him, spitting mad.

"It'll be over soon, Barbie," he purred.

Was he going to end me? Could he?

At his closeness, my heart fluttered wildly. My skin tightened as my body ached for him, craving for him to be closer. While I was terrified of what he was going to do to me, my body felt electrified, the need for his pure male flesh and his touch searing a path in my bloodstream.

Then his starlight washed over me, warm and cool at the same time.

I stared at him in confusion, until I felt it turning to invisible fingers that caressed my flesh from the column of my neck down to my breasts, slowly sliding further down.

My back arched at the sensation, a moan nearly escaping me.

Pleasure, anger, humiliation, lust, and fear

blended into a cocktail, until I couldn't tell which emotion dominated them all. I had no means to counter his kind of magic, and I didn't want to. All I knew was that I was at his mercy.

But then I decided not to roll over.

I pulled out Deathsong from the sheath on my thigh and waved it at the heir of the House of Chaos.

"If I go down," I pulled my lips back and roared, "I'll go with a bang! I'll open you up and see how black your heart is."

"That's a bad idea, and you can't mean that, sweetheart," he purred and lunged.

I stabbed the lethal dagger forged by my father toward Killian's chest, but he sidestepped, lightning quick, his darkness and starlight surging with him as he counterattacked. Next thing I knew, he had my dagger in his large hand.

"I can't allow you to harm yourself, can I?" He smiled at me and stepped out of the circle of darkness that still railed me in like a force field.

"I wasn't going to harm myself! I was going to give you a world of hurt!"

"That's not very nice, Barbie," he sighed. "There's a lot for you to learn, including being a nice...girl."

I wanted to spit at him.

Killian smirked darkly.

A blink, and I felt so light. I looked down in horror, my bare breasts perking up for all to see. During my stay in Mist of Cinder, I'd filled out. Now I had full bosoms, my nipples the color of flame.

Killian's starlight had burned away my servant's uniform along with my breast binding without leaving any burn marks on my skin.

All the princes stared at me, their jaws dropped, their gazes glued to my breasts and heat starting to rise to their eyes.

"Perfect tits!" someone shouted.

Sy preened.

Thousands of eyes fixed on me and my tits, then everyone from the spectator seats started to record with their tablets fueled by magic. Soon my shame would be all over Spinchat, the supernatural social media!

Killian sent me spinning over the ice for good measure so everyone could get a clear view.

"Ladies and gentlemen of Shades Academy," he shouted, his voice booming over the entire stadium. "That *is* Barbie, aka Little Bob's darkest secret. Barbie is a girl, through and through. We've all been deceived!"

The audience roared their rage.

I trembled, my mouth full of ashes. Tears of fury, hate, and fear burned behind my eyelids, yet I fought the urge to cover my breasts.

You make me proud, Sy encouraged. *We're not weak! Tits up and let them admire!*

The prince of the House of Chaos will fucking regret this, I seethed, swallowing my tears. *I'll make it my life's passion to destroy him!*

You got this. Sy cheered for me. *By the way, I like Barbie a lot more than Bobbi. The prince of the House of Chaos has given you a lovely name. Not all is lost.*

"Take off Barbie's pants! Let's see if she's got a cunt!" some dude bellowed from the center of the audience seats, his group hollering and chanting.

Killian snapped his enraged storm-blue eyes toward the spectator seats, homing in on them like a predator. A wave of formidable power rippled off him as he raised a hand. A spear of lightning shot from his fingertips, reaching far and razing the section with one precise strike.

Shouts and screams rose from the audience seats before silence fell as the prince of the House of Chaos spoke again.

"Show's over," Killian said, his gaze lingering on my breasts before he flicked his wrist.

Darkness and starlight covered my breasts.

"Barbie isn't an agent of dark forces or a monster prince." Killian let his sensual and cold voice carry over the ice. "She's a girl pretending to be a boy to avoid the obligation of the Brides Selection. Due to her unknown origins, she belongs to my house. From this moment on, Barbie is under my rule and protection."

I blinked hard at the turn of events, then glared at him more.

A smirk lit his cruel, masculine face as he turned to me. "You're to be enrolled in the Shades Academy as a bride candidate, which is mandatory under the rules of the Brides Selection of Mist of Cinder. Effective now, Barbie."

Pre-order House of Fae and Mists (Shades of Ruin and Magic #2)

Coming Dec 2023

Author Note

My, did I just leave another cliffhanger for you? It's necessary though, since book two is all about the cutthroat Brides Selection game. Don't expect any chick or dick to be nice.

I'm dedicating this series to you—all my loyal readers. Writing is hard, the journey lonely, but your kindness and encouragement keep me going. And many of you always rate my books, leave cozy reviews, and spread the word. I see you and thank you from the bottom of my heart.

I plan to pen six books in the *Shades of Ruin and Magic* series, even though there're only five houses in the realm. It'll be a surprise gift when I present you with the secret sixth house.

Things are going to be bumpy for Barbie in the Shades Academy, but I promise you one hell of a ride.

Thank you again for reading *House of Vampires and Flame*.

-Meg xoxo

Follow Meg on Amazon.

Don't forget to sign up to Meg's mailing list to hear about her new releases, giveaways, and fun stuff.

*** P.S. If you enjoy House of Vampires and Flame, would you consider rating it or leaving a brief review on Amazon? Hugs!

EXCERPT OF HALF-BLOOD ACADEMY

THE DEMIGOD OF WAR

The green-eyed human girl fought like a fiend against a large, vicious gang.

Her ferocity was the most stunning thing I'd ever seen.

But I didn't come for her. We came for the two supernaturals on her team. Rogues weren't allowed to roam the demigods' territory unchecked. They either joined the Academy or were put down.

Wrap it up, I ordered Cameron, the lieutenant of the Dominion of Gods, with a gesture. These soldiers had survived the Trial of the Blood Runes because they had gods' blood in their veins.

The fight in the street ceased abruptly as Cameron's men marched into the battlefield, gunning for their targets. The other combatants stepped back, fear of the Dominion soldiers sinking in their eyes—all except for the human girl.

She stepped in front of a teenage wolf shifter and an underage witch, blocking Cameron and his soldiers.

"Marigold, they're the Dominions. We can't fight them off," the shifter whispered, trying to pull her back to protect her, but she shrugged him off.

"Like Hell I'll let them take you!" she said, her hands twitching, ready for violence.

She was still running on adrenaline. I smelled her dark fear, though it was no match for her fury.

Cameron's jaw clenched. He hadn't met a civilian who dared resist an arrest or recruitment. And no one cursed in front of a Dominion soldier without suffering the consequences.

The lieutenant and his men were more than zealous to impress me, as a demigod rarely accompanied them on an enlistment mission.

"I don't give a fuck how pretty you are, chick," Cameron snorted. "Get the fuck out of my way, or—"

The girl attacked.

She planted a boot into Cameron's chest and kicked hard. At the same time, she nocked five arrows, letting them fly in blurry succession.

Her every aim hit true, but she was up against the well-trained Dominion warriors in armor that no human weapon could penetrate.

Our forces surrounded her. The girl yelled for the shifter and witch to run, but instead they pressed their backs against hers, ready to fight to the death with her.

I chuckled.

"Fun's over, little minx," I said, peeling myself from the shade and stepping into the battlefield before my soldiers terminated the trio.

My demigod power coiled, ripping the fabric of the air.

Every knee—the soldiers', the civilians', and the gang members'—dropped to a battlefield strewn with shells of bullets, bits of concrete, animal fur, and blood.

Yet one pair of knees refused to go down.

A flick of surprise flashed through my eyes. That was a first.

The girl braced her feet apart and glared at me, the fire of fury burning in her eyes, their color so vivid it was greener than any forest in any universe I'd passed.

A flame lashed out like invisible lightning,

striking the icy, steel walls that encased my careless, ruthless demigod heart.

Instantly, my cock hardened.

What the fuck?

The beast roared in me, awakening, as did my primal need.

I reined in the beast with effort so I wouldn't drag down that female, push her to the ground, and mount her from behind, right there.

I prided myself in not being a savage demigod, but without a mirror, I knew my eyes glowed molten gold with a crimson ring around the pupils.

My power increased, unleashing at the girl's challenge. Violent wind charged from me, wheeling and slamming into everything in its path.

The buildings within the scope of my power rumbled, glass shattering.

The wolves, hybrids, and humans whimpered as they were thrown backwards, including the young witch and the shifter who knelt behind the human girl.

She swayed before steadying herself.

Kneel, I commanded her.

Her lavender hair spread wildly, whipped by the electrifying power in the air. Beads of sweat dotted on her cute little nose. Fear and rage spoke volumes in her eyes as she endeavored to resist my power.

Her legs buckled, revealing her human weakness, and I waited for her to drop to her knees to pay me respect, like everyone else.

My faint smile wilted from the corners of my lips when she straightened her back and straightened her legs.

No human or supernatural could withstand my compulsion, except for the primordial Olympian gods and Lucifer. Even my demigod peers had to put on their armor and shield themselves against me with their power.

But this mere human girl stood her ground.

As if that wasn't infuriating enough, she flipped me the bird.

It was the first time anyone had ever given me that. She didn't know she was courting violence, then death.

My soldiers' gasps were audible, even over the gang's and her companions'. Hushed quietness resumed at my snarl.

Everyone waited for me to strike down the insolent human girl.

The minx smirked, the brightest, most gorgeous

thing on Earth, and every predatory cell within me swirled alive.

A thrill coursed through my veins.

My cock grew hard, jerking forward and rasping painfully against the fabric of my pants.

I clenched my teeth, willing myself to keep control and stay put, no matter how badly I wanted to claim this female now, over and over.

Fortunately, instead of tight armor, I wore a leather trench coat, which covered my erection.

My gaze roved over her sinfully enticing body before peering into her eyes to search for her secrets —how could a human oppose me?

What was she?

I stalked toward the deadly, beautiful creature, hands in my pockets as if I were strolling in the park. Despite my casual manner, another wave of whimpers from the soldiers and gang members indicated the effects of my rippling power.

The girl tensed at my approach, the knuckles of one hand white on her spear and her other hand ready to, I assume, pull out a gun from her leather jacket to turn on me.

I held her blazing gaze, daring her to try.

Her fear blended with hate and fascination,

wheeling in her fiery jade eyes as she kept glaring at me.

The minx wasn't entirely immune to me and my power, after all.

I held back an amused chortle. It was rare anyone could still amuse me, even though I was the youngest demigod walking Earth.

And I had never been so aroused.

She didn't back off but held her chin high and puffed up her chest, which drew my gaze to her perky breasts.

I strode around her, studying her as if she were a prickly kitten I'd cornered, and she wheeled accordingly, never showing her back to me.

When I'd annoyed her enough, she gave in, breaking the silence.

"What the fuck do you want, demigod?" she demanded. "And which demigod are you?"

Such attitude. Outlaws always hated authorities.

Everyone else held their breath at her lack of self-preservation. I would have squashed the offender had it been anyone less interesting.

I didn't bother to conceal a flick of surprise.

Everyone else knew who I was. She must be terribly isolated in this forsaken town. Yet she knew I was a half-blood.

I tilted my head and sniffed. A discovery made my eyes brighten, and I smiled. She wasn't the human she presented herself to be.

Yet she wasn't like anything I'd encountered.

This close, I could sense potent power in her bloodstream, but it was veiled.

She didn't even know, or she'd have fought with her magic instead of rudimentary bows and daggers.

Some force held her magic captive.

Then her scent hit me fully in the face, and waves of heat rushed inside me until they all gathered in my groin.

A firestorm of lust burned in my veins.

That instant I decided what she would be for me.

She was the puzzle I needed to solve.

A wilderness to tame.

A treasure I'd found.

A rare jewel I would possess and lock in the most guarded vault.

And a female I would ride every night, savoring her cries as she begged for the ecstasy I could give her. This girl I would claim as my mate.

The mystic wind passed between us, and she widened her stunningly green eyes as if she'd seen the most brilliant sunlight flooding the forest for the first time. She'd taken in my scent as well, and I watched her reaction in satisfaction.

Her soft, full lips parted with shock. She'd fight me with every ounce of her strength if I told her now that she was mine and her future belonged with me.

She recovered faster than I'd thought any woman could.

But then, she wasn't just any woman. Not even close.

"We're law-abiding citizens, mister. You won't take any member of my coven," she shouted, then swept her spearhead toward the werewolf gang she'd fought. "But you're more than welcome to round up those up-to-no-good scumbags! They should fight the demons in the frontier at your Dominions' command instead of harassing innocent small-town people."

The werewolves snarled, but stopped the instant Cameron shot them a harsh look.

"They're too old," Cameron said, thrusting his chin toward the werewolves before training his hard gaze on the girl. "Only the teenage wolf and witch will be enrolled into the Academy. We came for them, so I suggest you step aside if you don't want any more trouble."

He was nicer to the girl, though wary, after she'd put up a fight against me.

"No way!" the girl said. "Everyone knows Half-Blood Academy is actually Half-Death Academy. Less than half of the attendants survive the first ritual, and I won't let my people try their luck."

"How dare you!" Cameron hissed. "That blasphemy alone shall get you hanged."

I raised a hand to stop Cameron from cursing the girl further and quirked an eyebrow at her. It'd be interesting to see how the fiery minx survived her first day at my academy.

"I'll spare your friends under one condition," I said with a charming smile that every woman ate up.

She narrowed her eyes, but I could feel her pulse spike.

Her every reaction provoked mine, exciting me.

The girl arched a long, elegant eyebrow, relaxing a little and ready to bargain.

"And what is your condition, demigod?"

Read Half-Blood Academy Complete Series

Books by Meg Xuemei X

SHADES OF RUIN AND MAGIC: Brides Selection

House of Vampires and Flame (releases on Oct 2, 2023)

House of Fae and Mist (Coming Dec, 2023)

House of Shifters and Smoke

House of Mages and Ravens

House of Demons and Bones

House of Chaos and Dreams

MONSTERS AFTER DARK

Shifter God

Vampire God

Death God

UNDERWORLD BRIDE TRIALS

Playboy King

Rejected Queen

Hellfire Crown

Hidden Court

CROWN OF THORNS AND SINS:

UNDERWORLD BRIDE TRIALS

Hunted by the Dragon

Ruined by the Dragon

HALF-BLOOD ACADEMY SERIES

Magic Trials

Magic Secret

Magic Fury

Magic Unchained

Magic Flame

DARK FAE KINGS SERIES

Book 1: Fever Fae

Book 2: Frost Fae

Book 3: Night Fae

Book 4: Blood Fae

THE WAR OF GODS SERIES

A Court of Blood and Void

A Court of Fire and Metal

A Court of Ice and Wind

A Court of Earth and Ether

COURTS OF UNDERWORLD SERIES

The Burn of the Underworld

The Rise of the Underworld

The Dragonian's Witch

The Witch's Consort

About the Author

Meg Xuemei X is a USA Today and Amazon Charts bestselling author of paranormal and fantasy romance. She loves writing badass heroines and hot psycho alphaholes.